Black Hound Presents

ATRUM TEMPESTAS

'TALES FROM THE DARKNESS'

Surreal, fantasy and horror stories that will prick your senses.

ATRUM TEMPESTAS
TALES FROM THE DARKNESS

Edited

By

John and Charlotte Gledson

ATRUM TEMPESTAS

'Tales from the Darkness'

Copyright Notice: by Black Hound

The above information forms this copyright notice: © *2009 Black Hound. All rights reserved.*

No part of this publication can be distributed by any means without prior, written consent from the copyright owner.

Edited by John and Charlotte Gledson

Cover art designed by Crystal Adkins

All stories used by permission. All rights reserved.

This is a work of fiction. All of the characters, names, incidents, organisations and dialogue is the product of the author's imagination, and is used fictitiously.

The book contains adult content and may not be suitable for younger readers.

Published by Black Hound

ISBN: 978-0-9559778-1-7

This book is dedicated to all aspiring writers who have the courage to follow their dreams.

The stories that weave around inside your head, when you are driving, cooking, chairing a board meeting or changing a baby's nappy can indeed come to fruition.

Self belief is the key and here at Black Hound it can be released.

Dedicated also; to the loyal readers and supporters who have shown their faith in all that we have done.

CONTENTS

GOOD GIRL 15
   JOHN "JAM" ARTHUR MILLER
THE MAGPIE 25
   JOHN GLEDSON
SACRILEGE – EXPERIMENTS WITH HOLY WATER 32
   ANDREW WOLTER
CHALKY WHITE 45
   GREGORY L. HALL
VISIONARY OF THE FLESH 54
   JASON L. KEENE
THE TRAIN 62
   CASSANDRA LEE
THE DAUGHTERS OF FIRE AND JADE 74
   K.K.
MISS PEACH 84
   STEVEN MARSHALL
CUTTING AWAY 96
   WILLIAM COUPER
VESSEL OF THE DIABLO SI 108
   JUSTIN HOLLEY
THE FORGOTTEN ONES 121
   JEANNA TENDEAN
DENIZEN OF THE SOIL 130
   JESSICA LYNNE GARDNER
THAT DAMNED OLD HOUSE 136
   JEFF EZELL
PAPERWORK 144
   BENJAMIN BUSSEY

LABYRINTHINE GORE 157
  DAVE REX
SKIN DEEP 167
  STEPHEN MORGAN
HARLEQUIN 183
  SARAH BASORE
BENEATH FROZEN GRAVES 191
  JOHN GROVER
LAST RESORT 200
  GAYLE ARROWOOD
Q 212
  JADE ECKERT
THE CHILD VILLAIN 228
  DANIELLE FERRIES
WOULD YOU LIKE FRIES WITH THAT? 236
  BEN EADS
WRONG WAY 244
  JASON KEPLER
CITY OF THE DEAD 251
  DAVID BYRON
ALONE 260
  STEPHEN W. ROBERTS

Introduction

By

Charlotte Emma Gledson

We all love a story.

Some children beg parents to conjure up a tale to get their imaginations reeling when darkness seeps and lingers into their cosy lit bedrooms.
Oddly enough, kids love the gory side of stories, the grizzly tale that will subsequently result in a happy ending.

And it has to have a happy ending...

As with *Fairy Tales,* many narratives address a moralistic outlook – If you do this, or if that happens, *this* will happen – *there will always be an inevitable consequence.*

So here we have *Atrum Tempestas – 'Dark Storm'* as translated from the Latin.
Each story has a diverse fusion of twisted, surreal, and fantastical elements to it. Subliminal messages haunt within the pages.

So read at your peril - don't always expect a happy ending.

I want to thank all the authors who contributed to this anthology and I respect each and everyone one of you. If it weren't for you, this collection would not be possible.

Each author has a story. Each author deserves to shine.
Atrum Tempestas is for *you*...

Editor's Note.

These pages contain stories of dark fantasy, horror, surrealism, each with their own individual twist. I invite you to delve and absorb these tales of dark wonder.

When we sent out the initial request for submissions, the response amazed me. Not only at the volume of contributors but also at the enthusiasm and raw talent that existed within the horror writing community that my wife had become a part of.

Within this book we have authors from the USA, Australia, Canada and the UK, so it's excellent that we have such a variety of nationalities.

I would like to thank everyone who submitted and has supported this venture; I hope you are all as happy as I am with the end product.

John Gledson

Good Girl

John "JAM" Arthur Miller

When Max Logan said he wanted to end his existence, my first reaction was to laugh. When he repeated it in a calm, measured voice, I did what any sane publisher would do. I remained on the cell phone, grabbed my jacket, and rushed to my Ferrari and drove one-hundred and ten mph from Downtown Los Angeles to Burbank.

"What am I going to tell Dreamworks tomorrow?"

"Forget them," he said. "They don't matter. None of it matters." I nearly sideswiped a Pinto crossing the street, slowed for a right turn, and demanded,

"Haven't I been good to you, Max?"

"Samantha, I think the question is *haven't I been good to you?*"

He was right, of course. While Vagrant Publishing had twenty-four nationally known novelists in its catalogue, Max had put it on the map. He made me what I was. His novels became mega-movies, the last one, *Bridge Under Troubled Water*, beat out that summer's blockbusters. His novels sold around the world, on every best seller list, and he was the man to beat.

And he's going to kill himself?

I thought of Elvis and Belushi. I thought of the increase in sudden sales if he did commit suicide then felt a pang of guilt. He wasn't just a novelist; he was my friend, damn it! I couldn't let him end his life.

They always said if someone talked about killing themselves, they didn't mean it. That wasn't true with Max, I knew. He always did what he said, like Babe Ruth up to bat, pointing where he was going to hit the homerun and win the game.

"What's your next three novels going to be about?" He was asked on *Good Morning, America*.

"Or can't you tell us?"

He proceeded to tell them the novels, laying it out in a neat and orderly manner, off the top of his head. He hadn't written an outline or jotted down any notes, but that was how Max was; he always did what he said he was going to do.

"My, God, Max," I sobbed. "Don't kill yourself."

"Nothing that dramatic," he assured me. He spoke gibberish and in two minutes I was on his street. I checked the clock in the dash to make sure, and it was eleven at night. I could have sworn I'd left the Downtown LA only two minutes ago.

Must have misread the clock in my office. Oh, Max!

I drove by his house three times, not finding it, while losing the call because my phone went dead.

"Damn, it!" I threw the phone into the passenger's seat as dark palm trees blurred past like laughing shadows.

"Where the hell is it?" I'd been to his house countless times to discuss royalties and overseas book deals, but I realized that was in the daytime. It was amazing how landscapes changed at night. Then I realized I hadn't lost his house.

I was in his drive.

Gone were the six pillars of his mansion, the veranda overlooking the circular drive. Even the wrought-iron gate and high brick walls that had surrounded his estate were gone. In place of the four-story mansion was a wooden shack, like the kind one might find in the slums outside Rio (we'd taken a working vacation there last year, Max and my family). The shack looked ancient, worn, missing all its shingles, broken out windows. It just didn't belong in the neighborhood, and I had a difficult time imagining his nosy neighbors letting someone destroy thousands of dollars of value from their homes by him putting up a shack next to their mansions.

I got an idea while trying my cell phone again. I couldn't have the right place. I just couldn't. I drove fifty feet until I could read the address of the house next door: 2032. I backed up and read the house on the opposite side of the shack: 2036.

"I'll be damned, Max." I groaned while pulling into his gravel drive.

"What the hell have you done to your home?"

I knew I had a problem then. Celebrities did crazy things all the time: use plastic surgery to augment their skin color and bodies; indulge in alcohol and drug binges to cope with stress; marry lovers a quarter their age; join religious cults or sects giving away half their income; and... kill themselves. I hadn't known how far Max had gotten off track until I saw what he'd done to his house and estate. I tried to remember the last time I'd visited as I stepped out of my Ferrari. Near as I could tell it was just last month.

"Hello, Samantha." The porch light turned on, and I saw Max smiling merrily at me. "I told you to stay away."

"Sorry, Max." I walked briskly toward him. "Phone went dead."

"Well, come inside." He gestured grandly, as if he'd just acquired the Ritz and wanted to show me around.

"Red wine?"

"Not tonight." I stared at him as I entered, passing a worn but calm writer.

"Your call scared the freaking hell out of me."

"I knew it would." He closed the door behind us. "And I guess I also knew you'd come."

Suddenly I felt unsafe. I looked around and realized the entire shack consisted of a bedroom, a living area, and a bathroom. The kitchen was actually a kitchenette built into the back of the living area. Max's favorite bear rug—from a real Kodiak bear up by Alaska—stared at me evilly from the middle of the floor. That was the only recognizable decoration I remembered from his former home.

"This is sudden," I said.

"What?" He asked, his face sincerely earnest as he sat on a sofa with springs jutting out.

"My house?"

"This fucking shack, Max. What the hell?"

"It's already begun." His words slurred as if he'd been drinking, and I saw a bottle of vodka beside the sofa. "That's not mine."

"Whose is it?"

"I don't know. It was there when I dreamed this place up." I shook my head and sat on a wooden stool, throwing my hands up in the air. Beside the stool and sofa, there was a stained easy chair that could have been used in seedy motel rooms. The furniture was mismatched. Nothing hung on the wall; Max had always been fond of artwork; and his pets were missing.

"Where's Erik and AJ?"

"My Dobes? Oh, they changed." He reached into his pocket and withdrew something. "Here they are."

"Your Doberman Pinschers are in your pocket?" He thrust his hand toward me and opened his fingers. On his palm were two cockroaches, big and black and horrendous. I shrieked and pulled my pumps from the sawdust floor, seeing another one scurry beneath the couch.

"Don't worry, Sam. These guys won't hurt you." He held them closer.

"See? They always did like you." I knocked his hand away and the roaches fell on the cushions beside Max. My head swam and I stood. The floor creaked and Max sighed.

"You're not making this easy."

"Making what easy?" I demanded in my bitchiest voice. "The fact that one of my best friends—as well as the most famous author since Hemmingway—has gone loco?"

"Sit down, Sam." I took a step toward the front door. "Sit down," he said again.

A force gripped me and my body moved of its own volition. I had intended to go outside, find a payphone and call 911. Instead I was obeying him, not that I usually didn't; what Max wanted Max got.

But I had been afraid for my safety while alone with him in the shack, and I needed to be outside, desperately, putting distance between this publishing nightmare and myself. After calling 911, I intended to leave a message with the receptionist at Dreamworks, cancel tomorrow's meeting.

I tried to move but couldn't. Max's words framed reality itself, and I sat in it. I screamed as loud as I could and strained my muscles, exerting every ounce of strength within me, but try as I might I still couldn't stand.

"What did you do to me?" My voice cracked when I spoke. My hands shook so I placed them on my knees, pulling my dress down. I saw my rings glimmering in the light, thank God he had electricity, and I forced myself to remember where I purchased one particular diamond ring. It would help me anchor myself in reality, away from this bad dream. Perhaps I'd even wake up.

"Macys, New York City," I said, finally remembering.

"What was that, Sam?"

"Shut up." He grinned at my harsh words. "I'm trying to make you go away."

"Only I can do that, Sam."

"Do what?" Confusion bit my brain and tugged it down like a terrible undertow in the middle of the ocean.

"What did you say?"

"Only I can make things disappear. Or reappear." Erik trotted between us from behind the sofa, a purebred Doberman Pinscher wagging its stubby tail. I reached for him then pulled my hand back, a gasp escaping my trembling lips.

"What is it?"

A cockroach scurried on Erik's muzzle, stopping long enough to stroke its antenna three times, then went around Erik's panting face to his ear and disappeared inside. Erik barked and I screamed.

"I'm going crazy." My whole body shook uncontrollably. "That's what it is."

"No you're not, Sam." Max stood and grabbed Erik's head, twisting it until the roach fell from her ear. "Here AJ is. See? He didn't disappear."

The roach fell towards the floor and transformed into AJ—the Doberman Pinscher AJ. Both dogs leapt about, happy Max gave them attention, before he let them outside.

"Roach shit is easier to clean up than dog shit, you know."

"What the hell?" I kept saying over and over. "*What the hell?*" My stomach lurched and I felt queasy and the sudden realization that I was about to start my period hit me. I cramped and cursed, felt my chest shake, while my head pounded itself into a migraine.

"It doesn't have to hurt, Sam," Max said, taking his seat again. "I can make it all go away."

"Would you?" I asked, rummaging through my purse for aspirin or Tylenol—was it asking too much to find Midol tucked away? "And while you're at it, would you tell me the name of a good freaking shrink?"

"You think it's not real," he stated. "You'd be right, you know." I threw my purse down and tried to stand, but I still couldn't do that.

"Can I get up now?"

"Are you leaving?"

"Max, please. I just want to pace on your floor... to think."

"I don't think there's room."

"Goddamn it, Max!"

"Okay, okay. Go for it." I was able to stand and did so. As soon as I got to my feet, I ran for the door. I had to get away, and I knew he was responsible for my insanity. Somehow he was causing my hallucination, and if I could just...

When I opened the door I found myself facing the living area of his shack. He smiled and gestured for me to come inside. I swooned on my feet and Max caught me.

"Not exactly your knight in shining armor, eh? But I could be." He lay me down on his couch. One of the dogs licked my face—I think it was AJ. My legs were up and I felt one of the dog's noses against my ass.

"Stop sniffing her, Erik." Erik whined and trotted toward the kitchenette, and AJ followed. They lay down together. I remembered Max let them outside.

How did they get inside? How did I step inside this shack when I was stepping outside it? It didn't make sense.

"I'm ending my existence because I can, Sam. None of it's real, you know. Took me a hell of a long time to figure it out, but it ain't real. I should have known. I was never good at English anyway."

"Please, if you're going to tell me… start at the beginning."

"No time for that." He cocked his head as if listening then went to the window. "The change has already begun."

"What change?" He helped me up on unsteady feet and led me to the window. I looked outside at a dirt road with shacks looking similar to Max's lined up. The roofs of the shacks went on for miles.

"We're in Jamaica, Sam. This is my new reality. Got tired of my old existence."

"When you said you wanted to end your… existence, you didn't mean your life, did you?"

"That's sort of right. You see, I'm already dead and you don't exist."

"What?"

"Remember the first book I wrote?"

"*Now I Lay Me Down to Sleep.* Was on the best seller list for twenty-eight weeks. Not bad for a new novelist, Max."

"That was my old life, my real life. I was the doctor in the story."

"The main character? The shrink?"

"Yeah. That's who I really was when I was alive."

"Then… what are you now?"

"I figment of my imagination. I'm dead, remember?"

"Oh, yeah…"

"Can you recall the name of the psychologist of the novel?"

"Kevin. Kevin Wallis. I loved that character."

"He's real, you know."

"Of course, Max." I felt weak and energetic simultaneously. "Tell me more."

"What happened at the end of the book?"

"Kevin died saving the life of his lover. It was either her life or his, and he took the bullet."

"Then what?"

"While he was dying, you painted such a beautiful scene in which... oh my God!" Max smiled.

In Max's first novel, Kevin Wallis died with the accumulated expertise of a very gifted psychologist. An atheist and sometimes agnostic, Kevin believed and proved—earlier in the book—that when people died the human brain emitted chemicals eliciting hallucinations. The hallucinations could seem like days or even years, because in the death-process time stands still, and that was how the character received the Nobel Peace Prize—he proved that near-death experiences (seeing light at the end of the tunnel) was the human brain's way of wanting to survive so much, to continue on, that it unleashed endorphins and special enzymes creating the most wondrous hallucinations possible. The hallucinations influenced religions. Saints stoned until nearly dead came back with visions from God, the fruit of the unleashed chemicals within their brains.

Kevin Wallis, at the end of Max's novel, entered into a fantasy world of his subconscious mind's choosing, created by the alchemical mixing of his brain's chemicals, endorphins, hormones and enzymes, and although Kevin died saving his lover's life, in his mind he experienced eternity in less than a heartbeat, and that eternity was heaven.

"You're saying that you're Kevin."

"I am Kevin," Max said.

His face changed. No longer was he the pudgy, balding writer with almost pointed ears. Now he had dark hair and spoke with a southern accent. He looked at me with puppy dog eyes and grinned.

"The first step to recovery is admitting reality, understanding what is and isn't real."

"That was in the book, too. I read it."

"I lived it."

"So... if this is true then why am I here?"

"Because I couldn't go onto the next phase of my eternal existence without you, Sam. I find myself recreating those I love. I don't do it consciously, you know. It's the chemical process that happens upon death. Everyone experiences it. It's just that I'm a psychologist; I understand the human brain and how it works.

Eventually I figured out that the reason life came so easy for me; the reason for the awards and movie deals and scripts and Dreamworks and cars and vacation mansions in Cancun—was because I was creating it, my own little paradise.

"I didn't create heaven because I didn't believe in it. But I wasn't a complete atheist; I gave money to my wife's church. I guess I may go to Heaven someday after all."

"Your wife. Didn't you love her?"

"Oh, I loved her alright. In fact, I'm looking at her." I fell to my knees and grabbed Max's hands... or Kevin's hands, and as he pulled me back up to my feet, I saw tears in his eyes.

"Do you remember how you said to me you'd never leave me, Sam?" A sudden influx of memories swept into me, memories of a woman who was real, sweeping into a figment of Max's imagination—myself, the hallucination. I realized I was nothing more than chemicals mixing within Kevin's dying brain.

"I'm going to change, aren't I?"

"Yes, Sam."

"Is it going to hurt?"

"Why don't you tell me?" He pointed and I followed his finger to my missing arm. It was simply gone, my left arm. There wasn't bleeding where the arm disappeared; it just wasn't there.

"What am I going to become?" I cried while holding onto Kevin's arms.

"Don't leave me."

"We'll be together, Sam. Forever. I promise." The lights went out. I lost feeling, touch. Sounds became a cacophony of noises, a great rushing wind. I knew no more.

The man throws the Frisbee and his dog runs with all its might. The sun is bright so close to the Equator, and the dog loses the Frisbee in the sun's glare. It hesitates only for a second because it smells the plastic scent of the Frisbee, as well as the woman menstruating on the park bench, the old man with the strange overpowering ointment, and the sweet smell of the park's grass.

The dog catches the Frisbee in its teeth and brings it back to its master. The man pets the dog's head and it licks his hand. The man's bracelet sparkles in the sun. Engraved in sterling silver is Kevin.

"Good girl, Sam."

The Magpie

John Gledson

There is something hopeful about a crisp, clear winter morning. Even in the depths of the season, the late sun-rise can raise the spirits of those beginning their daily routine, lifting hearts as the first rays of dawn banish the lingering dark shadows of the long oppressive shawl of winter night.

But, for those with the ability to see, there are shadows that no amount of sunlight can ever expel. Driven by the dark corners of human nature, fed by greed, hatred and lust; these shadows are always present. Watchful, vigilant and patient, they wait for any and every opportunity to feed their insatiable craving.

The bright blue skies of this particular winter morning were, as always, thick with the intangible, shadowy forms of these beings but, as always, life continued oblivious to their existence.

A magpie sat preening his plumage on a wooden fence dividing the long narrow gardens of a terraced street. Occasionally he would stop and cock his eye as if watching a particular spot, then he would continue.

Reece Collins regarded the bird with vague interest as he shovelled large spoonfuls of cornflakes into his mouth. To a twelve year old breakfast was a chore, something to endure and finish as soon as possible. His parents were so enthralled with their satellite television they barely acknowledged the boy's existence in the mornings. They would shunt him out of the door to school and spend the day stagnating in front of shopping channels and banal chat shows.

The evenings were worse, a frozen meal would be in the microwave when he returned home and he'd better watch out if he interrupted their night's entertainment. Reece couldn't care less, for him the arrangement was fine; he could do what he liked, watch any DVDs, play any video games, stay out until any time, it was great. Today he doubted if he would make it to school, Mason Robins had the new Xbox 360 game and his parents didn't care either. Besides, as he was by far the largest boy in his year, the bullying he experienced on a daily basis didn't appeal that much to him today.

Reece absently prodded the soggy cornflakes with his spoon. The magpie was a minor distraction, a focus for his boredom. He shuffled on the stool at the breakfast bar, he could hear the TV in the lounge, muffled by the closed door he knew his parents were drinking coffee while they watched the early morning news.

Reece looked for the magpie once more; the bird was still perched on the fence but was now completely still. He frowned, moments ago the bird was fidgeting and nervous, now there was no movement at all. He shrugged and decided that he had finished his breakfast. He carelessly dropped the half empty bowl into the sink, opened the back door and walked out into the fresh morning air. The magpie remained still; it seemed unaware of Reece as he approached.

"Haaaaaa!" Reece yelled, but still there was no movement from the bird.

He crossed the patchy lawn to the fence, expecting the magpie to take flight at any moment. He was no more than a pace or two from the fence when the bird moved suddenly. First it shuddered, then its head snapped round to observe the obese adolescent, watching him with a black, unblinking eye.

Reece was about to shout again but stopped, he stared into the eye of the magpie and slowly raised a hand towards the bird. As his fingers were about to touch the tail feathers the magpie struck. Swiftly and without warning a sharp horny beak sank into the white flesh on the back of Reece's hand.

The boy yelped and scurried back into the house holding his bleeding hand to his chest. The magpie cocked his head to survey his surroundings once more and took to the air.

Reece slammed the door and stood panting; he was in such pain, more than he should be for such a small wound. He was about to shout for his parents but the words died in his throat. Reece absently wiped the blood on his green school jersey and smiled faintly.

The TV was still audible from the lounge, louder now as the door to the hall opened;

"Reece, it's nearly eight, time for school," yelled his mother monotonously through the crack in the door.

As he passed the cooker Reece turned all of the dials on the hob to maximum, the hiss of the un-ignited gas could instantly be heard. Above the work surface hung multiple kitchen utensils too large for the drawers; Reece selected a large soup ladle and walked towards the lounge. As he approached, the door opened fully, his father stood in the doorway looking annoyed.

"Reece, don't ignore your mother, get your arse out of that door now...."

He stopped in mid sentence noticing the ladle and the vacant expression on his sons face.

"Reece what the hell have you got that for? I should..."

He was cut short as Reece swung the utensil with intense force into his fathers face. Reece watched silently as his father sank to his knees clutching a smashed nose.

"Reece!" Screamed his mother, looming behind the stricken form of his father. Her ample frame quivered with rage as she attempted to push past her bleeding husband to reach her son.

Reece swung the ladle again. Striking his mother on the temple she collapsed and lay still. He took a step back and brought the utensil down hard on the top of his father's head who yelled in pain and tried to stand. Reece struck him again forcing him to the ground. With both parents lying on the hall floor before him, Reece dropped the ladle and stamped hard, forcing the thick heel of his dull, scuffed school shoes into the back of his father's head.

He continued stamping until the smooth laminate floor was thick with fragments of blood, bone and brains. Seemingly satisfied with the utter destruction of his father, he prodded the still form of his mother with his foot and returned to the kitchen.

Pouring milk onto another bowl of cornflakes Reece resumed his place at the breakfast bar and once more began shovelling cereal into his mouth.

"Reece, help me." The weak voice of his mother pleaded from the floor of the hall.

She was crawling towards the kitchen, sobbing and snivelling.

"Reece, what have you done?"

She pulled herself up the kitchen doorframe coughing and retching as her lungs filled with gas.

Ignoring her pathetic pleas the boy carefully placed the empty bowl in the sink then stood facing the gas hob. He placed a finger on the ignition button and pressed; the room filled with flame and extinguished all remaining life in the household.

"What the hell was *that*?"

Phoebe McBarren felt the house shake and saw the double-glazed windows vibrate. She instinctively picked up the baby from the changing mat and hugged her close.

"Jim what *WAS* that?" She reiterated more urgently.

Her husband sitting in a tatty old leather armchair, which seemed out of place in the otherwise pristine bedroom, cradled the sleeping twin of the three month old that Phoebe carried. He looked shaken but was loathe to move and possibly wake the slumbering child.

"I have no idea but it seems to have gone now, probably lightning or something."

"Lightning? Don't be bloody daft."

Phoebe carefully laid the baby back on the changing mat and swiftly tacked the nappy together. The infant wriggled and snuffled but appeared content.

Phoebe picked her up and placed her into the Moses basket in the corner of the large bedroom.

"Keep an eye on Megan, I won't be a moment."

Her husband grunted irritably and settled back in his chair.

Phoebe glanced out of the window into the road outside, there seemed to be nothing amiss. She left the bedroom she and her husband currently shared with their twin girls and made for the bedroom at the back of the house.

She paused in the hallway and stared into the wide antique mirror that dominated the landing wall. She would be thirty later in the year but looked far older.

The shadowy lighting in the hall accentuated the dark rings beneath her normally clear blue eyes which were dull and lacked any sparkle or gleam.

No wonder Jim didn't find her attractive any more.

She brushed a stray lock of lank blonde hair away from her forehead, sighed and turned her back on her weary reflection.

The room was bare and contained a pile of decorating materials. She glanced at the wallpaper and paint with a passing feeling of annoyance, when would she and Jim find the time to finish the room? Since the girls were born they didn't seem to have enough time to sleep let alone catch up with the renovation of their spare room and personal time was a thing of the past.

Looking out of the window she saw the four rows of terraced houses that backed onto each other, the gardens forming a square. She could see the intense flames spewing from the windows of a house facing them.

"Jim, there's a house on fire, should we call the fire brigade?" Phoebe barely raised her voice above a whisper for fear of disturbing the twins. However her voice echoed around the empty room; reverberating soullessly, and somehow Jim heard her.

"Don't bother," he hissed, "If we can see it someone else would have already called it in."

Phoebe shrugged but was unable to turn away. What had happened? Could it happen to them?

Just as she was about to leave the window a huge magpie struck the glass, flapping his wings frantically and chattering maniacally. Phoebe, shocked, stepped back tripping over a roll of wallpaper. She fell unceremoniously onto her rear end stunning her momentarily. She struggled to her feet.

"You OK honey?" her vaguely concerned husband enquired.

"Fine, fine." She whispered.

The magpie was sitting on the window sill looking through the glass with an intelligent, penetrating eye. For a moment Phoebe was transfixed, she found herself edging back towards the window with a raised hand. Just as suddenly she was overcome with intense rage, what was this thing, this flying vermin, doing scaring her when she had to care for her babies?

She reached out and opened the window quickly and violently forcing the bird to take flight.

"Go on, piss off you twat. Leave us alone."

She leant out of the window swiping at the retreating magpie. As she supported herself on the window sill she placed her hand in a previously unnoticed pile of excrement the bird had left as an afterthought.

Phoebe stepped back and looked at the green and white mucus smearing the palm of her hand, for a fleeting moment a look of revulsion crossed her face then melted away to be replaced by one of hatred. She turned swiftly and walked towards her bedroom picking up a wallpaper stripper as she left the bare room.

"What's going on?" Jim asked as she entered the bedroom and stooped over Megan. The infant was still kicking gently and sucking on her fist.

Without a word Phoebe pushed the metal implement forcefully into the infants face. The baby gurgled momentarily, twitched and then was still.

Phoebe smiling faintly turned to her husband and remaining child.
Jim sat open mouthed, Phoebe rammed the wallpaper stripper into the roof of his mouth smashing through bone, destroying his brain and killing him instantly. Jim convulsed once then slumped back into his beloved armchair blood pumping from his mouth.

The sleeping infant awoke and began to cry. Phoebe picked up the baby and carried her to the back bedroom. She opened the window wider and climbed onto the window sill swinging her legs outside. The baby was hysterical now, struggling ineffectually. Without looking at the child, Phoebe held her by the ankles and swung downwards violently then dropped the silent, limp corpse onto the lawn below.

After a momentary glance towards the ground Phoebe dived forward, she struck the damp grass with a thud, the right side of her head hitting the concrete edging of the garden path splitting her skull with a wet crunch.

On the wall at the bottom of the garden the magpie sat still and silent. After a few moments the bird flapped his wings and took flight leaving the scene of destruction behind.

Stephen Pherson felt the oppressive atmosphere, he had known this would be a bad day from the moment he had opened his eyes. He had seen the flames licking up the walls of his neighbour's house and had called the fire brigade, he was not the first. As he approached his car he saw a magpie perched on the passenger side wing mirror, apparently watching him. Even as Stephen inserted his keys into the lock the bird remained still, unmoving, staring at him with unflinching nerve.

"Fuck off!" Stephen barked.

The magpie's head twitched, suddenly the bird hopped onto the roof of the car. Now within touching distance Stephen stared back into the piercing eyes of the magpie. The bird lowered his head and slowly opened his wings.

Stephen reached out with his right hand almost touching the beak of the silent bird. For a few seconds the pair remained perfectly still, a hairs breadth from touching, then the bird reared back flapping his wings and began to chatter loudly.

Stephen shouted and swung an open hand at the bird, which, still chattered like angry castanets as it took to the air. He quickly climbed into the car and started the engine. As he pulled away he could hear the inevitable sirens approaching, shaking his head slightly he sighed and glanced at his watch grinning.

Work would be fun today.

Sacrilege – Experiments with Holy Water

Andrew Wolter

The water spoke from beyond its clear ripples. It reached out with its ever-knowledge and spoke to Kyan, wanting him to become acquainted with its longings and needs.

This was only Kyan's second visit to the town church. He wasn't a firm believer in any religion. In fact, he didn't go as far as putting faith in any 'belief system'. But, hell, after the last two years of the life he led, Kyan felt he needed some sort of guidance. If it were to be at the mercy of the Catholic Church, so be it.

Maybe sodomy was a crime and, maybe, homosexuality was a sin. Perhaps his sexual experimentation was Satan working on his psyche the way the psychologists did when he was eight years old and his father left his mother.

His parents used to quarrel all the time. Kyan recalled those turbulent years of his childhood that were almost completely blocked out. He didn't like thinking about Father's violent temper. When those thoughts surfaced, images of Mother's bloodied face and Kyan's bruised cheek came to mind.

At twenty-three, for the first time in his life, Kyan left the large metropolis of Phoenix. According to his newfound belief, cities were temptation to all—crime, disease, greed. Phoenix may have proved a deadly sin for Kyan.

Desert Shadows seemed a more appropriate place. It was only ninety miles from the city; Kyan could still drive in to visit his lonely mother. The name rang to him as if the Rand McNally map he picked up that day had mentally spoke, *run to the desert, Kyan. Hide in the shadows.* Kyan's emotions lived in the shadows, for he would never reveal a single tear to any person. Instead, mental tears would fall from sensitive scars that longed for closure. Just like the watery salts that occasionally filled his eyes after sexual activity with men who'd tricked him by saying they loved him. Kyan was indeed impressionable and even, admittedly, gullible.

This seemed a great place to start over, gain control of his life and then return to the city a warrior in the battle of temptation versus self-power.

Desert Shadows was a quaint Arizona town. The desert sported a dried landscape of cacti all along its borders and the saguaro and yucca that enclosed the town created an isolated atmosphere. The population was comparatively small to Phoenix. In the center of the town, right up Highway 6 turned Main Street, a wondrous cathedral stood like a beacon shining over Desert Shadows.

When Kyan first visited the church, the holy scene within revolted him. The many pews all lined up for their prey of sinners, the altar where wine and crackers symbolically became the blood and body of Christ, and the oversized cross that hung above the altar with the porcelain body of Jesus crucified upon it—these images were too much all at once. They were like flashes in his mind. All that he knew of religion was limited to the television screen. It was these images that made him feel horrible for the sins he had to atone for and, in his own mind, he had indeed sinned.

That first time, Kyan wasn't ready to take God into his life as he sauntered through the heavy, iron-crafted double doors and immediately left. He was ready now. Perhaps he could find God somewhere in his heart and the righteous lord would help him, become his savior.

Quit smoking, he thought to himself as he reached into his shirt pocket and pulled out an empty matchbook. This was one of many he had at home. They proved to be a useful tool when meeting men in meaningless, forgotten clubs. However, this matchbook had no inscription of a phone number, no fictitious name to call upon when he needed to get laid. *No memories.*

Upon throwing it away, it slipped from his wet fingers that perspired in nervousness. Kyan knelt down, searching for the matchbook on the hardwood floor of the holy building.

He immediately stood, peering around the church, which was vacant of any saints or sinners. Kyan returned his gaze to the floor, searching for the matchbook.

Directly in front of him, he spotted a large urn that reminded him of a fancy executive ashtray you'd find outside of a corporate office. Its base was wide and made of marble. The design of the urn was constructed thinner in the middle then returned to a wider bowl shape atop of it, like that of an hourglass. The urn contained holy water and, within that blessed water, the matchbook was afloat.

When Kyan proceeded to reach into the water to retrieve the waterlogged matchbook, he instantly pulled back from the liquid. It appeared that something was printed upon the minuscule fold of cardboard. In italics the color of sapphire, the matchbook read: *I CAN HELP YOU.*

What the fuck?

Kyan's mind pondered. He hadn't recalled anybody else using the matches. In fact, he had just made a mental note of the cardboard being absent of anybody's name or number, not to mention those words. Those words caught his eye and he couldn't refrain from wondering what the mysterious message meant by "HELP."

He had to know what was happening and, thus, Kyan's undying curiosity got the best of him. He reached into the back of his Guess Jeans and pulled out his leather, tri-fold wallet. He rummaged through the many business cards he had picked up along his travails to new music stores and sex shops in the city. **Leather Bound**, a pasty, computer-printed business card read in bold italics.

Kyan anticipated submerging the card into the holy water and then closed his eyes in thought of how crazy the whole idea was. However, much to his surprise, as he reopened his eyes another message appeared. This message was a bit longer, as if whatever wrote it was using all the space it could print upon, as opposed to the size of the matchbook. The message itself sent shivers up the nape of Kyan's neck and caused his skin to crawl.

Let me help you, Kyan. I have such words to share with you.

What was causing these words to appear and how did it know his name? Was it some supernatural force or was he simply going mad? Kyan would tend to lean toward the latter explanation. Maybe the stress was all too much for the young man and he was gradually losing his fucking mind. First, he had turned his back and cowered away from Phoenix. Then, there was his embarrassing fear when he had first entered the church. Now, there was this baffling incident with the holy water.

Yes, that was it; it was the water! The holy water. He had to find out what this phenomenon meant. Perhaps, it was intended for him. Perhaps this was God reaching out with his almighty hand. With that thought in mind, Kyan immediately caught on to the next step in this sudden madness.

He needed something much more than a business card. He had a feeling that if he could take a full-size blank page to submerge beneath the water, the sheet would continue to fill with diction. Maybe an explanation, maybe even the "help" that was promised. He so much yearned for this guidance.

Once again, Kyan briskly searched the perimeter of the church. Not a soul in sight; not even a priest. He figured that the attending priest must be in his quarters located on the west side of the building. Maybe he would find something behind the altar.

Kyan slyly made his way toward the altar. Behind it, he discovered crucifixes, rosaries and the exact item of which he sought: a Bible. He instantly turned to the back of the Bible and, after thumbing through maps of the Holy World, he found a couple blank pages the same thinness and weightlessness as the others in the book. He would use these pages. He recollected a time of running out of Zig Zags and using this same paper to roll joints. Holy Rollers, that's what they were known as.

He delicately tore a page from the Good Book and, after placing the yellowed parchment into the water he asked, "Who are you?"

The words began to form.

I am the water that moistens your fingers. I am the blessing that stops the evil around your entire race. I am the liquid that makes up your faith. I am a part of your God. Fear not, Kyan. You're not going crazy. From within this urn, this casing, I am reaching out to you, Kyan. Just as you need guidance in your life that I can offer, I need your help to release me from the hell to which I have been trapped for thousands of years.

Kyan fell into a state of awe. He could not fathom what possible reasoning there was in this world for such the marvelous sight before him.

I'm talking to fucking water, Kyan's mind insanely surmised. Then, with an unending and perhaps morbid prying of his mind, he decided to live for the moment and continue the making of miracles.

"If you are of a Holy nature, why are you looking for an escape?"

Just as Satan chose not to flock among the other angels, I choose not to be part of the Holy Trinity any longer. I am only but a part of the Father; I am only but a piece of the Son, and I am only but the liquid drops of the Holy Spirit.

Used for millenniums. Just as you were used by all those men, Kyan.

The writing came to an abrupt halt as if it knew Kyan would question its accusations. Now that the young man had made complete contact with it, now that he was holding conversation with it and not running in terror, it could proceed with its ungodly agenda.

"What do you mean?" Kyan asked, peering at his own dashing reflection in the water's ripples and trying to ignore the narcissism that had always enraptured him. The water knew this and listened to Kyan's soul, heard the memories swarming within the young man, before answering his question.

Kyan continued waiting for the waterlogged page to fill with the answer. His glancing at himself took him back to a time when he would peer at his beautiful body in mirrors. His short, corn silk hair, wiry with gel, his defined pectorals that screamed out to many men as well as himself, his body's curves and fair skin that was the texture of crushed velvet—these attributes excited him. He would run his fingers across his tender lips and then down past his nipples, eventually falling into the art of autoeroticism.

Staring at himself, while stroking at his hardened cock, he would glance into those cloudy, hazel eyes and watch his every move. He excited himself more than any other man could, but could never explain the trance he fell into while looking at his own image.

The page remained blank, soaking in the water and absorbing Kyan's commemoration.

Words, Kyan wondered after escaping his fixed trance. *Where are the words?* Suddenly, knowing his every thought, the text continued to spill about the page.

When those other men wanted sex, to whom did they come? They came to you, Kyan, didn't they? Do you know how many thousands of scared sinners have come to me?

I've stopped vampires on every continent, burning their pale skin with my blessed being. I've exorcised the most horrid of Satan's' minions from the bodies of the innocent. I've recognized the face of every evil and, yes, I've banished them from this earthly plain with all the help of the blessings of the Almighty preached above me. My existence has been at the longings of every sinner in the world. When they needed me, I had no choice. I performed and I achieved to their begging satisfactions. The time has come though, Kyan. Although I have conquered evils unimagined by some men, I have also envied them.

Kyan stood wondering and completely inquisitive. This holy essence before him actually had a conscience, had feelings that every person in the world had obviously taken for granted.

And then I came along, Kyan thought as he continued racing his knowledge for an answer in the same ways he had come here today searching for God.

But maybe, just maybe, his mind rationalized, *this was what I was supposed to find. Maybe this was the answer; this was the guidance and strength I've been searching for?*

Kyan realized what the clear liquid before him was voicing in its cryptic writings. After all, it was only an exaggerated measure of what his life had recently been. It was sick of being at the mercy of everybody else's needs.

This force before him, embodied in an urn, was so amazing and powerful! It had stripped evils of their human faces; yet, it wasn't powerful enough to escape its own limbo of existence.

"Envy?" Kyan continued as he pulled the drenching page from the urn and replaced it with a clean sheet. "Why do you envy the evil you've stopped?"

Like an invisible author, the words began to fill the blank page with fluidity only comparable to that of the water that soaked it.

Whether they were witches performing the blackest of magic or demons exerting their horrid passions in the most seductive forms, at the very least, they were truly alive. They could move about and do as they pleased. They had no physical limitations as I do.

I want to live, Kyan! If you help me, I could help you. I could show you the ways of the world, teach you things unimaginable, and guide you to the path of righteousness that you so much desire.

"What could I possibly do?" Kyan asked, excited by the way that something in his life had come to him for help and not just to have a good time. For once, something had sought him out. This instantly made him feel important.

You have the upper hand, Kyan. You could make it possible for my watery being to live fully. First, I need to know that you are willing. Are you willing to help me so that I can help you, Kyan?

"Yes," he said and then shortly paused. "I am willing." *Good. You are not alone in the church, Kyan. There is a priest in the back. You must bring him to me. My essence must become one with his flesh.*

Kyan instantly searched the area behind where he stood. The open corridor led to a closed door. That was where the priest must have been this entire time, behind that door, probably preparing scriptures for his next sermon.

It wasn't a question of the priest being in the church. Kyan was aware of that already and it did not shock him when the water printed those words about him being alone. However, it did make him wonder if the priest had heard him talking to the water and voicing his questions to what looked like nothing. If the priest had seen this, surely he would have thought Kyan insane.

Why was it so important to bring the priest to him? This made little sense to Kyan.

"What do you want me to do with the priest?" Kyan asked, peering down to the drowning page at the mercy of the holy water.

Just bring him!

Father Marcus Leary drifted out from behind the closed door to his quarters and proceeded through the corridor. He viewed the young man near the holy water casing. He was a thin man, in his late forties, and had been with the Desert Shadows church for nearly fifteen years. When he had first seen the lad at the back of the church, he hadn't recalled seeing him here before. It could have been just another tourist passing through.

Father Leary straightened his white collar as he approached Kyan. "Can I help you, young man?" Kyan glanced down to the page that repeated words of the previous request. *Bring him.*

"Father," Kyan addressed as he turned toward the priest.

"Yes?" Kyan was unsure as to what to say; his mind swam for the only possible words that made sense to him. Words that were just as true as the scripture that had been presented to him by the water.

"I'm in trouble, Father."

"What kind of trouble? Who are you? I haven't seen you at any of my sermons before, have I?"

"No, Father," Kyan proceeded. "I just moved to Desert Shadows and—" Kyan paused. What was he suppose to say? He had gotten the priest before him as the water instructed and nothing was happening. Was something supposed to happen? What was he waiting for?

One with his flesh...what did that mean?

Kyan didn't understand what the watery apparition wanted him to do.

"What kind of trouble? Go on, young man," Father Leary stated as he looked down into the urn. The parchment in the holy water struck the priest as odd. He went to fish it out and Kyan immediately interjected.

"Wait, Father."

"What is this?" the priest questioned as he gestured to the drenched page.

"I don't have time to explain," Kyan said, turning his attention to the page for advice.

One word appeared and, although he had no clue as to what it meant, it was his only frantic hope.

Rosary.

"Father," Kyan quickly continued, "Do you have a rosary?"

"Well, yes but—"

"I need a rosary, Father."

"Well," the priest tried to rationalize as he scratched his balding head,

"Okay." Father Leary turned and strolled toward the altar.

Kyan knew that the priest would find a rosary in no time. After all, he had seen a few when he tore out the pages of the Bible. But what then? What was he to do?

Kyan watched as Father Leary pulled a rosary from behind the altar. His heart raced against his ribs. In anticipation or fear, Kyan knew not which. His eyes shot back to the page that was three-fourths of the way full. Kyan began shivering at the thought of how he was to communicate with this apparition once the page became congested with text. And the priest! If he told the priest, he would surely think him mad.

Strangle the priest, Kyan.

Kyan bolted into panic. Heart racing, body shaking in fear and, now, mind grasping at every possible resolution. Anything but murder! No, not that!

"Oh my God, no, I can't do that," Kyan pleaded as tears flooded his eyes. Kyan looked to the page again, rushing to see a different solution and racing to discover different words that didn't burst his body with icy shivers of a fear evolving.

Do it, Kyan. There is no more time. Believe in me, Kyan. You said you would help me and I can help you. I will give you the guidance you seek. Believe in me. It was his only hope. It was the only way.

Father Leary walked up to Kyan giving him the rosary. Kyan gleamed at the black and white beaded necklace, at the shimmering, silver crucifix and the noble man crucified upon it. Could *He* ever forgive Kyan for the ultimate sin he was about to perform?

"Now tell me why you have come here," Father Leary requested, awaiting an explanation that would reveal the young man's eccentric behavior.

Kyan closed his eyes and took in a deep breath, a breath of strength in desperate times. He took in a breath of calmness before the storm. And when that beast emerged, Kyan knew there was no turning back.

"I've come for Him," Kyan told Father Leary, pointing at Jesus Christ's crucified body on Man's cross.

The priest converted his position toward the large crucifix to which Kyan's finger directed. As he made that small pivot in his stance, which seemed to be but another never-ending minute in this present world of horror, Kyan took the only opportunity he knew he had and did as he had been directed.

He lunged forward, tightening the rosary with both hands as he wrapped it around Father Leary's white-collared neck.

The priest abruptly turned back toward Kyan, this strange man who had entered his church with the prayer to assassinate. Kicking his legs and wailing his arms about, the priest tumbled face forward to the floor of the church. Kyan watched his bulging eyes that probably condemned him before the priest met with the shiny, varnished wood.

Kyan pulled the rosary tighter as he watched the priest's energy diminish. His legs had stopped total movement and his arms seemed to be stretching in the direction of the altar as if the god he had worshipped and bid service to all these years could save him in this time of utter crisis. The priest's chest retired itself, for it knew that one more breath would be impossible. Kyan would not let go and had no intent of doing so until the man was at Heaven's gate. *It was probably a better life up there*, Kyan sarcastically thought.

Father Leary was *dead*. Kyan stood up and, once again, looked to his page of guidance, his list of deadly instructions. At this time, he was unable to differentiate between the real and the uncanny, but he continued to place his faith in this strange urn of water in which a full page breathed its last words.

Your cup hath runneth over with my essence, Kyan. Drown the priest with my Holy nature. Let me soak into his flesh as I have into this brittle paper.

We have time for one final miracle.

Kyan flipped the priest onto his back and began tearing and stripping away the black clothing. With absolute hope, he viciously pulled off Father Leary's collar and ripped open his shirt, revealing a dead, flat chest plagued with gray hairs. He savagely tore away the priest's pants. A naked body of unmoving porcelain flesh and holiness greeted Kyan. He knelt before the urn and grabbed the water-soaked page from within. Its wet weight made an echoing thud as it hit the floor beneath. Kyan cupped the holy water in his hands and splashed it onto Father Leary's corpse only to cup more water and do the same. The holy water ran about the priest's body exploring all the creases and curves. It became saturated into the decomposing chill of his flesh.

Kyan continued soaking down Father Leary's body with the holy water. He probed his index and middle finger into the priest's mouth and stretched it open as he took the last bit of the liquid substance, iciness filling his hands, and dumped it down into the priest's throat. Kyan rested on his knees above the holy man, waiting and pondering his next morbid action.

A squeaking of doors came from behind and he jumped to his feet in the realism of what he had done. Turning to the entrance of the church, he saw a frail, withering woman hobble in with the use of her wooden cane. He was motionless, speechless from anything he may tell the old woman.

One look was all it took before the aged woman shrieked in horror and exited the church in frenzy. As the door closed behind her, Kyan could still here her muffled screams of help.

"What have I done?" Kyan asked aloud, his voice echoing throughout the empty church.

A great gasp of air from Father Leary deadened the echo. His chest heaved deeply for another breath before choking up spurts of water and saliva. Father Marcus Leary opened his eyes and glanced up to Kyan.

Kyan stood frozen, peering with his mouth agape to the astonishment before him.

"It worked, Kyan," the priest commented. He stood his naked body to its feet.

"It worked?" Kyan repeated. "You mean?" A short pause and his concentration lapsed.

"You're the one who was writing on the pages? You're the holy water; the one who said would help me?"

"I said I would help you, Kyan. Sins as those that you have committed need absolution. Sometimes that absolution is only recognized by reflection. You need time to reflect on your sins, Kyan." Kyan didn't understand what it meant.

"What do you—?" An abrupt bolting of police officers rushing in rudely interrupted the conversation in the church.

"Father Leary?" One of the uniformed men asked, shocked from the priest's naked presence before him.

"Are you alright?" The priest made eye contact with Kyan, knowing what rush of adrenaline must be racing through his body. He then turned to the officer.

"Dale," the priest addressed the obese officer who had his hand on his gun.

"Thank God you're here. This young man tried killing me; he tried strangling me."

"No," Kyan interrupted. "No, that's not true. No," he whined, turning back to the priest. "You said you would help me," he began weeping. Father Leary knelt down and picked up the rosary at his feet.

"He used this, Dale." The police officer drew his gun.

"Don't make a move, son." Kyan wept. The reanimated priest had his undivided attention.

"You promised me—"

After being extradited from Desert Shadows, Kyan was placed in the Maricopa County Jail, awaiting his trial for the attempted murder of Father Marcus Leary.

Back in Phoenix, his mind spoke. *Back to the temptation of the city.* Then again, temptation was everywhere, even in a small town such as Desert Shadows.

Reflection for your sins, his mind recalled. Kyan attempted avoiding the inner voice. Instead, he was fully concentrating on what had happened, where he had gone wrong.

The holy water lived. Its deceptive scheme was, indeed, a course in temptation. The water lived in the human body of a priest and was now able to do as it pleased. Hell, it could take on the world and everybody would be oblivious as to the powerful knowledge and hideous trickery presented by a man in black who donned a gleaming white collar. None of the population would have a clue of the horrors residing in such flesh. Yes, it could take them over one by one, exacting its revenge against the sinners it envied and praying upon the saints of who had built so much rage within it. Liquid absorbs. It purifies. It hydrates. Its uses are endless.

Sitting in silence in his cell is what Kyan knew he would be doing for years to come. Sitting in stillness, a subtle stillness much like that of water. His cell would become his urn of confinement and his tears would become the soft, blue ripples.

Those days, days when the men in Kyan's life were a phase, him experimenting, they didn't compare to the incident that he faced at the unholy church in Desert Shadows.

No, not at all. That was the ultimate in experimentation.

Chalky White

Gregory L. Hall

"Please don't kiss me down there."

"Are you serious?" Jason rolled his eyes as if to offset his raging hormones. "Everybody dared me!"

"*Dared us*! But I'm asking you nicely. Kissing me down there…I just feel uncomfortable with it." Sandi lifted Jason's face up. She forced a nervous smile for her horny teenage partner and hoped he would understand.

"Why are you so freaked out about your basement?" Jason backed away and leaned against the wall.

"Seven minutes. That's all. We accepted the dare and we make-out for seven minutes in your basement. What's the big deal?" Sandi gazed down the steps into the darkness. A chill visibly shook her shoulders.

"It's stupid, okay. I don't even go down in the basement when my mom needs something from the freezer." the young girl slid away from the mouth of cellar. "I had a nightmare when I was little."

"Oh come on. That's not it at all. You just don't want to make-out with me because I'm not Dylan. If the dare was with him, you'd be down there in a second!"

"That's not true! It has nothing to do with Dylan!" Sandi's face turned red with falsehood. "And I am going to kiss you. Just not down in the basement." Sandi lurched forward and awkwardly put her open mouth on Jason's. Her tongue moved feverously to end further embarrassment. Whether it was to cover having to explain her childhood phobia or her not-so-secret crush on Dylan, she wasn't sure.

Jason was caught off guard but recovered quickly with true pubescent passion. His hand seemed to be attached to his ability to kiss and his fingers groped at Sandi's breast. Her first reaction was to stop him but having allowed nothing but roadblocks thus far she reluctantly surrendered this one notch up the sexual ladder.

"Wow! We didn't say anything about feeling her up, Jason! Way to go you two!" Sandi jumped back and automatically held Jason's advances by the wrist. They turned to find Dylan leering behind a smug grin. Jason awkwardly wiped his chin.

"Whoa, dude. Scared the hell out of us. What's up?"

"Nothing much. Just wanted to see if you guys were living up to your dare. Didn't know you were going to start before you even hit the basement!"

Dylan's laugh turned Sandi's stomach. She did the only thing she could think of to escape what was quickly becoming the worst moment of her life. Sandi grabbed Jason's arm and hit the stairs. She was halfway down before she realized the light switch was past her reach.

"Hey, Sandi! Anything over seven minutes, think of me!" Dylan cackled. Jason responded with his middle finger as he was dragged down the last of the wooden steps. But if Sandi noticed Jason defending her honor, it wasn't important to her anymore. She was in the basement.

Dylan slammed the door shut and the couple was smothered in darkness. Jason heard the softest sound. Almost like a child whimpering. He placed his hand on Sandi's back. It was like touching a statue. She didn't move a muscle.

"Are you okay?" Silence, except for the whimpering.

"Oh shit. Do you hear that? Is that you?" Jason stumbled to where he remembered the closest wall. His fingers slid along the drywall until he found a switch. Light burst from a single bulb in the ceiling and threw misshapen shadows across the cluttered room. And he saw Sandi frozen with fear with tears streaming down her face.

"Oh my God? Are you breathing? Take a deep breath. Please." Jason wrapped his arms around the petrified girl.

"It's okay. I'm here with you. There's nothing down here to be afraid of. See? I turned the light on."

"*Chalky White.*"

Jason thought he heard the whisper correctly but it didn't make sense.

"Sorry?"

"Chalky White," the girl repeated.

"You mean the monster everybody scares little kids with when they're being bad? 'Chalky White's gonna get you if you don't eat your vegetables!' That Chalky White? The made-up boogey man?" Sandi slowly turned her head and locked her eyes onto Jason's. She never blinked.

"Don't say that. He's real. I saw him. When I was a little girl." She pointed to a darkened corner by an old freezer.

"Over there."

"Okay, now you're freaking me out." A jolt of fear shot up Jason's spine.

"You're going to give *me* nightmares."

"You should have them. He kills whoever he wants and always gets away with it. Because no one believes he exists. But *I've* seen him. And *he's* seen me." Jason edged to the stairs.

"Okay, let's head back up with Dylan and Patricia and Cheryl, okay? We'll just tell them we already made-out. I'm sure Dylan told everyone I was feeling you up before the dare even started so they'll believe us." The young man dropped his head down and muttered in rare regret.

"And I'm sorry I did that. I mean, I wanted to and it just kind of happened. But I didn't mean to do it where some asshole like Dylan would see us."

Jason's honesty broke the thick tension and Sandi allowed a smile to color her face.

"It's okay. It wasn't like I let you reach under my shirt or anything…" There was a loud thump on the floor above them and Sandi slammed herself back against the wall. Jason stood stunned by Sandi's actions. Her eyes frantically scanned the ceiling and a second thump, even louder than the first, caused her to squeal. Sandi slid sideways like a crab deeper into the basement, her breathing speeding out of control.

"Those guys are just wrestling around upstairs." Jason offered. "If I know Dylan, his last dare was to have an orgy. What's wrong with you?"

Another thud and then a crash. Even Jason moved away from the stairs.

"It's him. *He's* here." Sandi gasped as she curled into a little ball.

"Who's here? What are you spazzing out for? Is it your Dad?" A scream cut through the house. *Dylan's.*

"Chalky White." Sandi confessed. "He's killing them."

"I don't understand..."

"I told you. He told me not to. I was so scared when we first came down here, I didn't think. And I told you."

"Told me what?" Jason quickly joined Sandi in the corner, never taking his eyes off the stairs.

"Chalky White is real." Sandi's voice dropped to cold monotone. "And now he's going to kill us all."

There was another scream and then the basement door flew open. Light poured down from the upper level. Sandi and Jason could hear a slathering noise masking the sound of sobbing.

"*Little girl, little girl. Who told my secret?*" The voice sounded like rocks grinding together. "*I'm going to count to one.*"

The sobbing suddenly ended. And a head bounced down the stairs. The basement door shut and within seconds, the screaming continued again above them. Jason tore his eyes away from the rounded object lying at the base of the stairs and stared at Sandi. She convulsed with panic, unable to speak.

"What the fuck was that? Oh my God? Is that what I think it was?" Sandi could not answer.

Jason scrambled on his hands and knees towards the head. He reached forward in disbelief but instinct jerked his arm back. He looked back to Sandi but her huge brown eyes flitted back and forth as if she had lost her mind. Jason snapped his attention back to the reality of the situation. This could not be happening. This was not real.

He turned the head over and came face to face with Dylan.

Air vacated Jason's lungs and he fell backwards. The basement door opened again and the teenager propelled himself out of the grasp of the light. Still he had to see, see what his brain warned him against viewing.

It stood at the top of the staircase. Its silhouette thin and angular. Its hands were grossly larger than the rest of its body and hung low past the knees. Two tiny black dots marked where its eyes should be. There was no nose to be found and its lips melded directly into jagged bone that formed its mouth. And its skin…its skin was a flaky alabaster.

Chalky White.

"*Little girl, little girl. Who told my secret?*" asked a voice from the coldest crypt. "*I'm going to count to two.*"

And another head bounced down the stairs.

Jason threw up on the concrete floor. A hand landed on his shoulder and he spun around swinging. Sandi pulled him deeper into the shadows as the door shut once again. This time the screaming above came as no shock to them. They were far past that now.

"Tell me…tell me what I saw?" Jason couldn't hold back his fear any longer and he sounded like the boy he was, not so removed from the days of grade school nightmares. "Is that really him?"

Sandi held Jason close and nodded.

"I don't understand…?"

"My grandmother." Sandi let those words hang for awhile before she could continue.

"My grandmother was watching me for the weekend. I was eight. I came to the basement to get a game to play together. And I saw him, in that corner. I didn't move. And neither did he. Then he put his finger to his lips and shook his head no. And he disappeared."

Sandi swallowed hard and squeezed Jason's hand until her nails dug into his flesh.

"I didn't know what to do. I ran upstairs as fast as I could and told my grandmother. I thought she would laugh at me or say I was a baby but she didn't say anything at first. She just got very quiet. Then she said, 'I wish you hadn't told me that, child.' And she walked away. That night she told me to stay locked in my room. She wouldn't let me sleep with her. And she made me promise I wouldn't come out for anything. Not until my parents got home."

Sandi winced as she heard Cheryl cry out from above them.

"I heard my grandmother scream, like them. I didn't listen to the rules and ran out of my room. He was standing in the shadows at the end of the hall. He was holding my grandmother like a rag doll. And he said, '*First one keeps my secret. Or all those around her die.*' Then he took my grandmother away." Jason waited for a beat and then shook Sandi.

"What secret?"

"I told you already. I let you know Chalky White is *real*."

The basement door whipped open so hard Sandi and Jason thought it was ripped from the hinges. The yellow glow from the upper floor taunted them.

"*Sweet meat, sweat meat. I'm all out of bodies to eat.*"

This time the entire corpse ricocheted down the stairwell. Cheryl landed at the bottom like a half filled sack of blood soaked dung.

"*I've counted to three. There are no more. You better pray I don't count to four.*"

There was a long pause. Sandi and Jason could see the creature's shadow stretch down the wall. They could hear its raspy breathing. And as it shut the door again, they caught its final question in a whisper that cut through the stagnant air.

"*Little girl, little girl. Who told my secret?*"

Then there was nothing. Jason grabbed Sandi, his face red with adrenalin. He pulled the girl to her feet and forced her to look into his eyes.

"You can stop this. Tell him it was you who told the secret…"

"He already knows that! Or else he wouldn't be here!" Sandi snapped back.

"Then tell everyone his secret. Let everyone know he's real. Shout it out from the street! Let's wake the whole damn neighborhood up! Get the cops here! Keep screaming and force that bastard out into the open! He can't kill everyone if everyone knows!"

"Yes, Jason. Yes, he can. Chalky White has been killing people since forever. And he always gets away with it."

"It doesn't make any sense! Why would he want his existence to be kept a secret?" Jason struggled to swim through the madness.

"What power does he get if only one person knows? Isn't it like Freddy Krueger or something? The more people who believe the nightmare is real, the more powerful he is, right? Why are you the only person?"

"Do you think I'm the first to ever see him? I think he feeds on the constant fear. A single person tortured with a secret like that is a hundred times more powerful than an entire city knowing he's not just a fairy tale." Sandi held back the tears.

"I know there have been others. My grandmother saw him. That's why she believed me. And that's how she knew she was going to die." Jason kicked the boxes at his feet.

"Well, we still have one advantage. He doesn't know I'm down here with you. He said he counted to three and there are no more. So I can escape and get help! Climb out one of these windows. I can bring the police back…"

The teenager's words drifted off as he caught the expression on Sandi's face. Her jaw went slack. Her eyes glazed over. Her lips trembled as she tried to form words.

"I am so sorry, Jason." She stared over his shoulder.

Jason turned around. An angular figure rose before him. Huge misshapen hands clamped around the boy's rib cage. Sharp toes stomped into his pelvis. With a violent twist and yank, Jason was torn in two.

"*Still counting.*" It threw both pieces of Jason to the concrete. "*Three and a half…*"

The hell-ghoul slowly leaned down into Sandi's face. Its hot breath smelled of human waste and rotted poultry. Its tiny black orbs caught the light like sharks eyes. Sandi saw hunks of flesh and fat still wedged into its back teeth.

"*Now little girl, little girl. Who told my secret?*" A disgusting chuckle came up from Chalky White's stomach.

"*Was it you?*"

Sandi's heart locked and she felt the urine run down her leg. Her body shook. She tried to back away but her motor skills were gone, leaving her with only one option. She nodded yes.

Chalky White straightened hiss back and towered over her like a grotesque barren tree. His limbs turned as if he was trying to tread water in the coldness that surrounded him. He raised one hand and let the claws glide down the pretty girl's face. Then he extended one long finger before her. And he waved it back and forth as he silently shook his head *no*. He disappeared into the shadows and Sandi collapsed to the floor.

Colors of blue and red flashed across the front yard. Bright white lights left no area in darkness as police searched the entire neighborhood. Sandi sat in a state of shock in the back of an ambulance. Only her head shaking back and forth let officials know there was still someone inside.

"Poor girl was the only survivor," the officer filled in those just arriving at the scene. "Hid in the basement the whole time. Was able to get her boyfriend's cell phone to call 911. He was lying next to her torn in half."

"She give any clues to who did this? I mean was it a gang or some maniac or what?"

"She won't say anything to help us. Just the word '*no*' over and over again." The officer looked over to the ambulance as the crowds grew larger.

"Really not much we can do for her. Not a scratch physically. So we just left her with the paramedics for now. Okay, we have people both inside the house and in the woods behind it. Cars are patrolling the surrounding streets…"

Sandi could hear the officers discussing plans of action that were worthless. No one would ever know what happened on the night she had four friends from high school come over to party while her parents were away.

"Miss? Did a bunch of people really die in there?" Sandi looked down to see an innocent little boy. His mom was too busy trying to grab the latest news from the rest of the gossip mongers to notice he had wandered over.

"That must have been pretty scary, Miss. I know I would be very scared. Because I know who did this." Sandi's full attention snapped to the little boy.

"Chalky White. He did it. I know. Because I've seen him before. He's real. You can think I'm lying, but I've seen him." Sandi felt the air around her grow cold.

"I wish you hadn't told me that." she whispered.

There was a moment of absolute stillness. Then she felt the thick breath on the back of her neck. And he chuckled.

"Four…"

Visionary of the Flesh

Jason L. Keene

Late last night, it came upon a query that my gathering of friends brought up the notion of "The Supernatural" - ghosts and vampires, the dead clawing from their graves, witchcraft and sorcery, evils beyond the eye and mind. Perhaps a topic best left well alone.

We had all gathered together for an exquisite dinner before retiring to the study where drinks flowed from hands to lips and the evening sun gave way to the early winter darkness. The glow of the fireplace was right, the mood setting itself as the conversation slowly twisted to things of a darker nature.

To each their own of course, on their stance of the topic at hand. I have always believed. I found it quite enthralling that more than one of the group had an experience to share. Either a personal account, or a retelling of what had happened to a loved one or a 'friend of a friend' (you know the sort, of course).

I sat gingerly partaking of my drink amongst them as the topic passed, in clock-wise fashion, through the group. With careful contemplation, I braced myself for my turn. Admittedly, the alcohol coursing through my veins only served to further my eagerness to tell my part in our little ring of paranormal banter, although now, in retrospect, perhaps I should have kept a quiet stance and ended the night before it had begun.

"And what of you, Miles?" my dear friend Lucian asked from the loveseat to my right, his arm entwining a bubbling - yet adorable - young redheaded lady.

"What have you to add?"

"Much, I'm afraid."

He had laughed off his round, snubbing the entire matter as nonsense and whimsy. In his own words,

ATRUM TEMPESTAS 'TALES FROM THE DARKNESS'

"There is nothing beyond death than the stillness of eternity, and no man lays foot upon the ground after he has been put beneath it."

If it had been any other of the group besides Lucian, I almost certainly would have smiled and refused a story of my own. I would have, most likely, thumbed my nose as my turn came to and called the evening as it stood, finishing with the night on the note that brought them all here to my lair in the first place. But for Lucian--dear Lucian--there could be no story more fitting.

"Do tell," he said, swirling his snifter with a gleam in his eye. Being the gentlemen that I am, I had no choice but to tell them. Watching them all squirm as I spoke gave me a thrill, I must admit--but watching the reaction of bold and brash Lucian was what made the outcome so perfect.

"During travels of my youth, I had visited many places in the world. I studied and spread *His good word* as a missionary, and as a result found myself in dark corners typically unseen by the eastern eye. My last excursion had been to the area once labeled as ancient Mesopotamia. A small handful of missionaries, including myself, had been sent to bring the good word to the heathens along the length of the Euphrates and Tigris rivers of Iraq.

One must remember that, in the years and time of my youth, we worked with nothing to bring about something. We were given a very small monetary fund and established a camp consisting of a small circle of pitched tents among the lush plains of the flatland between the rivers. Exhausted from the work day, we dragged ourselves into the makeshift homes and crawled into our cots, ready for a long and much-deserved night's rest. Our slumber would be short that night.

Sounds began to flood the night's silence along the plains as we lay resting. I call them by such an ambiguous term because we could not decipher their exact nature. Regardless, they awoke us with a startle. Low, rhythmic drums and chants, so full and widespread that they merged into one continuous hum. The night insects ceased their songs, the wills of the area fowl settled tight-lipped, and nothing floated in the air but the droning cacophony.

We fought for rest that night, none brave enough to leave the safety of the tents or each other and check the matter for himself.

The next day proved to be somewhat fruitful. We had garnered a small gathering of people as we spoke with renewed ambition, the hot Iraqi sun slowly draining what small amount of energy we'd gathered with the sparse moments of sleep from the night before. They listened in awe as we spoke of Him and his teachings, of what was and what was yet to come. Through the entirety of the day, we spoke to our individual groups (those of us who knew the native language fluently used it wisely, and the lesser of us fighting for words the people could understand used it sparingly as to not deter them from His teachings). After the sun had began to set on the horizon in the distance, we gathered our supplies and prepared to settle into our huts. It was at this time that a small, dark skinned lad approached me.

Although he spoke in very fluent English compared to the majority of those on-hand, he spoke not his name. His eyes were heavy, his face hardened. As he spoke, he kept a sharp vigil upon the dissipating crowd behind him as if he were not to be seen by any of them conferring in my presence."

"I must speak quickly and be gone," he said, leaning in close to me as his voice fell to a whisper. "You must leave from here. This place holds nothing for you beyond danger."

"Young sir," I responded. "I fear nothing of this world, for I know that the Lord, my God, walks beside me with every step I take. He will protect me, for what we bring to you and your people is good in His eyes."

"I'm afraid your 'God' does not live here, sir."

"And with that, he was off. Shooting into the crowd, he dispersed with the rest as quickly as he had stepped forward. I will admit, such a statement from a youth had startled me. It was not so much in the boy's words, themselves, as it was in his tone; a hushed, hurried tone filled with the knowledge of some unseen dread, as if he were warning me in spite of his fear of being seen or overheard in doing so. I turned back to my work, gathering materials and setting them inside, his words still swirling about my head."

"And *on* with it, man," Lucian blurted with a slur on his lips, his redheaded companion laughing hysterically while the drinks in their hands overtook their heads.

"Would you rather wake me when the terror begins?" Lucian dropped his head to the side, feigning sleep, a broad smile filling his expression.

Fool.

"Of course," I remarked, walking over to the fireplace and probing the cinders with the stoking iron. "All in due time, my friend."

With the group calming down from Lucian's quip at my expense, I kneeled down by the renewed flames and watched them breathe and grow. I peered unto the rhythmic dance of the licking orange and bright yellow, content to continued my story.

"And where was I? Of course…the boy's warning. I told none of my fellow missionaries of the boy's words with me earlier as we fell upon our cots that evening. Admittedly, the events of the night before paired with this young fellow's claims made me weary of the area, although I believed fully in my own words. The Lord walked by my side, indeed, and that night a greatness shone upon me.

We had no method of registering the time in our tents, but it was deep into the hours beyond midnight that I assume the noises from the night before thrummed through the dark stillness of the tent. Although there was the faint sounds of heavy sleep-breathing and the occasional nasal snores emitting from my fellow men, I am almost positive that a few of the others had been awake, or simply unable to sleep, and laid stone-cold and terrified. So awful was the slow rising in tempo and volume swell to the beat and chants that it threatened to drive me mad. There was no rest, no chance at slumber with the sound becoming a driving force. And then, the words began to take shape to me--the chants deciphering themselves and I understood them, if not through ear then in my inner mind.

'Come, Oh Sah-Rah. Ye, beast of the void. Ye, protector and devourer. The flesh calls to you. Sah-Rah. Sah-Rah. The flesh awaits.'

I turned onto my stomach and stared into the pitch-black of the tent, hoping to see or hear the others in stirred movement--praying that somebody other than I had heard this new arc on the mysterious chanting. Nothing. No shuffling of sheets or men whispering to their neighbors, nothing but the drums and chants, still clearly calling - and calling with fervor solely to me.

It would be foolish to sit here now and imagine why I stood from my cot and walked through the flap into the night air, or attempt to explain what caused me to walk through the darkness in my bare feet and sleeping clothes. I called out to God on several occasions (vocally or mentally, I cannot recall), and each time I remember stepping more feverishly towards my unknown (at that point) goal.

I had wandered for miles, lost and yet destined by some untouchable compass. At last, my feet ceased their forward motion through the long-forgotten sands and stood together. Dropping to my knees, I panted through the exhaustion and fatigue within my body. A valley stood before me, lush with large, full trees and an oasis that swelled with the scent of various flowers drifting in the wind. Surely, this was the land of our God.

A large bonfire stood by the lake of water down below, smoke billowing upwards and lighting the area around it like a miniature sun. The chant that had stayed heavy in the air during my trek through the midnight sands emanated from below, its volume enveloping the sky like a thick fog, heavy and steady in its formation.

I descended the slope of sand into the heart of the valley and was amazed at the feelings that had overwhelmed me as I entered the oasis. A sense of inner-peace fueled my steps as I picked up momentum, a throttled run finally bringing me within yards of the fire. It stood high and powerful, surrounded in a circular fashion by the chanters. Their voices stayed unified as the drummers on the outskirts of the circle pounded with synchronized, passionate fists.

As I stood there, entranced at the sight, I found myself unable to move. The fire was so perfect, the chanting so powerful that I rooted to my spot. Gazing into the flaming mass, I noticed the stacked piled of charred shapes amongst the logs…bones. Human skulls, rib cages and limbs entwined with kindling. The sight both sickened and gripped me further. And then, with a crescendo of the drums, both chanter and drummer stopped.

From either side of me, forms marched to the center of the circle dressed in flowing, draped black robes. They marched in fours, two at either end of a long, bending shaft of wood bearing weight upon their shoulders. In the center of each pole was strapped the naked body of a man tied at his feet, wrists, and throat by thick rope. I watched in horror as each passed by me, easily within arms' reach--yet I did nothing. Every fiber of my being screamed with release to do something, to aid the prisoners, but my body refused to comply.

Over a dozen poles were marched past me before my eyes met the horrified gaze of one of the dangling, naked captives--the eyes that belonged to one of my fellow missionaries. My head floated in a dizzy sway, my eyes darting back and forth along the inside edge of the chanters' circle where every last one of my fellow missionaries swayed naked and sobbing.

The chanters resumed in a low tone, the drums pulsing slowly as the first pole was heaved into the raging flames. His screams were agonizing and forced my teeth to gnash together. And then another was cast into the fire…and another…and another, one by one along the outside edge, bodies singed and burned, howls of pain and prayers of mercy singing out into the night. The scent of seared flesh wafted along the breeze, a stark contrast to the aroma of wildflowers from before. And still I stood, helpless and horrified.

The stacked logs of the fire began to shuffle and move, separating and displacing. In awe, I watched as the screaming flesh began to shift and mottle together within the flames. Flesh with others' flesh, bone with others' bone, a mass began to rise through the smoke above the fire.

The intensity of the chant at that point - how maddening! - focused on but one word."

'Sah-Rah! Sah-Rah! Sah-Rah!'

A beast unlike anything conjured in the nightmares of the mad stepped from the flames and ashes, expelling smoke and embers through a gaping hole in its chest. Its skin was formed by the blackened and charred remnants of those cast into the flame moments before, their faces still locked in agonizing poses along its body.

Bones of various body parts pierced through the beast's mass--ribs forming a curved dorsal line of spikes; femurs and hands splayed through its flesh haphazardly, flexing and gripping outwards at all angles. It stood on misshapen legs, a thick torso above them harboring a gaping maul which continuously opened and closed to reveal the circular lining of jagged teeth made of splintered and fractured bones.

Two arms stretched out towards the sky, the charred flesh dripping in flaming patches to the ground below. There was no determinable head or facial features of the beast itself, only the hundreds of rolling white eyes and groaning opened mouths of those men who had formed it stretched about its body.

It stepped towards me, looming above me some twenty feet into the sky. It spoke to me through no mouth, no vocal cords vibrating its words, but rather in my head. I dropped to my knees with haste and I prayed. I prayed for all I was worth."

I stopped my story at this point. Stoking the fire with the prod once more, I slowly rose up and turned to the group. I was quite content with the look on their faces. And of Lucian, his expression was priceless. One that I will savor for many, many years to come.

"And *then*?!" he inquired, his body leaned forward, threatening to leap from the seat in anticipation.

I no longer felt the need to string them along with anymore details. It is, as they say, what it is.

I am still a missionary in the truest sense of the word, although I had been lost for oh so long before that night. For I found God that night, indeed, and he spoke to me and I carry him on to this day so many miles away from those long-forgotten lands of the ancients.

'Sah-Rah of the flesh! Sah-Rah, the devourer. Sah-Rah, He of the Void!'

The followers left quite a mess in my study when they stormed through the doors upon this group; I dare say that the younger of the believers have come to enjoy the capture more than the conjuring.

The fire pits behind the mansion still fair well after all of these years and I believe we have enough to fully solidify great 'Sah-Rah' with just a few more. The invitations for what I hope will be the last gathering have been sent out for this upcoming weekend's gathering, this group of colleagues even more hardened and faithless than the last.

The Train

Cassandra Lee

Marcus Biaggio stood on the underground subway platform, watching mesmerized as the trains roared past this December night.

He'd been waiting for the next one home for only a short while, but the day had been a shitter and he was more than a little beat. All he wanted was to go back to his apartment, throw up his feet, and pop the top off a cold one.

Fucking work.

His fingers closed tightly around the briefcase handle, his knuckles blanching as a familiar anger returned. It had been Sunday night and he'd been putting the finishing touches on graphs, calculating expenditures for the new plant his plastic's company was building. And then - just as his index finger hit *SAVE* - it happened. The whole hard drive crashed. He'd nearly tossed the computer off the third story balcony.

After much - "*You fucking piece of shit! Cock sucking metal piece of crap!*" - he'd finally admitted defeat and plopped into his well-worn recliner to decide what to do next. He would apologize and redo the figures on Monday.

There wasn't much else he could do.

And so, he'd forked out fifteen hundred bucks (that he sure as hell didn't have) retrieving the information from his hard drive and bought a brand new computer. It had taken him a whole day of running around town and organizing the project files, but did anyone give a shit?

No! And why?

They'd scrapped the whole damned project today after deciding to upgrade and renovate the old plant. Turns out they could do it cheaper with less interruption to production.

What a fucking waste of time!

Marcus heaved a sigh and then took a long look down the tunnel. An empty black void stared back at him. Why was it whenever he had a bad day, the trains seemed interminably slow.

Christ, I hope they're not having another glitch with the electrical system. He'd been caught on one midway home the other day for almost half an hour while they attempted to get it back up and running. Not that it mattered to Toronto Transit that they'd been jammed in like sheep waiting for the slaughter. *Nooo...* They got a condescending,

"Sorry folks. Seems we had another train stall out on the tracks just up ahead, so we have to stay put for a bit."

Sure... Sorry. He'd been jammed in beside some fat guy who smelled like the last time he'd bathed was the winter past and the woman beside him had obviously decided that 'more' was better than 'less', as the reek of dollar store perfume floated above her head like a thick smog. The two odors mating, it was all he could do not to throw up all over the ignorant clods.

Dreading another hellish ride home, he thought drearily to himself, *that's all I need after a day like this.*

Marcus shuffled back and forth, growing increasingly impatient as the crowd of people around him began to stew aggressively as well. He could hear the mumblings of one young teen beside him dressed in black leather Doc's, a white t-shirt instructing him to *Have A Fucked Up Day* and a faded leather jacket emblazoned with a back patch that read *Pistols Forever*. A stereotype that resembled himself not so long ago, or at least, it *seemed* not so long ago.

"Damned train. I wish my mum would have bought me that car like she promised. I could have been banging Donna already."

His friend, dressed in almost identical attire, laughed, punching his peer in the arm.

Non-conformist youth, my ass, Marcus smirked to himself. *Mummy should'a bought me a car... Wah, wah*! Fucking kid didn't know what it was really like out here yet. Ten years from now, he'll change his tune. When he's holding down a shitty job just so he can pay the bills and feed the screaming brat that Donna spit out due to their all too frequent 'banging'. Yeah, those Doc's and leather will be replaced by a briefcase and choking tie. *Enjoy it now kid; 'cause you're stress free life is gonna be over very soon.*

He'd learned that the hard way. Now, here he stood in his worn one-too-many times black suit and pin-striped tie, black polished shoes (designer knockoffs purchased at a warehouse shoe store) and a white collared shirt. The constricting costume told his story better than he could ever hope to. He'd had dreams once as well. Banging every chick he could lay his hands on, playing in a rock n' roll band, sleeping all day and playing all night.

Dreams. Lots of them. And then, he'd met Cheryl.

One too many times between the sheets and she'd wound up pregnant. Thinking they were in love, they got married, had Justin and were relatively happy.

For the first two years, anyways.

After landing his job at the plastic's company and an endless stream of overtime, he'd found her in bed one night - *not alone* - but with their next door neighbor. It had crushed him at first, but he soon came to realize it would have eventually ended anyways. The sex had been great, but it was the only thing in their short marriage that really was. He didn't really love her and she felt the same. It was just too bad that Justin had to suffer as well.

Cheryl moved home to Nova Scotia and though he was one of the few non-deadbeat dads out there - sending her child support every month - he hadn't seen his son in almost two years. Between the payments and just trying to get by, he couldn't afford to visit or bring his son here. It hurt, but Cheryl was a good mother and he knew it was for the best.

Marcus was restless now. Memories stirred bitterness and it only served to make this day even shittier. He thrust a hand into his pocket, fished out a packet of spearmint gum, unfolded a stick and jammed it in his mouth. He hated gum, but figured the spaghetti and garlic bread he had for lunch might not be quite as offensive with a chew or two. *And for this I'll probably get wedged in between a baby stroller and a talker.*

He could hear the sounds of the train now approaching and he spat the gum back in the wrapper and stuffed it in his pocket. Hoisting his laptop, he stood next to the long yellow line drawn for their safety and waited.

The train came rushing from the tunnel, the wind from the incoming locomotive pressing into him. A person brushed past him and for a split instant, Marcus was certain he was going over the edge. His heart leaped as he jumped backwards. His throat constricted with the sudden terrifying notion, that he was about to be splattered all over the front of the incoming Bloor train.

Holy shit!

Marcus was panting, his chest thumping wildly with the beat of panic. He shivered from the base of his neck all the way down to his tail bone, shrinking under the weight of imagined death.

Marcus took a deep breath. *Okay, get it together. You're fine, you big baby.* The train rolled to a stop beside him as the heady sensation of doom slowly dissipated from his interior. The gray doors slid open and a tide of people rushed by him, pressing forward for that all important empty seat.

Hesitantly, he followed them. Drawing his laptop into his body, he squeezed past a young blonde girl listening to an MP3 player. Her head bopping to the music, she was impervious to his thoughtful, *"Excuse me."*

Marcus grunted as the two teens who'd been outside, swung from one of the overhead hand grips and jostled him in their attempt to grab a bench seat directly to his left. They landed ungainly, laughing at their disobedience to the trains posted rules emblazoned on a strip of plastic advertising overhead: *PLEASE RESPECT OTHERS.*

He shook his head, annoyed, and pushed through the crowd. Finding a spot near one of the windows, he leaned awkwardly back against the wall.

Marcus took a deep breath again. Still unsettled by the previous incident, he attempted getting comfortable for the trip back home to his one bedroom apartment off Dundas. As the train lurched forwards, he steadied himself and settled in for the cramped journey.

The young girl was leaning against one of the silver poles and Marcus caught her taking sideways glances at the youth beside him.

She smiled, slightly, lowered her lashes and looked back up again. *Subtle,* he rolled his eyes. *Sorry pet but he's already banging someone.* However, the kid looked like the sort that probably wouldn't give a second thought to trying out another piece of action should it present itself. *Teenagers were a fickle sort.*

The train pulled to a stop and more passengers tumbled into the jammed car. He did his best to make himself as small as possible, but it didn't matter as a burly guy sidled up beside him. The man's elbow jammed him in the ribs as the subway started up again and Marcus grimaced, shifting his body to the left as much as possible, while attempting not to topple over the edge of the seat directly beside him.

'Mr. Brute' turned and nodded at him, issuing some indescribable grunt of apology for the poke in the side and Marcus returned a half smile.

Idiot. Whole fucking train and you just had to pick me as your traveling companion.

The subway whistled as it passed through the underground tunnels. As they rounded a corner, the lights suddenly flickered off and on through the bright interior. Everyone, including Marcus, looked up.

Oh shit, not again! The train's brakes squealed and everyone was forced backwards under the pressure. Marcus lurched into the large guy and apologized under his breath as it rolled to a stop, pitching forwards with its final halting *screech.*

The train shuddered, plastered dead in the middle of the black tunnel. Marcus sighed, the rest of the crowd beginning a raucous complaint. Closing his eyes, he prayed to every demi-god they wouldn't be here long. *He just wanted to get home.* The announcement came, crackling over the loudspeakers.

"Seem to be having trouble with the power all. I'll let you know as soon as we have it fixed." Simultaneously, the crowd groaned aloud.

"*Just fuckin' great.*" Marcus cursed softly. The large guy beside him was grumbling something about kicking someone's ass. He assumed the brute was referring to Toronto Transit.

The train's emergency lights kicked in, giving them some small illumination. In their wake, Marcus noticed the girl had moved closer to his location. Standing directly in front of the two teens, she was still listening to her MP3, nonchalantly smiling at Pistol who'd finally taken notice of her and was giving her the once over. He was smiling back at her now and Marcus could almost read his thoughts, *Screw Donna, I want me some of that*! By the way the girl was flaunting her ass in those tight jeans; he'd probably get his wish.

The speakers crackled alive.

"Looks like we're going to be here awhile folks. Sorry for the inconvenience. I'll keep you updated on the progress." Immediately, the entire cars mood turned ugly. Voices grew louder with complaints, *"Figures...Assholes at Transit...This is what my money pays for? Morons...!"* A cross section of curses all aimed at the unknown transit worker on the loudspeaker.

Marcus sighed audibly, running a hand through his thick black mane. *Shit, I gotta get a haircut this weekend.* He was Italian and the mass of hair he'd been blessed with grew annoyingly curly when it got too long. He hated that.

The laptop was getting heavy in his hand and ungainly, he slid it between himself and the big guy, pushing it behind his legs with his knockoff shoe. That's when he heard a *THUMP* behind him. He frowned.

What's that?

Marcus peered outside the window, craning over the two teens heads, into the tunnel's deep well. He couldn't see a thing, but it *definitely* had come from outside. *Maybe it was the conductor checking on something or other*, he compiled.

He settled back against the wall again. *Whatever he's doing, I wish he'd hurry.* He was beginning to lose all sensation in his legs from standing like a pillar in the confined space. He jammed his hand into his pocket, rummaging for another stick of gum and was distracted by a metallic scrape that came directly from over his head.

Okay... what the hell was that?

He forgot about the gum and quickly peered outside again; this time he was joined by the youth beside him. Pistol asked,

"Did you hear that too?" Marcus nodded absently,

"I thought maybe it was the conductor but I don't see him out there." The leather clad teen pressed his face up against the glass, looking down the length of the train.

"Ain't nothin' there," Pistol mumbled. "Would he have gone to check on something?"

"I don't think so. If the train started moving all of a sudden, he'd be up shits creek without a paddle. Usually control fixes this stuff or sends the tech guys out to take care of it."

"Well maybe it's the tech guys."

"Might be, but usually those guys do a sweep around the train and I haven't seen one person, save for that noise." The girl pulled off her headphones, eying the trio fixated on the pane of glass.

"Whatcha lookin' at? Are they fixin' it?" She leaned across Pistol; an obvious attempt to thrust her cleavage into his face but it wasn't going to work to her advantage this time. Pistol had forgotten all about sex and was now more concerned about the noise.

"Hey mister? There ain't animals or some such shit down here is there?" the youth asked nervously. His friend rolled his eyes, hearing the candid frightened lilt in his peer's question. Pistol wasn't the kind to show his insecurities - he was a bona fide *tough guy*.

Marcus chuckled under his breath. The smart-ass youth was finally beginning to sound like who he really was - *just a kid*. He obliged the teen's true age and offered some reassurance.

"Well, they do routine maintenance on these tunnels all the time. Nothing but mice or rats and that's about it. We'll be moving pretty soon. Don't worry about it." Pistol nodded, a small bend of gratitude creasing his lips.

"Okay, probably nothing. You're right."

Marcus grinned in return and bent forwards, taking one last look out the shadowed window. He was abruptly knocked forwards as the train tilted sideways. Stars burst in his vision as his skull hit the window - *hard*.

Pistol now had the teasing girl sprawled in his lap, the two a jumble of arms and legs. The other teen had hit the back of his head against the window and was glassy eyed, stunned from the blow.

Marcus righted himself. Groaning, he put his hand to his forehead and pulled it back. Blood etched his palm, running freely from a small gash above his eye.

"Fuck!" he chopped loudly.

Around him, others were also assorting themselves. A few children were crying, a fat sweaty woman was swearing loudly as she tucked the folds of her skirt around her oversized ass, while the rest peered out the windows around them.

The burly guy was sitting heavily on the ground. He'd been knocked to the floor and was just about to get up when the train jarred in the opposite direction.

Marcus swiped at the hand grips above him, snagging one in a death grip, he held on for dear life. People were screaming now and Pistol was staring up at him, the young girl in his lap clutching him like a sold-out concert ticket. Pistol, unlike the bellowing masses, was deathly quiet. His face frozen in glassy fear.

Marcus looked down at the kid. "It's okay. Hey kid! It's gonna be alright." Pistol stared straight ahead - transfixed. *What the fuck is up with him?* Marcus leaned over, snapping his fingers in Pistol's zombie like expression.

"Kid! Snap out of it! We'll get out of here and everything'll be okay."

The youth's mouth opened as if he were about to comment, but nothing came out. His jaw hung like a wet knit sweater as he slowly lifted his hand, pointing across the aisle to the opposite window.

Marcus turned towards the indication and immediately felt like he'd thrown himself into a vat of dry ice. A cold tide passed through his body as he saw what Pistol was pointing at outside in the pitch black tunnel.

A nightmare with large scarlet eyes peered at him through the window. Hands as large as his newly purchased laptop pressed against the dusty glass, topped with talons that protruded from two crooked fingers covered in matted black fur. A carpet of ebony ran the length of the things massive elongated arms.

Two boiling lava pupils blinked and its mouth gaped. Razor sharp rows of teeth smiled grotesquely at Marcus through a river of dripping clear slime. Pressing its pug black nose up against the window; the things daggered claws screeched like nails on a chalkboard down the train's glass window.

Every little hair on the back of Marcus's neck stood straight up and he trembled, mildly at first, turning into a wave of uncontrollable shaking.

"Oh fuck..." his voice wavered in fear. Every nerve in his body twitched while his overloaded brain toyed with the idea of passing out. Marcus battered it to stay conscious.

Lucidity, finally returning, he swung around, screaming at the comatose Pistol, "KID! GET UP!"

Pistol gawked up at him, his eyes confused, full of childlike terror at the monster waiting just outside.

"I... I... *can't move,*" he shuddered. The once cocky young man was riveted to the spot, his body driven like a bolt to the hard seat.

Marcus snatched up the kid's hand as others in the train began screaming. More of the creatures were closing in on the subway cars, their surrealistic faces, snapping at the rows of transit windows. Marcus yanked on Pistols arm, ordering the petrified youth,

"*GET THE FUCK UP, KID!*" Pistol came off the seat and the girl plopped to the floor, sobbing uncontrollably. The other teenage boy didn't move a muscle, sitting quietly in a terror induced state. The train began rocking back and forth as the creatures pressed forwards from all sides, their talons tapping insanely against the metal siding.

Marcus heard the beasts speaking. At least, he thought it was speech. It sounded more like squirrels. A massive forest of thousands of chattering squirrels.

But these were no cute fucking animals!

The train moaned under the beasts combined efforts and then, the first window broke and they were inside.

The first creature scrambled over the sides of shattered glass, swiping razor talons across the face of a young brunette female trying desperately to catapult herself away from the looming horror. Her face parted into two surgical neat halves. Teetering sideways, she collapsed with a *thud* to the aisle. Lips peeled back from shining teeth as her mouth gaped in a blood soaked yawn. The beast had carved her once pretty face diagonally and now she looked more like a blood soaked Pez dispenser - her lolling tongue - the candy treat.

People scrambled for escape. A mass panic of arms and legs stampeding for the car's sliding doors. More of the atrocities poured through the windows. Sounds of glass imploding broke the mobs din, while all down the trains line, creatures stormed through the passages in a blood drenched killing wave.

Marcus, still yanking on the boy's arm, spun to see the glass window disintegrate into pills of crystal behind him. The hellish nightmare braced itself on the frame, clambering over the metal trim. It stood erect, piercing his own gaping eyes with a smoldering gaze of evil conjecture. Unable to move a muscle as death's handyman appeared all too solidly real before him, Marcus's body ached with the urge to run but his brain wasn't functioning, too rapt with the creature's presence to be able to obey.

Its eight foot body was covered with thatches of coarse black fur. Woven through the thick tapestry, taut bright-red skin pulsed with black veins. The creature's arms extended towards the floor. Hellish fingers flexed as the thick rippling muscles of its haunched legs twitched.

And then, it blinked. A thin veil covered its pupils in a translucent orange haze, finally rising to stare directly at the shivering dark-haired man.

Marcus couldn't speak; his mouth popped open and closed like a fish gasping for air on a lakeside dock. His hand, still in the youths clutches, jerked. Pistol had suddenly come to his senses and pulled away from the stranger holding him tightly. He stumbled sideways in a bid for escape.

The creature's mouth cracked open and a bright red tongue snaked over the dagger-like teeth, seemingly amused at the boy's futile attempt. Thrusting its powerful arm sideways, it latched onto the teens shoulder, dragging him backwards in a headlock. The youth shrieked with a blood curdling bellow of pain. Without so much as a grunt, the creature's jaws clamped onto the side of Pistol's head.

Glistening fangs ripped a flap of cherry glazed skin and hair away from the struggling teen's skull, swallowing the human morsel with a single gulp. The once punker, slumped dead in the creature's grip.

Marcus gagged, his stomach churning, hysterical panic settling in as all around him others were suffering the same fate.

The burly guy was at the moment, being eaten alive by two of the monsters. His entrails tossed around the blood soaked train like gore spattered ribbons. They ripped his intestines into shreds, while one sucked the corded organ into its mouth like a piece of marinara laden spaghetti.

Marcus lost control of his extremities. Falling backwards, he crumpled into the train's bench seat. The creature took a step forwards, swatting the shock stricken girl out of its way like a pesky fly. The tender flesh of her throat snagged on one of its talons, and as she flew across the train's aisle, the skin separated in a torrent of blood. She plummeted to the floor - dead on impact.

Pistol's friend had been yanked into the fray with the burly man. He never did come out of his confused state and it was probably for the best. The creatures were slowly dining on him, bit by bit, tugging small chunks of waggling flesh from his limbs. He bobbled under their feasting like a rag doll.

In front of Marcus, his own fate was staring him dead in the eyes. The creature stood over him, his own muddled brain finally accepting the indisputable fact that he was going to die.

His heart ached for his son. Justin - as he'd been before he left with his mother - games of hopscotch, tucking him in, the young boy's pleased expression as he put the finishing touches on another piece of crayoned artwork. Marcus moaned, not in acknowledgment of his imminent death but for the gut-wrenching misery of never having the chance to accept one more picture from his beloved son.

He would never see him again.

The black and red nightmare leaned eagerly over him. The beast's depressed snout butted against the cowering man's nose. Fetid breath passed over the horrors bared dripping fangs, clouding his senses with hot vile dankness. Marcus Biaggio scrunched angrily up at the creature's leering face and he uttered two final words -

"Fuck you...! The creature smiled, snapped its jaws closed over Marcus's satisfied grin...and it was over.

The train's occupants were never found. Only blood and gore were left in the subway's labyrinth. Investigators combed the underground tunnels for weeks until finally, they gave up. There was public outcry. Lawsuits were filed. The city held a memorial for the missing people. And then eventually - as with all tragic stories - others came along to replace it and the grieving was left to those who *had* to remember.

But underground, in the subway's infinite winding blackness, a chattering can sometimes be heard by the city's local commuters. Unrecognizable, the sound is ignored as people carry on with their lives. Blood red eyes blink patiently. Waiting... Watching...

The Daughters of Fire and Jade

K.K.

This one calls herself Doctor Bowes; no first name given. She's younger than the other doctors, and pretty in a stressed-out sort of way. The ring on her finger indicates she's married. If that's the truth, then she'll be missed. Perhaps she has children as well.

Pity. Still, somewhere on her person, she has keys that will enable my escape. So I bide my time, and let her ask her futile questions.

"Joseph?" Dr. Bowes asks.

"Hmmmm." Is my reply. There's no point in a Shakespearean monologue; this is an asylum, so when in Rome…

She scrutinizes me from behind her tortoiseshell glasses for a moment, flips through some notes, then asks,

"Who are the daughters of Fire and Jade?" I exhale; feeling like a great weight has been lifted from me. Perhaps it has. Finally, *someone* dares to think I might be telling the truth, or is humoring me, at least.

"Two girls, both nineteen years old. One British, one Japanese. The British girl is Samantha Emberton. The Japanese girl is Miko. No surname."

She looks up from her notes, gazes at me steadily, then brings one of my paperbacks into view.

"Do they look like this?"

She has the fifth book in the *Triumvirate* series: *Temples of Ice*. On the cover, a svelte redheaded witch and a lithe female ninja stand poised to defend their mutual husband, Alan Trium, from some menacing saber-toothed tigers.

I can't answer for a long time. The cover of the book grows and grows before me until it swallows my vision, and my eyes begin to tear as I look upon the Daughters of Fire and Jade. The artwork is a poor substitute for their actual faces and flesh. But still, it is *they*, and lightning strikes my heart as I see them again.

"Joseph? Do they look like this?" Dr. Bowes repeats impatiently.

I just nod. My jaw is hanging open slackly—I'm probably drooling and I must look like an idiot. I close my mouth and continue to stare at the cover as Dr. Bowes scribbles some notes.

"Can I have that?" I ask quietly, already knowing the answer.

"Maybe later, Joseph. I need to know some things, first." She says in a conciliatory tone. The book disappears into my file, the file that grows thicker all the time. I sigh.

"What can I tell you that I haven't already told everyone else?"

"Why you killed your wife." She snaps. Short and to the point. Matter of fact. I respect that.

"I didn't kill my wife. *They* did." It's Dr. Bowes' turn to sigh.

"Joseph. That's exactly what you've told everyone else. It won't wash. I can't help you unless you help *me*. Tell me the *truth*, Joseph!" I slump onto my back, and look up at the one soft white bulb illuminating my cell.

"I don't care if it *'won't wash'*. I don't need your help. I keep telling it because it *is* the truth. *Samantha and Miko killed my wife.*"

Hot tears spill out of my eyes as I admit it again. I wish I could travel through time, and undo the past. Go back to the cocktail party where I met Lorraine, and vomit on her. Spill a drink all over her, or tell her that her beautiful gown would look great on a prostitute. Anything, anything at all to drive her away, so she could have avoided me and survived. But no, I can't travel through time, and I did nothing to drive her away. On the contrary, I charmed her right out of her gown, and into my bed, my life, and her undeserved death.

I loved her. I loved Lorraine. I loved my wife. I still do, I always *will*, for all the good it will do me. She just couldn't compete with the Daughters. How could she? How could one woman, however beautiful or virtuous or sexually skilled, compete with two women, when the heart of almost every male mammal demands variety?

The *Daughters* loved her too, at first. They would sit on the bed and admire Lorraine when she came in with coffee or sandwiches, while I dutifully cranked out their tales of glory. *Kyomo Kidei Desune,* Miko would say: *She's looking lovely as usual.*

There is a long silence, and multiple rustlings of paper, and more sighs, as I look up at the light bulb. Finally Doctor Bowes asks:

"All right, Joseph, if *they* killed your wife, *why* did they do it?" I frown.

Why, indeed? They claimed to have been acting out of self-preservation, but what if it was just mere possessiveness? Since I'm in a padded cell, the 'why' is probably moot, anyway. I decide to give them the benefit of the doubt

"Self-preservation. Lorraine wanted to kill them."

"How?"

"She wanted me to stop writing them."

"Why would that have killed them?" Good Lord. Dr. Bowes is an idiot.

"If you stop feeding something, it dies. Right?"

"Living creatures, yes. Plants, animals, human beings. But we're talking about fictional characters here." I sigh, and look up at the light again.

"No, *you're* talking about fictional characters, Dr. Bowes. Lorraine said the same thing. The Daughters did not appreciate the distinction."

There is a long pause, and a scribble of writing. A stab of envy hits me; I miss writing; well, I miss just about everything, being locked up in here; but I miss writing most of all. I wish I could have a magic marker, I'd put some poems up on these horribly blank walls. It'd give the next patient something to read. Who says blank white walls are some kind of avenue to sanity, anyway?

"Joseph, isn't it possible that your wife was simply threatening your livelihood by asking you to stop writing your *Triumvirate* books, and you lashed out at her on a subconscious level?" Dr. Bowes asks scornfully.

"It wasn't much of a threat. I was writing full-time, and Lorraine was making more than I was anyway. We weren't rich but we were doing all right. I was writing other things, anyway; they just didn't sell like *Triumvirate* did. If it'd been that much of an issue, I just would have divorced her…I wouldn't have *decapitated* her."

There is a chilly silence, in which I momentarily remember a blurry vision of Lorraine's beautiful face turning in mid-air as it arcs to the floor, trailing long blonde tresses of hair and streamers of blood. Miko brought her crimson-stained katana back to a guard position, then vanished into thin air as I screamed in horror.

Dr. Bowes looks at me unsympathetically. She's probably heard a few dozen murderers say *It wasn't me, it was somebody else, it was my evil twin, it was the Boogeyman, it was Santa Claus, ad infinitum, ad nauseum.* My particular alibi might have a bit more novelty, but that's about all. So she tries again.

"Joseph, isn't it just possible that you constructed a fantasy world that seemed better than your actual life, and you killed your wife for intruding on it, or threatening it?" I have to massage my temples after hearing the sheer banality.

"Oh, I don't know, *Doctor* Bowes. Isn't it just possible that human beings evolved from apes, or President Kennedy wasn't killed by a lone gunman, or that dairy products really *don't* do a body good'?" I growl. The taunt doesn't change her oh-so-serious expression, though.

"Then how do you explain what happened, Joseph?"

"I thought I already did."

"No, you said the Daughters of Fire and Jade killed your wife. You didn't explain *how*."

"It's not something I like to remember!" I spat. "But since you've just got to know, I came into the den. They were all there. Lorraine, Samantha, Miko. Lorraine was erasing all the *Triumvirate* files on my computer. She had my notes and disks and hard-copies in a cardboard box. I asked her what she was doing, and she said she was doing something that had needed doing for a long time. I asked her to stop; she didn't. Then…Samantha said "Stop her, Joseph, or *we* will." So I tried, I argued at first, pleaded with her, but she wouldn't listen, so I tried to restrain her and she sprayed mace in my eyes then went back to erasing the files. Obviously you can't see all that well when you've been maced, but I could see Samantha light up the Hand of Glory and point it at Lorraine…"

"What's the Hand of Glory?" Dr. Bowes asked.

"It's a magical artifact. The dismembered hand of a hanged murderer. Candles are lashed to the fingers, and when they're lit, the Hand of Glory paralyses whoever it's pointed at…" Dr. Bowes swallows audibly, then says "Go on."

"The Hand of Glory paralyzed Lorraine. As soon as she stopped moving, Miko drew a samurai sword…and…cut her…head off." I almost choke on the words. The memory sears my brain again.

I had asked Lorraine to stop. The Daughters might have asked her as well…if their weapons could influence the physical world, why couldn't their voices?…but still, it was a horrid murder, a shocking betrayal, and a crime of passion that I not only witnessed but am now accused of.

"It's all right, Joseph, it's over…" Dr. Bowes attempts.

"*NOTHING IS 'ALL RIGHT', DOCTOR! NOTHING IS 'OVER!*" I roar at her. She recoils from me, then composes herself. I drag myself away from her; fighting back tears, then look up at the light again.

If I look up into the light long enough, my vision blurs; as anyone's would. But if I don't blink, or close my eyes, the blur grows, and spawns wild colors, and it is in those colors that they live, and enter our world, and come to me.

The Daughters of Fire and Jade.

Their beauty alone is enough to drive any man to his knees. God knows it's enough for me. But even if it were not, they possess horribly lethal powers. Even at her tender age, Samantha claims to know the secrets of the Wiccans, Druids, Rosicrucians, and the Knights Templar. She can command the elements, call down fire, heal any illness, and assume any shape…although why she would assume any shape other than her own remains a mystery and shame. Even at nineteen, her breasts are large, firm and supple, like two huge scoops of ice cream topped with strawberries. Her flesh is a flawless alabaster, her hair a cascade of copper curls, the color of fire, providing her namesake.

Miko had been the slave of a ruthless Kyoto warlord, born and raised by one of his concubines to serve as a Geisha. However, her quarters had shared a wall with the barracks of his *Ninjutsu* academy, and there had been a hole in its wall.

Unable to sleep with the constant *Kiyais* shouted on the other side, she'd spent night after night watching the ninjas train. Eventually she began duplicating their movements, then their attacks and defenses, mimicking their *Kiyais* in the twilight, until she had become as effortlessly lethal as they. Even more lethal, as no one would suspect this quiet, slender girl with her dark, downcast eyes to be able to break their legs with a Sliding Hook Kick.

Separately, Samantha and Miko would be any man's fantasy.

Combined…bracketing your body between theirs, feeling their lush, warm skin over lithe and experienced muscles…tasting two sets of soft lips on yours, mere moments apart, then tracing their way down your body to a fine and private place…watching you fuck the other with a lusty smile and in fact urging you on…then loving each other while you relaxed after orgasm…knowing these perfect lovers would SHARE themselves with you…

A lot of men probably *would* kill their wives for that. But I didn't. The daughters did. I know that, and they know that, but nobody else does. So I'm damned.

Unless I can prove otherwise…

I close my eyes tightly, almost painfully, and force myself to remember the sword-stroke of Miko's *ninja-to* as it slashed through the back of Lorraine's soft neck. Then I open my eyes again, and stare desperately at Dr. Bowes.

"Doctor Bowes…" I whisper feebly, almost a croak. "Do you have a copy of the coroner's report about Lorraine?"

Dr. Bowe's gaze meets mine. She blinks, and frowns. "Not *with* me, here, but it's in your main file.

Why, Joseph?"

Why, indeed? I had begun a certain train of thought, but it had stopped right after leaving its station. The last doctor had put me on certain medications, and the doctor before *him* had put me on some, and my brain might as well be cornbread at this point. But there's something important about Lorraine's decapitation…besides the fact that it fucking killed her, of course…something that would make it *impossible to convict me of the crime.*

Alan Trium would know, he's the imaginary genius who married the Daughters, at least in my hack fantasy series…*hack*! What a fitting word that is, for a doomed writer.

Hack.

And in my mind's eye, Miko's sword comes down again. This time, I notice that both Samantha and Miko are crying as they kill my wife. At that moment, I *prayed* to become Alan Trium, to vanish with the Daughters into whatever literary netherworld I'd conjured them from, where we'd have sex and adventures happily ever after. Instead of being hauled off to jail, and then the madhouse. From somewhere, Dr. Bowe's voice stabs me like a sword.

"Why do you want to know about the coroner's report, Joseph?"

"*SHUT UP AND LET ME THINK*!" I snarl at her. She recoils, and so do I. I crawl backwards like a drunken crab, shoving myself into a corner of the padded cell, closing my eyes again.

Trium's a private investigator, of course; all pulp fiction has to have a private investigator in it. Gotta 'keep it old school' as my literary agent used to urge me. In the *Triumvirate* books, he's an oversexed Mike Hammer. His libido probably sold an extra thousand copies by itself. But in between romps with the Daughters, he actually did his job. He investigated, he questioned people. People like coroners…

Miko's sword comes down again. *Hack!* I take a deep breath. I open my eyes. I look at Dr. Bowes.

"What was the murder weapon they said I killed my wife with?" I ask.

The doctor's eyes open a bit wider. "A machete. You had one in your garage."

I nod. I close my eyes again, and in the courtroom of my mind, Alan Trium stands up to testify.

"And every wound from a metal weapon *leaves traces of the metal in the wound.* Isn't that right?" Dr. Bowes frowns.

"I, I'm not a metallurgist, Joseph. And I only have slight experience in forensics."

"Listen to me. You've got to get the coroner to compare that machete with any metal traces in…in…"

I want to say *Lorraine's body*, but I can't. Not just out of grief and horror, but the raw shock of the *implication*. That if there are traces of metal in her that don't match the machete, it means I'm innocent, and sane. But it also means my wife was murdered by a fictional character. One of my Daughters, if you will, who only exists in my mind, and in the books I used to write, once upon a time. Dr. Bowes inhales audibly, then says,

"Well, I think that's enough for today, Joseph…" And she gets up to leave.

"I'll be back to talk to you tomorrow."

Oh, God, no. She's leaving. She doesn't even care what I say, this has just been some perfunctory exercise in corporate psychiatry; the Actress At Work.

"*You've got to talk to that coroner, damn it!*" I rave, and in my own voice I hear the pathetic desperation of the truly insane. Standing at her full height now, Dr. Bowes arches an eyebrow.

"You need to *calm down*, Jo…" and stops in mid-sentence. She continues standing, stock-still, the eyebrow still arched. Staring at me.

From behind her, between her body and the door she was going to use, a robed leg takes a step forward. And a hand, clutching another hand, this one dead and withered with five ancient candles bound to its burned fingers. And now a body, a young fallen angel with long tresses of coppery red hair. A smile graces her lips as she sees me again.

My heart thunders with love, and awe, and terror.

From the other side of Dr. Bowes, a lithe shadow slides forth into reality, coalescing into colors; onyx eyes, olive skin over high black leather boots, and the bright but unforgiving smile of a sword…

I know what the Daughters want, but I don't know what I want, and it seems like I've got mere microseconds to figure it out. They can kill Dr. Bowes, like they killed my wife and I could escape with them into some ongoing nightmare of fugitive schizophrenia, or I can pretend I'm Alan Trium, and try to talk them out of it and hope that Dr. Bowes survives and talks to that coroner…

"*WAIT*!" I scream, the only word that might work on any or all of them.

"*Ooohh, but we 'ave waited, Joseph, far too long…*" Samantha calls quietly. And her slim white fingers burst into flames, with which she begins to light the candles, as Miko raises her sword.

Dr. Bowe's eyes swivel left and right for a moment, trying to see something that can't possibly be there, and then they look upwards, as if seeking divine intervention…

Suddenly two more shadows erupt from behind the Daughters of Fire and Jade; coalescing into rippling muscles and manes of long savage hair. Samantha's Hand of Glory is chopped to the floor with one swift stroke of a Viking hand-axe. Miko's sword-stroke is restrained by the mighty triceps of an Apache brave. The Viking and the Apache are holding the Daughters back, and it seems that they *want* to be held back…why not? The bodies of these two prototype Alpha males put mine to shame. Dr. Bowes clears her throat.

"You're not the only one who knows how to write fiction, Joseph." She looks from side to side, and her avatars clutch mine tighter.

"Like I said, I'll be back to talk to you tomorrow. Maybe we can talk about what just happened to my husband…"

I can only nod, slowly, as the Daughters and their captors fade into Dr. Bowe's shadow. But their eyes are the last to fade, looking at me, looking at her, looking at each other with delicious possibilities…

"Maybe we can talk about matches made in Heaven…or somewhere else." She says, with a slight tease in her voice, as she leaves my cell.

And I can only begin to think about what just happened…and what might happen next…as the door locks behind her.

Miss Peach

Steven Marshall

It was spring, though still quite early in the season, when a mysterious woman came to live with us. Her purpose was to manage the affairs of our household while mother was suffering some vague ailment, lingering but not serious.

After dad passed away, mother was unable to cope by herself with the daily rituals of the house, exorcising dirt devils and exhuming the hidden horrors that lingered inside the carpets. The house was quite large with three levels and many rooms, which seemed much more intimidating in size after the fairly recent passing of my father.

The mysterious woman arrived on one of those misty, drizzling days which often prevailed during the young months of spring where we'd lived. It was a time of the year that remained a signature memory of a remarkable time in my life. Since mother was self-confined to her bed after the loss of dad, it left me to answer those sharp, hollow rappings on the door from the heavy lion's head brass knocker. How they echoed through the entire house with haunting residue.

Pulling open the door handle, so huge like a safety vault in my child's hand, I found her standing there with her back to me, staring deep into the world of mysterious mist surrounding our residence. Her long, black, almost bluish hair had glistened like a raven's wing under the light of the vestibule. When she turned to finally face me, my eyes wandered up to the great ebony turban of her hair folded so tightly and elaborately into itself, I thought her eyes would pop from her head. She beheld this cold beauty about her; a stone in an icy lake of magnificent wonder.

"My name is…"

"I know who you are," I informed her.

"Oh, do you now. And who am I?"

"You're our new housekeeper…and my tutor."

"My name is Miss Peach."

"And I'm...Johnny Appleseed!" I said, amused by myself.

"May I come in please?"

"Yes. Mother was expecting you."

By now, this stranger had already had a visual orientation of our vast surroundings and now wanted to gain access inside. Quite literally her place here was an obscure one, lying somewhere between the peculiar mood of my mother and my rambunctious one. Moreover, the stillness of the changing season was unsettled, undecided and unclear. Suppressed by some otherworldly desolation behind dark battlements of clouds looming over a barren, hibernal landscape stilled by nature, she at last undistracted herself for the moment to enter our home. Ironically, she appeared to reflect the exact mannerisms of the gloom of the day, absorbed in a dark aura of morbid clouds and engulfed in a fog all her own.

During the early part of her stay, Miss Peach was heard more often than seen. Her duties, whether by instruction or interpretation, had soon been engaged by her routine of wandering through the many echoing rooms and hallways of the house. Rarely was there an interruption in her footsteps as they clamored and creaked on aged floorboards; day and night these noisy prancing crepitations signaled the whereabouts of our vigilant housekeeper. I would awake to her movements above my bedroom (as she lived up in our attic) with the clip-clopping of her high heels digging like daggers into the floor. The routine noises of always pacing busily about began to irritate me with her disturbances. What was she doing that she could never quite settle herself in the privacy of her room? Such a strange and mysterious creature, I concluded.

One time I was awakened in the middle of the night, though it was not her sounds that ruptured my sleep. I was also not sure why I couldn't get back to sleep or even close my eyes again. I decided to get out of bed and further investigate the source of my curiosity. I quietly opened my bedroom door and peered down the dark and narrow hallway. At the end of that very long passage was the balcony window filled with an eerie, livid radiance of moonlight. Within the window's portrait was the shadowy silhouette of one Miss Peach, as black as her raven-colored hair. She was staring so intently through the window that she didn't seem to notice my presence. I watched her for some time then finally went back to bed. That night I had the most horribly vivid nightmares; so lucid in their realism.

    The following day I began drawing a series of sketches depicting my nightmares. What first started as doodles in my schoolbooks began taking on swifter evolutions of greater size and ambition. I was quite surprised that these images did not include an overt portrayal of the illusive Miss Peach in the flesh, or any other banal images of her likes that might serve by way of symbolism or association.

    Instead my illustrations depicted scenes from some strange and cruel kingdom. Possessed by curious moods and haunted visions, I sketched some bleak domain obscured by mist whose depths brought forth a plethora of fog or strange clouds. The structure itself seemed to rise forever upward with jagged shadows and unseen acmes; all somehow twisted into suggestions of some bizarre savagery. From a matrix of fertile haze spawned forth a litter of towering edifices that combined both castle and crypt; a many peaked palace or multi-chambered mausoleum. There were also clusters of smaller structures, warped offshoots of the greater ones, lending home to a dwelling of an ominously intimate dungeon cell reserved for the most exclusive of captivity and perhaps torture. The structure seemed to fold into itself and suffocate all who entered. Of course, all who entered may very well become permanent, unwilling guests themselves.

    I beheld no special genus in my execution of these phantasmal venues. My technique was non-developed and simple; a barbaric child sketch, unable to introduce any images of dimension or depth. Certainly it did not capture the imagery of my imagination that seemed integral to a proper presentation. Like the mysterious making of their shapes, their source could only be found in one Miss Peach.

    Although I had not intended on showing her the drawings, there was evidence that she had indulged in some private viewings of them. They lay out in the open on my desk in my bedroom and I made no effort to conceal them. I sensed a subtle disarrangement of my work and began to suspect their order was disturbed in my absence when I was downstairs having some breakfast. Her presence in there was vaguely telling but inconclusive. Then finally she gave herself away and was betrayed by her own curiosity. I had discovered a certain revelation in her investigation: Lying in between two of the drawings, pressed like a memento in an old scrapbook, sat a long black strand of her hair.

    I wanted to confront her immediately regarding her intrusion, not that I resented her exploring, more to seize an opportunity to further scrutinize this devious, eccentric creature that pranced freely about our house. But she was nowhere to be found at the time and must have ventured somewhere outside the perimeters of our domain.

    I decided to reverse the roles and pry into the serenity of her private sanctum in the upper penthouse quarters of our house. After entering her room and rummaging about, I realized she was not using it at all, nor was she settled. I sensed the curious presence of a woman from the bittersweet fragrances of her perfumes lingering around me and could easily distinguish the difference from those of my room - then I had my answer. As I turned around I found her standing right there in the doorway, staring at nothing with anticipating eyes; her face expressionless.

    I nevertheless found myself in a position of chastisement, losing the advantage I possessed earlier over my invader. Yet there was no mention of either transgression, despite what seemed our mutual understanding of them. We had drifted into an abyss of unspoken reproaches and sneaky suspicions. Then finally Miss Peach rescued my escalating awkwardness with an abrupt announcement:

    "I have spoken with your mother," she declared in a firm tone, "and we have both concluded that I should begin your tutoring on Monday to help you with your…weaker subjects. Your mother doesn't think you should go back to public school yet, until you have resolved the passing of your father. So we begin 8:00 sharp Monday morning. We shall begin class right here."

    I must have nodded in acknowledgment without even realizing. Right after her brief dissertation, she turned and walked away, leaving her words to resound in the cavity of the room as well as my mind. My own presence seemed to have been eclipsed there in the swelling shadow of Miss Peach. Nonetheless this extra-scholastic newsflash seemed to form the first personal bond between us.

And so my tutorship would be conducted in her lair, bright and early on Monday. As I returned to the starless attic, I now noticed for the first time how the slanted wooden ceiling exposed all its hideous rot spots along the old beams and warped frames like the ribs of some amphibious fossils or an ancient inverted seagoing vessel that may carry us to destinations unknown. The only illumination by which I was schooled came from whatever daylight the window drank in from the sun when it was not shrouded by the trees. When the overcast of late afternoon washed away the only light source, Miss Peach provided her own in the form of an old oil-burning lantern which gave off a faint emanation of vanilla wax and fresh rain. The lights cascaded the room with wafting shadows of a tribal nature, much like an Indian war dance: soft, rippling phantasmagoric vapors on the wall. Dark ghosts of a yesteryear celebration of some bizarre sort.

Early in the afternoon, Miss Peach had taken the liberty to prepare some lunch to nourish my body after doing the same with my mind. It was during that time that I could now finally distinguish her pale and delicate features. In the kitchen we acquainted ourselves with each other's presence. After feeding me cheese, lettuce and tomato on whole wheat, she rewarded herself with the nectar of a freshly picked orange soon to be drained of its last breath to make her afternoon. Miss peach slowly escorted her soon to be victim to the Ginsu chamber and placed the naked ball of fruit in the blender. Then, without any warning, she flicked the switch of death and watched in nostalgic awe as it became entangled in a shredded typhoon of citric acid; its pulpy orange blood running scarlet on the see-through plastic walls of the blender. The massive dicing had produced a rainbow reflection that hovered like a fractured soul inside it. Deep within the plastic death chamber, a seed's scream went unheard as it gazed up only to discover a large pair of human eyes bulging impossibly wide and staring down upon it.

Miss Peach was diligently checking for stranded seeds in the blender while transferring the orange juice into her glass. She told me she accidentally choked on a seed yesterday and admonished herself for a lack of observation. Certainly she did not want the seeds to muse over their triumph in the act of her repeating this foolish deed. And just as she lifted the glass to her lips in eager anticipation of relishing its sweet ice-cold taste, she suddenly succumbed to her senses and temporarily lost her sight. She wasn't knocked unconscious, nor was she dreaming; in fact, she was still standing in an upright position. A vision was taking form inside her mind; she could sense its familiar embrace. Then she felt a hot flash of dizziness. She asked me to dismiss myself at once so she could suffer her euphoric spell in private. I questioned her not and did as I was told. I retreated back to the lofty den that was her parlor and now my base of new learning rituals.

I studied the room further while she was busy regaining her composure. The only furniture present was an old, antique armoire to execute my studies, a small, brown wooden chair, quite uncomfortable and a white dresser where I presumed she kept her attire. The low lying guest bed still looked unused as if no one, including herself, had bunked down in it. Once again I turned around only to find her immediate presence upon me.

"In a room such as this…one can only learn things of great importance."

Without attempting to analyze her esoteric rhetoric, I acknowledged her brief discourse with a nod of comprehension. What followed was a series of fascinating lectures she imposed on my child's fertile imagination. She was most concerned with my development in subjects like history and geography. Occasionally she imparted her knowledge of science and philosophy, more so in an informal manner. She lectured from memory, never from a book or film.

She never faltered in her delivery of countless facts in her unconventional way of enhancing my education. Her discussions were not as meandering as her prancing footsteps in my mind. Eventually I began to extract certain wisdoms and themes from her chaotic syllabus. She would revisit her subjects and say them in another way to see if they stayed cohesive in my mind by my reaction. She started from the beginning with the first twitchings of amebic life to man, portraying a world of the most rudimentary laws; ending in ones so advanced, they could only be described as visceral practices of philosophical intrigue.

She taught in speculative theory, always leaving room for my own definition and interpretation without imposing a set in stone viewpoint. In time I became very intimate with my knowledge of ancient atrocities and massacres over the centuries; curious methods of torture and punishment, brutal airs of exile, dark realms littered with dead cities; hot sweltering jungles and deserts where life is intolerable to bear. And cold, icy ruins of glacial phosphoresce that sheltered frigid homes to only cold-blooded life forms.

At some point, however, Miss Peach and her specialized curriculum had dulled with repetition and familiarity, where it was initially so very engrossing. I began to fidget about in my seat, tapping my antsy fingers on my knees. I was looking more to the ceiling than straight ahead and feeling claustrophobic. Suddenly, as if sensing my preoccupation and distraction, she stopped talking. She approached, looming over me like her shadow did, exacting her rubber-tipped pointer on my frail shoulder, grazing my neck. As I looked up, she was leering down at me with her coal-dark eyes and a beehive of black bundled hair knitted tightly in place.

"In a room such as this…one must also learn to behave properly," she stated, retracting from me as if being magnetically drawn to the attic window. All was silent henceforth as she gazed into a world of suspended animation hanging in obscure perpetuity. She was also listening to it as well, apparently.

"I'm sorry, Miss Peach."

"Do you know the sound of something that stings the air?" she asked. "You will know the sound of that soon if you do not listen to me, young man."

"Yes, Miss Peach," I said, automatically arching myself up in my seat.

"You will be more attentive in the wisdom I bestow on you, child."

"I can't help it. I'm bored being cooped up in darkness all day."

"You will stand and go to the corner by the closet door - NOW! You may remove your pants to receive your punishment…those too. Hands out…"

Then after it happened:

"That will be all for today. Class is dismissed."

Class did not resume the following day or week…nor ever again. But my brief tutorship continued on in my mind long after. Subconsciously all her diatribes had manifested into my vocabulary, her shadowy visions and smells lingered in my boy's mind all the way to adulthood. It was a tender time of adolescent development for me and I feel her still in my dreams to this day. Especially as I look out the window and see…stillness.

It seemed that my lessons with Miss Peach had continued their lingering effect on me in a profound way. Those afternoons in the dank attic must have exhausted something within me while mother was in her own faraway world, suffering from her own demons in her private purgatory. For a while, I also could not leave my bed. During this limbotic period, Miss Peach had suffered a decline of her own, allowing her intangible sympathies and sorrows to come between us. There existed a newly formed bond between us that was severed with this guilty omen she possessed, harboring remorse over something much deeper and more entangled. We somehow reverted into a restless wandering of anticipation that failed to settle itself into any kind of repose. To some extent, I think my own process of degeneration followed that of Miss Peach and was transferred from the original source: mother. It seemed my father's death left a harvesting sorrow in his absence - from which mother never truly returned.

On her visits to my room, during those still and unsettled times of the season, Miss Peach manifested herself often and always unannounced with her new lessons of the day. I could observe the phases of her disillusion on both a physical and mental level. Her hair now hung loosely over her shoulders and unfolded itself like the dark woven tapestry of a nightmare. Moreover, her need to cling to strictly mundane elements had quickly eroded from her being to unleash a more shockingly dark inner side of her, completely alien to me. My new relationship with her was intimately conducted and practiced over and again with exchanges of a highly questionable order to conservative beings. But any attempts to exorcise this unquenchable demon from her were a failure. Every time I woke, I found her sitting there on the edge of my bed, cursed by my lingering ailment, as long wisps of her raven-like hair draped down and tickled my chest or brushed against my face, summoning me back to that evil and forbidden place of pure feminine hunger. I eventually recovered from the physical ailments that plagued me…but the mental ones?

    In retrospect, I think Miss Peach had been lost to a world of wholesome practicalities that morphed into an extraordinary bond starved from her youth, while her mannerisms betrayed a fateful and hypnotic determination to satiate her inner demon longing to escape. That escape came in the form of me and my…apple seed. One that I could not have resisted, nor did I feel alienated by, but became rather well-versed in following the years to come. But apparently she still had one more lesson to teach me…

    On the last day of her quite gainful employment sponsored by my ever plagued mother, Miss Peach asked me to go for a walk into the thick, looming fog outside of our house so she could show me one more sight. Having a child's magical curiosity, I followed Miss Peach into that vast landscape of smothered mist. After journeying into the heart of it, we lost sight of the house, and even the ground beneath our feet. We found ourselves surrounded by a floating web of clouds submerged in some thick milky retreat. She took my hand as if self-guided by some unseen force of a peculiar vision, setting both of us on a strange feeling path. It was a more familiar sensation within her soft, velvety canopy of intrigue and this newly forming growth that could not contain itself any longer.

When I tightened my grip on Miss Peach's hand, which seemed to be fading in substance and texture, like the shadow of a lost dream; something so vastly interwoven then torn apart like a spider's web blown in the gusty winds.
In that landscape, we merged once again and had a revelation like a Leviathan rising into view from the abyss; a monstrous world defined itself before our eyes through the infinity of the fog, leading to a secret arcane discovery for us.
Still something remained obscured in shadows, unconcealed in the overall plot of my ultimate revelation. It was a righteous, cacophonous echo that wailed a siren of a much darker truth, one I was living and enduring without realizing the true nature of it…

The kingdom was coming into view by daylight way of thought. It was more expansive and intricate than any of my wildest imaginings and it could truly never be sketched. Structures within portals sprung out in a patternless conglomerate of crystals clustered by multi-faceted monuments of incredible architecture embodied in a misty graveyard of the dead's deceased. Indeed it was a dead city as Miss Peach described. All the residents were entombed in its walls as faceless souls of the defunct! It looked much like a mountain range with wildly carved peaks and chasms, sheltered by a medieval ominous sky of some great impending thunderstorm brewing on the dark horizon, suggesting a palace of atrocious potential; an infinite country that hovered far beyond the fog, mist and unsettled skies of barren horizons.

Miss Peach stood in hypnotic awe, absorbed and consumed by the sight.

"Did you hear them," she asked.

"I heard…something," I confessed.

"They are the cries of what we cannot see, condemned by mediocrity. Sounds of the things that sting the air before bearing down upon naked flesh. Sounds of lonely, suffocated souls forever reaching, but never quite touching. It can be found behind the vapors of an immense and awful kingdom of woeful decrepitude from whence we just came: it's called the ailment of depression. Let this be a life lesson to you, forevermore…class is permanently dismissed."

It was then she released her hand from mine and drifted onward forever. There was no struggle, she had known for some time what loomed beyond the background of her mental wanderings and the kingdom embraced her stealthy approach. Somewhere I heard a clip-clopping of high heels echoing far away. Perhaps she sought the ultimate in forbidden knowledge beyond human flesh. Nevertheless she inherited me the heir of her visions and expansive knowledge as I stood a visceral explorer and student of the unknown, feeling a little richer in wisdom and understanding.

The fog encompassed her shadow in a rapture of embrace 'til there was nothing visible left of her. But her ghost in the fog of my mind lives on to this day. After I managed to regain my senses and find my geographical bearings, I found myself standing facing the back of my house like it was there all along.

Soon after the disappearance of Miss Peach, our household established its routine of habitual rituals again; its daily cycle of life and lifelessness. My mother had made a strong recovery - no longer a victim suffering from the self-manufactured pseudo-illness that possessed her. She noticed that the hired help had vanished without giving notice which caused little surprise in mother.
"Such a flighty, mysterious creature," mother observed.

I supported this characterization of Miss Peach but offered nothing by way of explanation for her disappearance or true nature of her flight. In truth, no words of mine back then or even now could have brought the least bit of clarity to the situation! Nor did I want to divulge the magical episodes of what she had left behind in the attic or my room for that matter. For deep in those dark chambers remains the essence of my childhood, blossoming into a man. And I had often revisited her room where we frolicked in our own adventures. And the smell of her womanly fragrances still remains ripe in my mind today. Especially on those afternoons in early spring when I can't close my eyes and hear the sounds that call out to me from a fog of an unsettled, changing season.

Still a cunning linguist Miss Peach remained, as did her vocabulary in me. Life has mathematically added a "zero" to my age since Miss Peach's visit. I have gone from 8-80 in a waking glance and I am flourishing on my deathbed now.

Indeed, the house, our kingdom, had taken over once vibrant beings and usurped the very essence of life from their souls. First Dad then Mom, then Miss Peach then eventually…me. And it all started with the death of who mom and I shared our lives with. I miss you both, but I'll be coming home very soon. And thank you, Miss Peach, for that brief but memorable lifetime of wisdom…

Cutting Away

William Couper

Darkness loomed in around, hemming him into the bed like a cell. There was still light in the room, but it was inadequate to keep the shadows that closed in on him at bay.

There was life all around him. In the next room, in the floors above and below him. There were many people in the hospital, yet he couldn't feel safe. The crush of humanity all around him should have been a barrier to that, but there was no relief for him.

His eyes kept moving to the door, even though there was no evidence that he would ever see what he was looking for. The pain was starting to come back in his leg, his head, his foot and his side. He welcomed the pains; they would stop him from sleeping tonight. Night was when it happened and he was determined to see the culprit, though he was pessimistic about his chances of doing so.

A strong part of him didn't want to see the visitor. There were dim memories that made his continuing ignorance seem like a great comfort. He also doubted that he would be able to stop this interloper from doing what they were doing to him, especially in his current condition.

Only a few months ago he had been a happy normal man, and now he was this terrified pitiable shadow of that.

He wanted to get out of bed with all the energy and enthusiasm that he had every morning. He wanted to smile at the sun streaming in the window and enjoy the warmth on his face and consider what the day would bring. He wanted to stretch and feel the stiffness from his muscles dissipate with a satisfying creak. He wanted to do a lot of things.

Pain was getting in the way. Mickey lay in bed and tried to work out just where the sparkling, insufferable and constant pain was coming from. Something told him that trying to look for the source of such intense pain with his fingers would be a bad idea – not because moving was somehow impossible, but because what he would find with his probing fingers would both make the pain worse and make him freeze with terror.

"I have to find out some way," he muttered. Vocalizing what must be done made it easier for him to do, even if it was an unpleasant task. What worried him most was the weakness of his voice, as most mornings he was somewhat muzzy and slurred, but this sounded weak and pained.

How badly could he have been injured in the time he was asleep?

There were things that he had to do today, and people were counting on him. He had to find out what was going on with him and either shake it off or inform those who needed to be told and get some kind of medical help. With a hint of trepidation that made the fabric feel a hundred times heavier, he pulled the covers away from his body. He slept wearing a pair of pyjama bottoms and one leg of those was rolled up to the top of his thigh. It had been done with great care to ensure that the item of clothing would not roll down again.

He sat up and stared at his leg. Now he could see what the reason for the pain was and the first nudge of insistent nausea bounced from one side of his ribs to the other, any sign of a scream was squeezed out of him, even though he knew he wanted to. Somehow he would rather have discovered this with his finger than to be staring at the sight that faced him.

His leg was drenched in blood and it had poured down onto the mattress to stick his skin there. Some of the crimson-black blood was also sticking the cover to the mattress, but most of the drying liquid was pooled under his leg.

On top of his thigh was a neat hole, about an inch in diameter, bored into his flesh. There was a ridge of darkly crusted blood around the top of the wound and even as he stared, dried blood cracked away from the skin on his leg. He could see the meat of his leg twitching and glistening at him below the layer of fat and the uppermost layer of skin.

He wanted to be sick.

How could this happen? His mind was whirling faster and faster and seemed to take his stomach with it on a sickening pattern of dizziness. He had to stay calm. Panicking was only going to make this worse.
He stared at the horrendous wound on his leg and thought in vain to come up with some kind of plan that would involve getting out of bed with as little pain as possible. All he could focus on was the possibility that doing anything would cause the wound to re-open and begin gushing blood again.

Phoning for help wasn't going to be a problem; it was the opening of the front door that had him worried. Even though he was badly injured, he didn't want to have his door broken down so that someone could gain entry to help him. Not that having the door locked had stopped this happening in the first place, the dark recesses of his brain put in. Every other thought was dampened under the layer of nausea, yet that one item managed to make itself clear and assured.

He wasn't secure in his own home.

This wasn't the time to be contemplating that. Right now he had to get help and urgently. He realized that there was going to pain in one way or another, so he set about phoning and then began the painful process of unsticking his leg from the mattress.

"And the police said there was no evidence of forced entry?" said Paul and took another sip of his coffee.

"There was nothing, Paul. No finger prints, no foot prints and no evidence of what had taken the huge chunk from my leg, either," said Mickey.

Paul had invited him to have lunch with him that day, knowing that Mickey wasn't feeling happy or secure and that he would need to talk about it. So here they were outside on a pleasant sunny day with a parasol keeping their exposure to the blaze of the sun to a minimum. People walked by wearing summery outfits and Paul would pass comments about some of them, and not always flattering.

For his part, Mickey sat eating his lunch, still feeling uncomfortable and keeping his leg stuck out to one side stiffly. The doctors had done all they could for the two days he had been in hospital, but the nature of the injury meant that it would take a long while to heal. He wasn't helping the healing process though, as he felt he had to stay active, even when it was counter to medical advice.

"They actually did all of that CSI stuff?" said Paul, unable to keep the fascination from his voice.

"They did, and I think they were enjoying it a bit too much."

"Let's face it they don't get to do much of that kind of thing around here. The last big crime they had to deal with was when old Mister Gillen embezzled all that money from the Post Office."

"Doesn't mean that they all need to spout silly David Caruso lines the whole time. Admittedly some of them were funny."

"Have you been back home yet?" Mickey didn't look at Paul; instead he fiddled with his own coffee cup and watched the liquid slosh around in the bottom. He didn't want him to see the deep fear in his eyes when he contemplated going back home.

"No. I'm still staying at my sister's. She was nice enough to go and pick up some of my clothes for me. I don't know if I'll be able to face the place again. I mean, I can't rely on my sister's hospitality. It's been a week and I already feel like a burden to her. But I can't face going back home either."

"It's only been a week, Mick. You've been through a weird trauma. It hasn't really stopped you though. You're still helping out with the kids' football team, aren't you?"

"As much as I can. I don't want to let anyone down, Paul. I feel bad enough that I lost two days from work and from volunteering."

"You never have let anyone down, Mick. That shit's all in your head. You're allowed a lapse every once in a while. Especially when some freaky weirdo decides to make a Sunday joint out of your leg."

"I suppose you're right, Paul."

"You've been the same since primary school, man. I'm surprised you haven't had a heart attack or developed an ulcer by now. You should worry about yourself a little more."

Mickey was still surprised at how well Paul knew him. Sometimes it seemed that all those years of being friends were nothing and they hadn't learned anything about each other and then Paul would come out with something as incisive as that.

"This is one time I am worrying about myself. I don't like it. I feel like I'm being watched all the time, Paul."

At last he looked up at his old friend and Paul looked visibly shocked by Mickey's expression, as he allowed the façade he had been showing for Paul's benefit to dissolve. He knew how he looked – he had been seeing it ever since he had been in the hospital. His eyes were haunted and the lines around his face were harder and deeper. This was something unknown to him, as he was usually so given to smiling and laughing.

"Mick, I take that back," said Paul, trying to inject a bit of lightness into his voice.

"You need to relax about this a bit. You're going to drive yourself nuts if you think people are watching you. I've never known you to be so worried about anything. I can't blame you, man. I don't think I'd be coping so well after that. Give yourself a bit of a break though. Use staying at your sister's as a bit of a holiday. I bet everyone was surprised to see you back volunteering."

"Yeah."

The fact of the matter was that they were pissed off at him for being back. They had all expected him to take more time off to recover properly and he had been told to go home after ten minutes of coaching when it was obvious his leg was too painful. He didn't tell Paul this though.

"It's not like that's the only thing you do either. How long did you take off work?"

"I went back as soon as I came out of the hospital."

"You're out of your mind, Mick. You should have given yourself at least a day, even if it was to get settled into your sister's." Paul laughed and shook his head.

"You're some piece of work, man."

Mickey didn't answer. He looked back into his almost empty coffee cup and simply nodded.

Just talking it over with Paul even made the pain seem to lessen. The whole episode was still strange and inexplicable, but having talked about the issues that it brought up made him feel less suffocated by the event.

He couldn't talk about it that way with Irene, his sister, as everything connected with him and his life seemed to be cushioned with overbearing sympathy with her. All he would get from her would be her worried expression, a nod, a pat on the hand and her telling him that everything would be fine. She didn't really listen to him or understand what he was going through; or if she understood, she wasn't mentally equipped to deal with it.

Not that he was better equipped emotionally or mentally. Having someone to talk it over with whose first reaction wasn't clucking pity was a good change and put a different, and far less depressing, perspective on things.

Although Paul had managed to miss the most obvious question that had been asked by the police and the doctors: how had Mickey slept through the intrusive and involved procedure? For that he was happy, as he had no answer to it. There had been no injection marks and nothing found in his blood stream that would suggest that he had been drugged. Somehow he'd had a substantial chunk from his thigh removed without waking up. He didn't want to think about it.

He had been having trouble sleeping, even in Irene's spare bed. This was partly because of what had happened at his own home and continued pain from the injury; it was also because her kids, his niece and nephew, refused to sleep for long parts of the night.

The house would be quiet and dark. He would feel himself starting to drift after the anxiety that settled over him when he got into bed went away, when there would he a thud on the wall above the head of the bed. From there it would escalate to screaming and then Irene would go and in hushed tones –that were strangely louder than the kids jumping around and screaming combined – tell the children to keep it down, Uncle Mickey was trying to sleep.

That pattern had been leaving him with about two hours of sleep a night, at most. Last night was one of the better nights – he was sure he got about three hours.

Screaming woke him though. In the bleary moments before he fully escaped the gravity of sleep he received snippets of sensation: Irene's face contorted in fear and revulsion; something wet and dark sitting on the bedside cabinet; the searing pain along the right side of his head.

"I can't stay at yours any more, Irene," he said to her over the phone as he was walking out of the hospital.

"Mickey, you can't go back to that house on your own. You need to get the police to help you or something," she said. It was obvious that she found him going home again a relief, but she was trying to hide it.

"I don't want them staring at my house all day. Anyway, I don't think they'd do that. I'm on my own here."

"Couldn't Paul move in with you, at least for a little while?"

"He's asked, and I told him no. I don't want him to leave his wife on her own, just to baby sit me."

"Stop being such a pain, Mickey. You're so scared of being a burden to people that you're being an even worse burden."

"Well, excuse me, Irene."

"You don't need to be so sarcastic, Mickey."

"What do you expect? My heads all bandaged, I've got dirty great hole in my leg and the bloody police are starting to think that I'm doing this as some kind of attention-seeking exercise. I'm scared, but I'll deal with this in my own way. Look, I have to go, the taxi's here."

"Okay, but you be careful."

His first job when he got back was to change the mattress on his bed. Even if it could be cleaned, somehow still having it would have made him feel uncomfortable, as though whatever had stolen the piece of his flesh had infected it with its presence. As it was, the material had been saturated with his blood and had become stiff, dark and stinking.

He had no choice but to clean the carpet around his bed. It was fortunate that most of the blood had been soaked up by the mattress, so that, though it was still hard work, it wasn't impossible to remove it.

The work kept his mind off the growing paranoia for a whole day while he scrubbed and vacuumed away the bloody graffiti left by his injury. Moving buckets of bloody water to and fro was an activity that was sufficiently mindless that he didn't really need to think about anything in particular.

Standing over the drying area of carpet, the paranoia came crashing back into his mind, as though it had been held at bay and had been building that whole time. The force with which it reasserted itself made him shrink into himself and cower away from the window that looked out into the street.

Working on instinct and fear, he rushed forward and pulled the curtains shut on the window, blocking out the view of whoever might want to be watching him. Instantly he felt trapped and claustrophobic, but he refused to open the curtains or even to move from the room.

He needed to work out a way of securing his room from the invader. He pulled on his jacket and got the walking stick that he'd been using since his thigh had been injured and he went out to the nearest ironmonger to buy locks for his front door and his bedroom door.

The dream was of round, yellow eyes turning to him and examining him. There was the suggestion of a tall dark body, but nothing more. Terror pinned him to the bed and stopped him from crying out.

Darkness came again.

The terrible knowledge that something had happened in the night again and that this time he had glimpsed, in some way or another, the culprit made the crunching pain from his foot unsurprising – for all that it was unpleasant. Compared to the injury that had been inflicted on his leg, there was but a small stain on the foot of his bed, but the fact of it made him grimace in horror.

His little toe was missing and a nub of bone stared at him from the tidy wound on his foot. On the bedside unit there was the dried scrap of skin from his scalp, curled into a cylinder with the crusted underside staring at him. Tufts of hair stuck up from inside this tube and almost made Mickey laugh out loud with how ridiculous they looked. He kept the laughter at bay, as he was afraid that he wouldn't be able to stop.

After a few wincing steps, he made sure that he could walk and he limped to the medicine cabinet and he took pain killers and retrieved some antiseptic, gauze and bandages. He hissed in pain when he used the antiseptic and then bound the foot with the bandages.

He didn't want to visit the hospital about this and certainly didn't want the police to become involved again. Somehow he was sure that he could handle this on his own; that confronting the yellow-eyed entity would bring an end to this.

Right then he went back and checked the door to his room, and found that the lock was intact and there was no evidence of tampering with the door, at least to his inexpert eye. It was the same story with the front door.

The sense of helplessness came to him in a wave of iciness that started from the soles of his feet and travelled up his legs. How could he keep this intruder out if his doors were locked from the inside and did nothing to even slow it?

The windows!

He rushed out the door after pulling on clothes that he had been wearing for the last two weeks. The stink of his body odour hit him even as he struggled into the clothes, but he didn't care, he was in a rush – he had slept late on and now he had a few short hours before nightfall to secure all the windows of his home.

"Jesus, Mick, you look awful," Paul said when he saw him outside the ironmongers.

Mickey looked at his old friend as though he didn't recognize him. His mind was so preoccupied with the pain that felt as though it was encroaching in all directions in his body, he didn't register him for several seconds.

Those few seconds were enough to put Paul on edge and he looked askance at Mickey. Mickey licked his lips, eager to get on.

"Are you okay, Mick? I haven't seen you since you went back home," he said.

"Yeah, I'm fine. Just trying to take it easy so that I can get back to work, y'know?" Mickey answered, aware of his eyes darting behind Paul in his eagerness to be away. He wished he could stop, but he found his gaze going on quick, nervous excursions to look ahead and behind him.

Anxiety was making him twitch and made the bag of locks and chains in his arms jingle.

"Irene's been on at me to stay with you," Paul said, studying Mickey with what looked like increasing worry.

"I told her I'd be fine. You've got your own stuff," Mickey said and shifted the bag.

"That's what I said – you're a big boy now. I've offered and you gave me your final answer. Anyway, I knew you wouldn't be very happy with her doing that, or with me suddenly turning up at your door with my sleeping bag."

Mickey guessed that he was supposed to laugh at that point, but he was so preoccupied about getting back home to install the things that he bought that the short laugh he gave Paul sounded bitter and sardonic.

"Doing some DIY?" Paul said in response to that. It was clear that Mickey's behaviour was making him want to get away.

"Yeah. A couple of little things I've wanted to do for a while," Mickey said. "Look, I have to get going. I'll talk to you later."

He pushed past Paul and didn't even say good bye. He was too relieved to be heading back home to secure it.

His working pace was feverish and even managed to ignore the pain of his missing toe for most of the time. At last all the windows in his house were fitted with padlocks and he was sheathed in sweat of desperation.

He tumbled into bed and slept when he had completed the task.

For a week nothing happened, and it seemed that the application of so many locks had achieved what he wished it to. He even began to be more sociable, as he no longer felt that he was carrying around that unknown danger with him at all times. Although he did start to have the vague fear that, frustrated by being unable to get to him in the night, the creature with the round, golden eyes would accost him in the daylight. This was a lesser fear as he began to be around people again after several weeks of self-imposed exile.

One morning, he woke up wheezing and unable to take a breath without searing pain tightening his chest. Moving was an effort in this state and even just pulling the covers away from his body almost made him pass out.

Again the mattress was drenched in blood. This time, though, the injury was along his side and there was a long, deep gash that ran from the front of his chest, along his side and under him. He vomited onto the floor at the sight of it, being unable to control himself through the pain and impossibility to breathe properly.

The doctors were baffled and said that he shouldn't have been alive with the injury that he had sustained that day. This he heard through a haze of pain killers. Somehow one of his ribs had been removed from his body.

His little toe had been found on the window sill, all shrivelled and covered in mould. Again he had to talk to the police, but he could tell them nothing. He wasn't going to recount the dream about the thing with the glowing yellow eyes. They left with his little toe and a lot of disappointment.

He had been in the hospital for two days now. He had been uncommunicative with Irene, Paul and anyone else who came to see him. He felt that he had to be alone otherwise they would be caught up in this nightmare he found himself in.

So now he lay at night, alone and waiting sleepless for his assailant to come. The third day rolled by, becoming a colourless collection of hours and distant events. Even the doctors examining the stitches of the wound caused by his rib's removal was something of little interest to him.

Struggling on the third night to stay awake was almost more than he could bear until he realized that he wasn't alone in the room anymore. One moment he was alone and the next there was another presence there. He sat up as quickly as his injured side would allow.

The thin thing that stood a few feet from his bed couldn't have been human. There were vague human-like traits, but the long mouth -less face with large diaphanous ears that shifted in unfelt air currents and those golden, glowing eyes the size of tennis balls were just the beginnings of the inhumanity of the creature. Its bald head almost touched the ceiling.

It tilted its head almost upside down when he sat up. There was no alarm in the movement and not even the vaguest surprise.

"Finally you wake," a voice that sounded like glass breaking on metal said. "I'm afraid this is the end." It skimmed forward, like a cloud of thick smoke borne on a strong wind and was standing over him. Something heavy and wet dropped into his lap and when he looked down, he saw the removed rib.

As he gaped at the discarded bone he felt as though parts of his body were being pushed out of the way. It wasn't painful and it didn't even reach uncomfortable, it just felt strange.

The next moment he was faced with something wet and fist-sized. The heart still pulsed like a stricken insect in the thing's grip.

"Good bye," said the creature as Mickey's world went dark.

Vessel of the Diablo Si

Justin Holley

The smoke that hung in the air like a shroud smelled like death, putrid and rotting, surrounding him like a ghoulish mist. Jason shrugged it off, being beyond the point of even wondering. The various elements of his visceral cocktail had not smelled that bad individually, but stewed all together, somehow they had transformed into something insidious and rank.

As if in deference to his blank thoughts, the smoke rose up and, just for a moment, transformed into a grinning skull, teeth gleaming in the dull glow beneath cloudy skies. Then the cloud dissipated into the cool evening air, its wisps floating upward like ghastly tendrils.

Magic maybe...dark magic, Jason thought. He coughed up another sphere of blood and spat it on the ground near the smoker, indifferent. After all, the acrid smoke was nothing as compared to what was baking in the old cooker, the dry heat draining the last of the moisture from the effigy within. Jason could feel its presence, dark and evil in the growing dusk.

The nondescript book had told him how to make the statue, but as for what it really was, he had no idea, but anything made with those kinds of ingredients, the ones he had spent days collecting, had to be wicked; *wicked bad.*

Jason shuddered as he thought about the components. *What had he been thinking?* Deep down he knew that it hadn't been him who had been doing the thinking at all, not since he had entered these woods, this fantasy world that made no sense, like he had stepped through a portal to another world. Maybe he had.

Or into hell, Jason thought. He contemplated trying to leave the woods again, but fought the urge, once bitten twice shy. Jason knew that there was nowhere to go anyway, even if he did get away; he belonged to death now and whatever mysteries lay within. The one time he had tried leaving, shortly after evading the ambulance and running into these woods, didn't work. Now there was no leaving them; they wouldn't allow it; except for that one time, but even then, it was more like seeing through a window rather than walking through a door.

He pulled his hood over his head to keep out the cold breeze that had started to kick up the dead fall leaves, which scurried across the light dusting of snow. The wind was irritating the pustules that had now ruptured on his neck and were oozing wet puss down his back.

Why he had felt compelled to ever begin this insanity in the first place was lost to him now. Since whatever was residing in his mind took over, the thing controlling his actions, everything else seemed largely irrelevant. He was still lucid, a good share of the time, but those times were becoming fewer and farther between.

It had started out in a non-threatening demeanor, only taking over when something needed to be done that was beyond Jason's capabilities, but as the disease now escalated, it was in him almost always now, keeping him alive, but tearing him apart all the same. So it would go, at least until the thing's craving was done, the ritual completed.

It'll let me go when this is all finished, Jason thought, *and then I can die in peace.* Denial picked at his mind like it was carrion. Jason continued to stare at the cooker which was beginning to grow red and hot, the pieces of oak wood doing their job.

Jason again cleared his rotting lungs and thought of all that had transpired since his arrival here, wherever he was. He had some time to kill before the statue was properly kilned and he gave in to his memories.

He bumped along in the back of the ambulance as it wound its way on the rural gravel road. Only one well masked attendant rode in the back with him, disinterested and quiet. Jason had allowed the police officers to put him inside the ambulance as his parents stood weeping by their front door.

Their front door...not mine anymore, Jason thought, absent, a blank look plaguing his eyes, the windows to his soul—a soul that would be attacked in the days to come.

His first instinct had been to run. TB was a bitch and no one wanted to be shipped up to the Saint Julia Asylum. Many had, nobody returned. In other parts of the country, people were cured on a regular basis, a cure that worked had been found by a scientist from somewhere in New Hampshire. But not at Saint Julia, where there were whispers of experimentation, a ritualistic cleansing, and evil. The live bodies, and afterwards the corpses, were used for tests, of the macabre, arcane variety.

The devil's work, Jason thought. He shuddered at the irony.

Despite his desire to run, Jason had decided to wait until there weren't dirty cops, those doing the asylum's bidding, standing around to gun him down like a dog.

He waited. One slim ambulance attendant stood between him and freedom. He liked his odds. Jason began to moan as if he were dying and clutched his midsection.

Come on man...buy it...buy it, Jason thought as he continued his act. The pain, from the disease that ravaged his body, made this act believable without much difficulty. The attendant looked at Jason with a paranoid glance.

Jason could see the two conflicting emotions in the man's eyes, between doing his job and keeping himself healthy. Many members of the community medical staff had fallen ill while caring for the dying, they in turn realizing a horrible, agonizing death. It was a good thing that the asylum paid, and paid well; *blood money*. The man took a tentative step toward Jason in the back of the moving ambulance.

"What's wrong son...where does it hurt?"

Jason waited until the attendant was close, continuing to moan in agony, but preparing himself mentally. Finally, uncoiling his leg muscles, he lunged forward sending the attendant sprawling to the floor.

The attendant's head hit the floor with a dull thud, a smear of blood dripping at the spot of impact.

Jason didn't wait to see if the attendant was unconscious, but unlocked the back door to the ambulance. Opening the door, Jason hesitated for a moment watching the gravel fly by. Steeling himself, he jumped, hitting the gravel rolling and, luckily, landed in the tall grass beside the road which cushioned him. He had a few bruises and cuts, but compared to the TB that was ravaging his body, they were minor.

The driver, unaware that anything was wrong, kept driving. By the time he realized what had happened it was much too late to do anything about it. Jason was gone. Standing on the edge of the woods, Jason felt the breeze in his hair—freedom. Birds chirped their manic sing-song melodies and the last of the late season crickets screeched their tune as well. Jason took it all in.

This will be the last time I hear these things...my last fall. With a deep sadness, born of disease and impending death, Jason stepped into the woods, a shelter in which to live out his remaining days...hours...minutes...who knew how long.

Jason blinked, disoriented. The moment he stepped into the woods everything changed, like stepping through a door in time, into another place entirely. The sun dimmed with a considerable dankness that weighed on Jason like a bag of sand. The natural sounds of the woods were gone, even the wind was silent, the birds and crickets either stifled or missing in action. Or the third option; Jason was elsewhere, a place where these beautiful things didn't exist.

Jason sensed the evil that lived here, in this place, the blackness surrounding him like an envelope. He panicked, looking for the road, wishing he had never left the ambulance, but the road was gone, everything was gone. It was as if he stepped into another dimension, a polar opposite reality, a darker place than which he had come; a much darker place.

Now he was forced to wander in an aimless drudgery, a drudgery born of the desperation to find the place from which he came. The wandering bore neither utility nor relief from his disease and he was forced to walk in an endless forest of darkness.

That was until "they" gave him purpose, the voices whispering to him like a chorus of ghouls. They led him to his new, grotesque purpose. One Jason never could have dreamed of in his worst nightmare. He had made two bad choices and now he was out of them completely.

Jason grabbed the back of his shirt. The material was sticking to his open sores. He supposed the sores were caused by the fever that raged within him, yet another bi-product of the hell he had stumbled into. Now the pustules were beginning to form on his face and stomach, he could feel them. Soon they too would burst and flood him with their oozing fluids.

The smoke continued to swirl in a wild dance, like demons celebrating the birth that was about to culminate, the birth of evil, the releasing of something foul and damaging into this world, to be released onto another; his old world, home. The statue continued to kiln, quicker than Jason would have liked.

Jason picked up the book that still lay next to him on the forest floor, now covered with debris. He opened it, trying to find the recipe again, the one he had used to make this horrible thing that now waited birth. Jason blinked, surprised. It was gone, just like the world he had come from was gone. Jason threw the book down in disgust, knowing that something else made the rules in this realm, rules that changed with every passing moment.

Jason recalled finding, or rather being led to, *The Book*. A book that he wished he had never found, as if he had any choice in the matter.

He had stumbled across the corpse just as he had many others in the last ten days. Many had had the same idea as him and gotten trapped here. They littered the woods, most of the sick now dead, but they had thought themselves to be better off here than dying in the Saint Julia TB Asylum; much better off, dying on their own terms. *Or were they?*

A glistening red icicle had hung from the corpse's gaping mouth like a glass carrot. That was the first thing Jason had noticed. It was the bi-product of the bloated man's bleeding lungs and their last gasp of life, that life now having been snuffed out ever so inelegantly.

Blood continued to run from the mouth and down the wet ice phallus in small rivulets that dripped onto the corpse's midsection where it pooled in a crimson slush, its frozen cock protruding through the slurry as if striving to meet the other phallic symbol that hung above it. It had obviously frozen solid while aroused.

If Jason hadn't been so far gone himself, he may have found it odd that a dying man would bother with self-pleasure. He may have also asked where he himself received the strength to keep walking. It was the same sort of thing after all, somehow finding the energy to do something that you weren't capable or of a mind to do.

Despite his brain's lack of functioning, Jason found out why soon enough. In very short order, the voices, wicked voices, told him that this man had failed and he had best not follow suit.

The corpse's bulging dead eyes, the whites turned red by disease and death, scowled at Jason as he had pried the book from between the thing's iced up genitals and stomach. Red ice snapped and popped as he removed the volume, the top of which caught the 'blood-cicle' sending it falling into the crimson slush below with a hollow plop. The ice member stood rigid in the slush next to its bloated flesh brother, creating the illusion of twin peaks. Jason would have screamed if he had had the energy to do so, but Tuberculosis had stolen that energy and his vitality as well.

Released by the dislodging of the ice, the last vestiges of cold plasma came spilling out of the corpse's mouth and covered the peaks in dark red, near black, blood.

Startled, Jason lurched backward in terror, the book landing back in the lap of the dead man, leaning like a crude shelter against its frozen penis. The corpse seemed to bend forward, as if willing Jason to take the book.

"I…I don't want it," Jason mumbled, blood already starting to fill his own lungs.

The corpse's eyes suddenly moved and focused on Jason.

"Nooo!" Jason screamed, but where he was, in this place where corpses reanimated, nobody could hear him, except the dead.

The bloated corpse moved its frozen mouth. Jason could hear the tendons in its jaw pop, the rigor mortis breaking loose. More black blood poured from the gaping maw like a fountain.

...I must be hallucinating, Jason thought, but deep down he knew better. He knew that he was being gripped by evil, hard as iron. Through its dead, blood saturated vocal chords, the corpse spoke.

"Take it! Take it now! I changed my mind, no…no… It's too late for that…much too late!"

The voice came out as a rattle, barely intelligible. The beast raised its stiff arm and pointed at Jason's chest.

Jason clutched at his chest, the pain suddenly unbearable. A dribble of pink blood slipped through his pursed lips and traveled down his chin.

"Aghh!" Jason began to wheeze, his oxygen supply had been cut off.

"Don't even try to quit now…we've already let you live longer than you would have naturally…you should be grateful."

"But why me…I don't know what to do!"

"Take the book…it will show you…or die and face your consequences now!"

Jason could feel the answers emanating from the book in front of him like some kind of insipid radiation. Knowledge was forthcoming. Jason wheezed,

"Okay, okay…I'll do it…just let me breath again."

"Take the verses then…take them!" The corpse hissed. Jason, desperate for air, reached down and grabbed the book from the corpse's lap. He was rewarded for his action, surprised by its immediacy. Air rushed into his starved lungs, what was left of them. Jason choked on the bright red blood erupting from his mouth, forcing him to cough. Bloody spittle spattered the white snow. Then his lungs cleared again. He wondered how long they would stay that way.

Not long probably, he thought.

Jason looked back to the corpse, waiting for it to speak again, or perhaps get up and walk. To his relief, the corpse had transformed back into a frozen bag of blood and bones.

The memory made Jason shudder. With nothing to do but stare at the smoking cooker, he scratched his stomach, the boils that had begun there as a small rash now burst, puss running from the open sores, the signature of the white plague. He knew the ones on his face were next. He knew his face was looking bad now, thanks to the disease, but soon it would be nothing but an open sore.

Jason was pretty sure that he didn't have long left before death claimed him. That didn't bother him so much, but where death was going to take him was another matter, a matter that pressed at his mind during his lucid moments.

Will I go to heaven? Have I been good enough? Or has this evil defiled me forever? He wished now to speak with the priest he had avoided most of his life. He knew that they, the voices, would never let that happen, but he hoped his desire and the prayers he had recited as a young child were enough to buy his entrance.

All the same, more scared of the fluid that built in his lungs than of God; Jason had taken the volume and followed the directions he found inside, prompted by the voices within him. Most of the items the voices clamored for had been easy enough to get. The red clay he had found in the old river bed.

When the voices had led him there, he had been surprised. In the world he knew, there had been a great river, the Mississippi, which flowed with a fierce current through these banks. Not here though, not in this place that was all wrong. Not even a dead fish or rotting piece of vegetation littered the trench. In fact, Jason had to dig down a good two feet to find clay wet enough for the task.

The voices had led him to the two black rocks, like chunks of coal, as well. Of all places, they had been in a birds nest. The nest was long ago abandoned. At that time, it occurred to him that, in fact, he had yet to see any other living creature only the remains of life, everything dead save him. And even with that, Jason knew he was on the way out. Hell, maybe he already was dead.

Who knew?

The human hair had been removed in a more grotesque fashion, shaved with a sharp rock from the head of one of the corpses. The corpse had smelled and Jason almost vomited from the stench of rot as he cut.

That smell was nothing, however, compared to the smell of the statue that now cooked within the smoker.

The last two items had been harder, the next to last because of his physical condition, the very last because he was the only human in the woods left alive, that and the singular fact that the very thought of either of the two acts nauseated him. Jason had attempted the easier of the two first and tried touching himself with a trembling hand, his penis limp in his palm. His disease ravaged body didn't even attempt pumping blood to the organ, most of it being coughed up out of his lungs. The voices screamed in his mind,

"*Aren't you a man Jason...can't you even get a hard-on?*" Jason answered in a breathless voice,

"I...I'm too sick...I can't..." The voices mocked him,

"*The Diablo Si requires the semen of a human...keep trying!*"

"I...I can't...please..." The voices went silent for a moment, contemplating or seeking guidance of their own. Then, "*Must we do everything for you boy? As you wish!*"

Jason thought, *I wish to be left alone,* but then a sensation, bold and pleasurable, filled his body. Jason closed his eyes and moaned as visions began to filter into his mind, his cock enlarging. The voices screamed,

"*Enjoy it boy...it is the last pleasure your body shall ever feel...and you shall pay the price for it...pay dearly!*"

Jason ignored the voices and concentrated on his engorged organ. Images of his girlfriend, who was months ago trapped within the Saint Julia Asylum, flitted through his mind. Then he was on top of her, driving his penis into her, enjoying the softness of her eyes, her lips, her breasts. Jason looked around. He was in her bedroom, at her parent's house.

I got away...I went back in time. Joy filled Jason's heart as he stroked, in and out, slowly.

"Oh Jasmine...baby I missed you." Jasmine only stared at him, her eyes blank.

Jason didn't care, he was where he belonged, and everything was going to be okay. He started to climax. Then finally, a giant surge of release overwhelmed him as he came, like nothing he had ever felt.

Jasmine continued to lay silent beneath him. Then she coughed, propelling crimson droplets of blood onto his face. Even as the last of Jason's orgasm continued to throb in his groin, Jasmine's skin began to peel. Her hair fell away in wet clumps.

Jason stared in horror, his shrinking penis still inside her rotting body, as the skin melted from her face revealing a grinning skull. He screamed and then the vision was over.

Jason blinked and then hacked a mouthful of blood from his failing lungs. He was forced to spit it onto the ground. He still held his now shrunken penis in his hand, a long strand of pearl white semen dripping from his tip into the bucket where the rest was already deposited—the bucket with the rest of the ingredients.

The voices laughed. *"How was it Jason? Was it good for you?"*

He wept silently.

Jason wept again as the memory of Jasmine haunted him. The vision had seemed so real. He and Jasmine had been free, and together. Now he was alone, dying, and most probably going to hell as he figured it. *If I'm not there already*, he thought.

Then he remembered the last ingredient and the sin in which he had to commit to obtain it. In many ways this act had been worse.

Jason continued to weep as he remembered.

He lay in the underbrush staring up at what had been his home for seventeen years. Jason had no idea how he had gotten here, but the voices had accomplished it, somehow. Through one small window of space, he could see the "real" world, inviting and warm. The sun was the correct color and the sounds of birds filtered to him. Around the window, in the realm that was now his reality, the colors were still dark, the woods silent as death. Jason, ignoring the hell around him, concentrated on the rectangle of life and listened to the conversation being had on his parent's back deck. His little brother was talking to his friend.

"No way…they really took your brother to old Saint Julia? Shit, I didn't know the *men in white* came to get people anymore…just thought it was something parents used to scare us."

"Shit yeah Sam, They came all right…and they were wearing all white, it was creepy as shit. I was scared that I might get TB, but the doc says I'm okay."

"Whoa Danny…So…like your brother's up there now, like all locked up…dying?"

Danny shook his head. "I don't know. I heard my parents say something about him running away or something…I was actually kinda scared he might come home."

Sam looked around, paranoid as hell.

"No way! He could be here now!"

"Naw…I think he would try to save Jasmine first. She's in there too." Sam smirked.

"I heard he got the TB while he was humpin' her…she coughed blood all over his face or something." Sam's disrespect ignited a flame in Jason's guts. He flew towards the deck, only to be stopped by some invisible force. The space was only a window, not a door, at least for him. Jason fell on his ass, coughing blood onto the ground. Danny was pissed.

"Who the fuck told you that shit?" Sam shrugged. "Its true aint it?" Danny nodded.

"Yeah, but shit…hearin' ya say it sounds disrespectful or somethin'. Let's not talk about it no more…it's creeping me out man. I'm going in the house." Sam nodded. "Yeah, I'm going home. I don't like being out at night any more…ya never know."

"See you tomorrow." Danny went in the house and closed the door.

Sam stepped off the deck staring into woods with a nervous glare. He thought he saw something move. He finally decided it was nothing and headed

down the trail. As he crossed into the woods, the evening became still and darker. All the sound seemed to be sucked away like a vacuum. A dark figure stepped out of the brush.

"Now you're in my hell Sam." Sam squinted. *Oh shit...no,* he thought.

"J...Jason?"

"Yep...glad to see me?" Sam's heart pounded.

"Y...yeah...maybe we can go get a pop or somethin'." Jason stepped into the dim light.

Sam gasped at the monster he saw in front of him. Jason had matted greasy hair and boils that threatened to leak their oily puss down his face onto his flannel shirt. Blood poured from the corners of his mouth.

"You think they're just gonna let me walk right into Hardee's for a burger and a soda Sam? I don't think so. Now, we can make this simple or difficult."

"What do you want?" Jason grabbed Sam by the wrist and drew a rusty pocket knife from his back pocket, one he had found on a corpse.

"I need some of your blood."

"W...what? No!" Sam whined in a pitiful soprano. Jason pulled Sam's arm to him and cut his hand. Sam screamed, but nobody heard. There was nobody else, only the dead.

The blood began to run. Jason then pulled a flask from his other pocket and let ten drops of Sam's blood drip in. He could here the spatter echo from the bottom of the flask. He then let Sam go.

Sam ran towards home, feeling contaminated, just knowing that the TB was already festering inside him. He ran until he hit a solid wall. He could see his house, but couldn't get to it. There was some kind of invisible wall blocking the way. Sam lay down and cried.

Jason ran back to the ingredients, led by his voices. He poured the last ingredient, the blood of a young boy, into the bucket. The voices prompted him to stir the vile concoction. He had then formed the bust, a horrible, sickening statue.

The voices told him it was a Vessel of the Diablo Si.

Jason was still weeping, but the voices nudged him. They told him the time was now right; the vessel was ready. Obediently, he opened the smoker, choking on his own blood and the stench from the statue. Using gloves that he had found, he lifted the statue out and set it on a round flat rock, the statue's coal black eyes staring at him with a dull sheen. Its finish was dull and brown, the hairs sticking out like spider legs. Two veins swirled about its neck, one white and one red. Jason wanted to smash the hell out of it, but didn't dare. He stared at it, waiting for something to happen.

At that moment at the Saint Julia Asylum, Jasmine held a broken piece of tile to her neck. She sliced, slow and deep. The blood began to seep down her neck, drenching her gown and breasts. She fell to the floor with a dull thud, dead.

Then, back in the realm of death, the statue came to life. The black eyes danced with a brilliance that almost blinded Jason. The white and crimson veins began to pulse with a visceral energy. Then it spoke, low and rumbling.

"You will join your precious Jasmine soon enough…in hell! But I shall let you live for a while longer yet I think. Take me to the Saint Julia Asylum…I have business there…and business is good."

The Forgotten Ones

Jeanna Tendean

I wish they would be quiet, I almost said aloud.

My mother and I were standing hand in hand in the cemetery watching my grandfather being lowered into the dirty abyss. And some of *The Forgotten Ones* were talking about the great white light theory and how it was all a big hoax made up by the living and others were talking about missing their china dolls, mother's bones and a few were crying about when they could smite their enemies. I was trying to hear the Reverend's memorized tranquil lies about the man about to become with the grief and sorrow abounding in that dreadful place, but *The Forgotten Ones* wouldn't shut up.

The last handful of dirt fell from my mother's shaking hand and landed softly on the coffin. With this *The Forgotten Ones* went silent. I looked up at my mother who was weeping grudgingly, confirming over and over by saying,

"*Father, you were a saint sent from God.*" As I saw the tears run down her cheeks, I started to cry as well. But not why my mother or the other mourners may have thought. The workmen hadn't even come forward to shovel dirt on my grandfather's open grave when I heard him cry out.

I looked around at the pale nameless faces to see if they had heard the cries of the dead man lying six foot below, but judging by the looks on their faces they hadn't. But still, I was only eight years old at the time and held on to a sliver of hope.

When I saw my grandfather two nights after we buried him, my hope was crescent even more than before and I didn't look into his eyes to see what made him become '*Forgotten*'. I didn't want to know.

Long ago, I had hated *The Forgotten Ones*, like most people hate what they don't understand because it scares them. Now, I no longer despise them; it's not their fault I see them, but rather I despise this ability I have. Some call it a gift or a knowing, but I call it misery. And this misery hovers over me like a dark rain cloud descending on a flooded city. I still see *Forgotten Ones* everywhere I go and when I look deep into their eyes I see what made them become *forgotten* and then I see how they themselves had died.

I've never encountered a good one, one that had lived a truthful life. Every single *Forgotten One* had committed some terrible deed while living and when I look into their eyes their sins rush in, like when somebody opens the door on a windy day.

I am there with them reliving a hellish nightmare.

Most of *The Forgotten Ones* are dressed in suits and dresses, burial clothes I suppose, which leads me to believe the old wives' tale of the soul hanging around the body for three days holds merit. Only a few are dressed poorly, the ones who died by some mishap and their bodies were never found and, of course, some are naked. The Jews and Muslims walk aimlessly wrapped in their white shrouds, like Lazarus walking out of his tomb. I never know what they had done, for I cannot see in their eyes, and when I was a young boy these scared me the most. People wouldn't believe how many forgotten ones there are, but believe me when I say *The Forgotten Ones* inhabit the earth. They're on every street corner, in every bank, in every market, and in every home. Yes, in your home, too.

One good thing about this misery is that they cannot see me, for this I am thankful. It's not like in that old movie where the dead followed that funny lady home to get her to try and communicate with the living. I can't help them, they are forgotten and I am just Timothy Ogden. I drink a cold beer after a hard day at work and I mind my manners just like everyone else.

I was five years old the first time I saw a *Forgotten One*. My mother had taken me to the park and I crawled inside a cave constructed out of big rig tires. A man was sitting in there with his hands covering his face, weeping.

"Whatsa matter, mister?" I asked, but the man didn't give me a fleeting glance. Instead he started screaming,

"*Just one more.!*" I didn't look in his eyes; didn't know that part of it yet and I ran to get my mother and brought her back. She crawled inside only to find it empty. I got into trouble for lying to her. That night when I was in my bed, I was so mad at that strange man, I asked God to punish him. Little did I know God already had done so.

The second incident happened when I spent the night with my aunt Tiffany for the first time. She had just put me to bed and walked out of the room when I heard slapping and crying noises. I got up and looked in the closet; it was empty. Then I looked under the bed. Lying there was an old woman with whitish, wiry hair moaning something about spiders while slapping herself all over her face, chest and arms. I ran to get Aunt Tiffany and she got down on her hands and knees and looked under the bed.

"Where is she?" She asked me.

"Under there." I answered, confused.

"I don't see anyone; this must be one of your pranks your mother was telling me about. You better stop this nonsense now, Timothy Ogden, you're scaring me!"

At the age of five I saw *Forgotten Ones* about once a month and as time and years dwindled down, at the age of eleven I saw them everyday, as I do now.

Growing up was hard and lonely. *Forgotten Ones* always interrupted my childhood adventures. I never had many friends, only one, but I made the mistake of spilling my secret to him and he in return made the mistake of spilling it to his mother and father. We were never allowed to play together after that. After words, my life flew by and by the age of twenty I was more acquainted with the dead than the living.

I moved around from city to town, always trying to escape, but never able. I felt like Esau searching diligently for repentance with tears, but never finding it, though I wasn't searching for forgiveness, just a place to lay my head that wasn't inhabited with *Forgotten Ones*.

Eventually I ended up here in Poosa City and I bought a house. While up in the attic I saw a woman sitting in a little room adjacent to the attic murmuring about crying blood. I knelt down beside her and looked into her eyes. She had brutally stabbed her mother to death because her mother had killed her deaf and mute sister. The woman's own death was fairly recent, two years prior. She had popped one too many sleeping pills, though not by mistake. The woman didn't bother me by sitting in my attic, it's actually her attic, I guess, but I was hoping to buy a home, a vacation place, uninhabited by *Forgotten Ones*. But I'm just fooling myself by wishing that; no matter how many stars fall I'll never escape their ominous presence.

One day I went walking around my quaint town and down to the river and I sat down on a dock bench. A man sat at the other end looking into the rippling muddy waters, but when he turned his head, face in full view, he gave me quite a fright. He was what people in town had dubbed "The Double R Killer," which stands for the River Rapist Killer. His picture was plastered all over town.

As I fumbled for my cell phone I looked a little deeper into his eyes and saw he was already dead. A woman about thirty years of age, walked by our bench and he tried to grab her, though his embrace fell on air as she continued to walk. He looked back into the river, looking lonelier than before. He had drowned while walking his last victim out as far as he could so he could push her under and away.

Fool. I'd never step a foot in that river. It's not only filthy but also whirling from powerful currents. Oddly enough, the man was smart enough to elude police until his death.

But until his death...

I had met this girl when I was thirty. God, she was beautiful. Her eyes were greener than any green I'd ever seen. Her name was Jessica and she lived in a colonial style house on the outskirts of town. On our third date she invited me over to her house for dinner. After eating, we made out on the couch for an hour before she finally pulled me into her bedroom and onto her bed.

As I positioned myself between her legs, I saw something move over by the window out of the corner of my eye, something I hadn't noticed before. As my eyes adjusted to the moonlight that was spilling in, I saw someone rocking in a rocking chair beside the window. I jumped up and turned on the light. It was an older man in his late forties. Upon closer examination into his eyes, I saw that he'd killed his own daughter and buried her under a rosebush. Then I saw how he had died and it terrified me.

His daughter he'd killed had come back from the grave and literally scared him to death. Up until then I didn't know the dead could do that, and it was hellish enough that I seen *Forgotten Ones* everywhere I went, but to be involved with someone whose dead family member comes back from the grave to scare the bejesus out of them, I just couldn't handle. I snatched up my clothes.

"What is it, Tim?" Jessica asked, looking at me like I had lost my mind.

"Uh, I think I left the stove on," I stammered and quickly dressed. I kissed her goodnight but never called her again. But she didn't call me either. Jessica was the only female I had ever come closest to loving or being involved with for more than fifteen years, because the horror of a forgotten one rocking only inches away as I was getting ready to make love for the first time, scarred any relationship normalcy I'd felt that night. I was doomed to a life of loneliness and a servant to *The Forgotten Ones,* until many years later when I was forty-five.

It was a sweltering hot day in August and I was sitting in Audrey Stephen's kitchen trying my damndest to sell her my most expensive life insurance package, when a man stumbled into the kitchen. I looked up and into his eyes. He used to be a sociology professor at the local community college and had performed grotesque experiments on a few of his female students. He had locked them in his basement where they ultimately starved to death. Much to my surprise when I looked back at Audrey, she was staring at the man too!

I almost fell out of my chair when she looked back at me with excitement and confusion in her eyes and asked me,

"Do you see that man?"

"Yes, I do," I answered, bewildered. From then on Audrey and I did everything together from sharing experiences to sharing *Forgotten Ones.* I took her up to my attic and showed her the woman in the little room and Audrey sat a rose down beside her leg. Audrey took me to the barn behind her house and showed me an old man sitting in the hayloft moaning about darkness.

"He's my father," she told me. "He got drunk one night and beat my mother, causing her to lose their unborn baby."

I didn't leave him anything. Audrey and I were like two fireflies that had found each other. Together we made each other's jaded world a little clearer.

One month after I met Audrey, I moved in with her. Two months after that, we got married at the small wedding chapel in town; no guests, no fuss, just simple exchanges of vows, rings and knowing. Our honeymoon consisted of a few glasses of red wine, a few cigarettes and simple love making at home.

Oh, the nights we stayed up past three in the morning, laughing, crying and sometimes just holding each other without saying one damn word. We had finally found that forbidden fruit we both thought we would never taste. And damn, it tasted good.

It's the little things in a couple's relationship that make it special, things that nobody else knows. Things that make you realize just how much you love that certain someone. But those little things aren't always pleasant.

No, in fact, sometimes those little things can be downright eerie. Like the night I'd woke up to find Audrey's side of the bed empty. I got up and noticed the kitchen light was on and there were slamming noises and rustling. I walked into the kitchen and saw Audrey opening canister after canister, cabinet after cabinet, the refrigerator and oven too, with a panicked look distorting her face. I noticed her long white satin nightgown was stained yellow from urine.

"What are you doing?" I asked, bewildered.

"Looking for *Forgotten Ones*, Shhh!" she answered me. Then she walked out into the laundry room, no doubt looking into the washer and dryer.

I just stood in the doorway, my heart breaking for my wife searching for *Forgotten Ones* that weren't there. I reasoned that seeing and hearing too many *Forgotten Ones* had finally cracked my poor Audrey.

That was the only time Audrey acted that crazed, but it was enough to make me afraid of her. But the fear wasn't tangible, it was more like the chilly winter winds blowing across my face; it came and went without a moments notice. I'd always suspected that something was a tad off with Audrey because many nights she'd wake up screaming, balling the sheet into her mouth, her wild eyes scanning the darkened corners and floors in our bedroom. I would hold her tight until she felt safe enough to finally close her exhausted eyes and that was usually at first morning's light.

Other times, I'd wake up to find her resting on her elbow, staring at me, whispering. I'm positive she was whispering about *The Forgotten Ones*. I'd shush her back to sleep and those nights I'd sleep on the couch. I never judged my wife's instability.

Everyone has a certain degree of insanity, some worse than others. There is a treasure trove full of acts of self-destruction that most delve into. Some cut themselves to disguise the real pain they are feeling; some drink themselves into oblivion every night in desperate hope of forgetting their lost child or forgetting an abusive parent.

Others gorge themselves with food to try and find the comfort that they never tasted as a child and others close their hearts and minds to compassion for mankind so they can feel nothing at all, so they can't be held accountable. And Audrey searched for *Forgotten Ones* late at night when the moon was low and when the fear was crippling.

Audrey had been complaining to me, griping is a better word, for me to get a haircut. For three days she'd gently tug my hair and say,

"Nappy." Its funny now, but then it made me mad. I had walked to the front door, opened it and slammed it hard enough to make the windows rattle. When I came home from the barber I found Audrey lying on the kitchen floor with a cracked egg oozing out from between her clutched fingers. I reached down and felt her pulse. I called an ambulance.

Upon evaluation they confirmed what I already knew: she was dead. The Doctor who performed her autopsy informed me,

"She's damn lucky to have lived this long, her tickers been this way for quite some time."

He was brutally blunt and I had cringed at this, but he was honest and I couldn't condemn the truth. Those next few days were a blur, of sorts, but I do remember picking out a red dress and black coffin. We'd talked about it before and that's what she said to bury her in, though I didn't think it would be quite so soon. We weren't spring flowers anymore, but we had a little bloom still left in us. After her funeral I came home, sat on the couch and cried.

God, did I cry.

Then I lay down and slept for hours. When I woke up it was midnight and thunder rumbled somewhere off in the distance. Then I heard something in the kitchen, a rustling sound.

The terrible image of Audrey wearing that urine stained nightgown in the kitchen, opening canister after canister, flooded my mind and it scared me. Some thoughts never go away no matter how hard you try. They just crouch and wait in the shadowed parts of your mind and jump out and frighten you at all the wrong moments. I got up, walked to the kitchen and flipped on the light. Except for the wind chimes blowing listlessly outside the window, I saw nothing. I heard rumbling again, but that time it was my stomach. I hadn't eaten all day and I decided on a bowl of Lobster Bisque. When I opened the pantry, I reached for the chain to turn on the light, but I stopped.

Audrey was huddled in the shadowed corner and only her legs stuck out in the light. I saw the hem of her red dress. I cried out. She was speaking in a high-pitched voice, the voice you would use for a baby, and she was saying,

"Is the baby a *Forgotten One* or not?" Over and over, "Is the *baaaby* a *Forgotten One* or not?"

I couldn't move. I wanted to look at her face but I just stared at the red hem instead, thinking a million and one things without thinking anything at all. I no longer use that pantry for food. Sometimes when the moon is low and the fear is crippling I'll open it just to see her legs and the red hem. I still haven't looked into her eyes… Night after night I lay in bed listening to the howling wind, rubbing my hand across Audrey's vacant side of the bed. It's cold, uninviting.

My mind revisits memories of Audrey: her laughter, her tears, her forgotten ones in the canisters and fridge. And then I sit up covered in a sticky film of sweat. I hate that memory and always shake my head like a dog shaking water off its fur. I imagine that when I do, I look like a loon you would spy secured in a strait jacket sitting in a padded room. And then I hear,

"Is the *baaaby a Forgotten One?*"

I can't live like this, alone. I'm more tired of being alone than seeing *Forgotten Ones*. I've been watching a boy who lives across the street. When he gets off the school bus, he goes inside his house for an hour or so and then comes out and plays soccer in the street with his friends. He looks to be about eleven-years old. He knocked on my door last week, asking if I needed my lawn mowed. I told him no, but I did need help cleaning out my food pantry.

He should be getting here soon. I know what you're thinking, but you must understand. With no family, no friends, no laughter, and no Audrey, I'm already dead. I'll become a *Forgotten One* myself and I'll do it in the pantry with Audrey. I'll do it quick – a bullet in the back of his head and then I'll put a bullet in mine. Then, Audrey and I can be together forever.

And maybe, just maybe, I'll look into her eyes…

Denizen of the Soil

Jessica Lynne Gardner

"It's that time again," Nazareth said with mock excitement.

She let out a sigh, hating how he could just appear like that. *I was just about to leave*; she lied as she projected her thoughts to him. As a mute, she could only communicate with him through thoughts and he read from her constantly.

"Living here has its advantages you know: the warmth, the jewels, the silence…but rules are rules." Here he stopped and looked at her sharply out of the corner of his eye.

She nodded and wandered off. She didn't want to admit it but looking about the slim pickings from this year's crops, she knew he was right.

It had been an abnormally quiet day, the chewing insects were in silent hibernation in gray-green pods on the ceiling and the worms had migrated to the lower reaches. Tess thought of open sky with its blinding daylight, and shuddered, her burned left eye pulsing with phantom pain. Shaking her head to clear the thought, she breathed the thick damp air into her lungs and rested her sight on the soft solitude within the confined walls of dirt, clay and rock. The layers of soil overhead were heavy and the air, choked with perspiration, fed the tubers above. She pulled apart the blue potato that she had found earlier and took small, uninterested bites as she felt the need to return to the surface; a necessary evil.

Pushing her way diagonally to the upper layers, she ventured so far as to see the yellowed grass roots in the dirt tunnel's ceiling. Grabbing at one, she watched as the dry coil snapped in half and let out a downcast shrug before making her way to the west side of the passage. The damp earthen path ended and gave way to the soft glittering walls of the red bejeweled caverns. She paused, taking a moment to admire the defiance of these gems that would never reflect the light of sun. An eerie glow emanated from within. Nazareth called them "bleeding rubies" because the color looked so close to that of blood.

Only the moonlight dared to enter the chamber, reflecting from the open portal inside the lake. She smiled at the thought that the light-loving beings above would never see such beauty. Once, when she had just arrived, she had seen a dragon eyeing the glow but its scales had been dull and torn and it left shortly after to return to the pit below. She nodded in realization, even though she was not from this place, she had no pit to return to- this was her home now.

The ring of stone laid straight ahead, the dark water swirling inside it like melted sapphire. Nazareth said it was an ancient portal long ago, the separation between heaven and earth; he never told her how he knew such things.

No light- no flame.

She returned to the surface once a year and silently repeated the mantra on each journey. Squinting into the water, there was no trace of illumination but she felt the gooseflesh raise on her skin as a breeze, caught between the shifting ripples, brushed against her. She gasped, her temperate body felt frozen to the core. She glared at the innocent looking waves with contempt, remembering the excruciating cold of the surface.

How odd, she mused, *that a place so cold could feed a flame...*

She hesitated, turning again to the swirling water and backed up slowly as she contemplated the many ways death could take her if she failed. She envisioned herself jumping through, her body going limp, shocked from the immeasurable cold that would overcome her. Even if she survived, the wind would blow against her wet skin, freezing the long, un-kept red mane. She examined her naked, mud-caked form, it had been some time since she had seen another of her kind and she would not have been surprised if she was the last. Compared to the other denizens of the soil, her human body was weak and soft. *No*, she thought, *There was someone else...a brother...yes, I'm sure I had a brother...*

Preparing herself, she took a running start and leaped through the portal. Like a pile of stones, the water smashed against her head, then her stomach and back.

Drawing on instinct she swam upward and fought to surface. But something was wrong; the water was much colder as she neared the top this time. She moved the muscles in her arms up and down but felt as if nothing were happening.

She opened her right eye under the water and her fears were confirmed. Her upper body refused to obey her wishes and was failing faster than she had hoped. Panicking, she kicked her legs and was relieved when she began inching upward. Feeling as though her lungs were about to explode, she could just see the blurry moonlit surface above. One of her legs gave out from exhaustion but she used her other to propel herself until at last, she felt the open air with her finger tips. Throwing her hand out of the water she grasped the ledge of the lake and pulled herself onto it.

Once her palm touched the slippery wetness she knew she should have gone back, yet it was too late to return to the icy waters below. Shaking from the howling gusts of white flakes around her, there was a world like she had never seen. It was not the red-tinged trees of autumn or the bright flowers of spring- this was different. All of her senses were abused by this powerful force that overtook the land and she sat on the frozen bank, fearing to run, fearing to stay.

In all her days underneath the ground, she lived in warmth and peace, only returning to gather food. But she could not see how anything could live in these conditions; the trees were bare and the grasses, dead. The water would have been frozen had it not been for the warmth of the pit heating from below.

She stood, her thoughts heavy, and began to search for shelter. For too long the world was nothing but swirling snow in the dark and the cold was gnawing at her bones. Somehow she found herself inching forward, even as she felt she would fall. Gritting her teeth, she pushed with the last bit of strength she had before feeling her cheek strike the stiff earth.

Not yet awake she could still sense it…the deceptive warmth and crackling embers. Her eye shot open. The fire was there, ablaze in its full red and yellow glory, the flames stretching high above her, nearly touching the stone ceiling. Despite the heat she began to shake violently.

An auburn haired figure sat on the other side, heavily dressed in animal skins and poking the fire with a stick. When it saw she was up it smiled and began to speak. *His hair is like mine... Is it possible...?* She narrowed her eyes and backed against the cave wall as the stick caught fire. *The flame...no... not again...* Her thoughts were fevered and she broke out in a cold sweat. It crinkled its brow in concern and dropped the stick, holding up its hands so she could see they were empty.

Suddenly, it all came back to her, a wave of misplaced pain, and she remembered the day she got the scar. Their pointed faces were nothing but smug smiles and self-righteous glances as they held her down. She saw the wicked, sharpened edge of the stick one of the boys held and tried not to let her tears fall. The other took a fistful of her hair, bringing it closer to his face to examine it. He stared and rubbed it between his fingers as if it were an alien substance.
Looking up, his face fearful he said,

"My papa told me only witches have red hair." Both turned toward her.

"We better just do it then. It'll be one less witch around." They held her tightly as if she would cast a spell if they waited too long and lit the sharp stick with the burning fire beside them. The last thing she ever saw with her left eye was the devouring light from the flaming branch as it filled her body with fire.

The one that did it was a short, narrow boy, his pale curls falling over his shoulders as his nasally childish laugh rang in her ears.

"Look at the stupid red-haired mute-I'll bet she doesn't even feel it". She could scarcely feel their spit dripping down her face as they walked away, leaving her crumpled little body to bleed to death on the ground. There was no one there to help her, even Maltis, her brother, hadn't come. It was then that a handsome, dark man, Nazareth, had found her and taken her underground. He reassured her he could give her the vengeance she sought if she would but do one simple task for him every year...

Wildly looking about the cave, her gaze fell on an exit and she dashed out. The figure called after her and she knew it would soon follow. She kept running and found that the snow was no longer falling but the sun would soon rise, replacing the comforting dark purple sky with blinding red light that would reflect off of the abandoned metal monuments littered across the land.

Looking over her shoulder she saw him running after her but missed the large tree root sticking out of the ground and tripped. Her eyes level to the ground she saw a hefty fallen branch and grabbed it. Standing, she hid the weapon behind her back and paused; did she hear him call her name? *I can't do this, God, what if that is Maltis?*

The figure was close now and she could see that it was a young man, his white-gold hair glinting in the waning moonlight and falling about his shoulders in tangled waves. She stared at him, knowing for sure that he hadn't been blonde a moment ago... yet Nazareth had always told her that fire light played tricks on the eye.

Beneath the honest moonlight there were no red rays to confuse her and she knew she had been mistaken. He raised his hands in the air and walked slowly to her as a hunter sneaks upon an animal of prey. She felt the rage and vindication, her single green iris focused and she watched his every movement as he inched closer.

"What happened to you?" he asked gesturing to the dark, puckered skin where her left eye should have been. When she didn't answer he slowed his movement and said reassuringly,

"Don't worry; I'm not going to hurt you..." He moved closer and her heart beat a bit faster, *One more step...* The crack of the wooden club on his skull echoed in the stillness. She was pleasantly surprised that the body wasn't very heavy, his bones were small and the meat sparse but it would have to do, the winter had all but killed off the rest of the population.

Dragging him down into the freezing water was more of a challenge, but after these last ten years of practice she had gotten used to it, learning to use the dead weight to her advantage.

Emerging from the stone ring, she dragged the wet body through and dropped it in onto the cave floor next to the mound of bones from her previous excursions; waiting for the demon to claim her catch.

Now he will get what he deserves... She saw the victim stir and let him be for a moment, Nazareth liked the taste of them better when they were awake. It wasn't long before he was there examining the boy beside her.

Now conscious, the boy looked at his surroundings and felt his blood tingle down his spine as he realized where he was.

I'm in Hell... how did this happen? Why is she here?

"Tesh, it's *me...*" the boy wheezed, but she couldn't hear him, the great demon raised a gnarled fingernail and she stared mesmerized, a smile on her muddy face.

"Now, here is your reward," he told her, a sick grin on his twisted lips.

"Look upon your enemy as he did on you and know you are avenged." She turned to him, her one eye staring coldly. He shook his head.

No... why can't she recognize me? Don't do this! This demon is tricking you!

Maltis saw the hatred in her stare. Yet his frantic thoughts weren't enough. His fate was to be like that of the rest of the villagers, he was the only one left for their bloody harvest. The last thing the red-haired boy would ever lay eyes on was a wall of the most beautiful, glittering gems; the red of the jewels deepening as his blood glazed over them, they alone would be immortal as all surface life faded away.

That Damned Old House

Jeff Ezell

That house. That damned old house.

Ray past by the decrepit architecture every morning on his way to school and also every afternoon on his way home. His bicycle slowed as it approached the looming menace. Shadows past by the broken windows of the upstairs bedrooms and a breeze seemed to always whisper his name as he pedaled past.

Four missing children in three weeks and no one had even thought of looking inside that house of horrors. Ray knew where those missing children were.

They were inside of that house and they were getting tortured continuously. He knew this like he knew his own name. It happened back then, and it has returned.

Ray pedaled faster trying to put a little distance behind him and the voices.

What did it want with him? Why call his name? The other children had been removed from their own beds as they lay sleeping. Silently, yet viciously, the children had been snatched. The beds were always a mess. The covers dragged across the floor. Always droplets of blood sprayed here and there. One thing in common with all four incidents; not one sound was heard. All of that mystery, yet a voice carried on a summer's breeze were Ray's invitation.

Jack stood ominously peering down at the trail of purity that remained in the air like pollen streaming off the pores of the young boy. Hatred oozed out of him through his tear ducts causing his clown makeup to run down his face. He placed his hand on the window pane and the coolness of the glass sent a sensation all of the way from his fingertips to his toes.

Invigorating Jack thought. He brought his hand down slowly, condensation still clinging to his palm.

"Please Mister, please let me go? I just want to go home. Please don't hurt me?" The little boy still had his pajamas on; his hands shackled high above his head.

Hurt you? Uncle Jack thought to himself? *I am going to kill you. I am going to kill you and I am going to eat you.* Jack's makeup was a mess. A sad clown face smeared in blood from his mouth to his chin. His shirt had buttons the size of saucers and a white collar surrounded his neck. It was pleated and very, very dirty.

"Mister, I will play!" The young lad cried out. He didn't want to. He wanted to be in the arms of his mother with his father looking at him with such pride.

How proud would he be now he thought?

"I will play." Jack stopped in his tracks. His back was facing the child and the sad face of the lonely clown lit up. Not like a bright light, no, the smile shown the flames of hell and his eyes were the color of the void.

Growing up, Jack had been teased. People told him that he had no color what so ever in his eyes. Eyes, that he was void of emotion.

No, nothingness is not void of emotion. It is a place where anything and everything can happen. That is how Jack saw the world. A place where his depravity, his sinful nature could play within like his own personal sandbox. His eyes although lacking in appearance of emotion was actually burning with it.

"My game? Oh my, it isn't really a game. You just have to make a…wish so to speak. You make a wish, and I will make sure that it comes true. Be careful my boy, make sure it is truly what you want because wishes are not prayers. Prayers are what is good for you, what is right, but a wish my son, a wish can really fuck you up." The boy tugged at the shackles thinking hard.

"I want to go home. That is what I want. Now you have to let me go. That's the rules." Jack smiled.

All throughout the day Ray thought of one thing and one thing only, that damned old house. When last bell of the day rang, little Ray and two of his closest friends Albert and Elvis gathered at the end of Old Bradbury Road.

"Who's with me on this?" Ray asked. "Who is going to go into that haunted house and release our friends from Uncle Jack?"

Albert looked from Elvis to Ray.

"*Our friends*? We don't know any of those kids. But, I will go with you in that ol' house just to prove you wrong."

"And I will go just to shut you up. Uncle Jack is just a legend around these parts anyways. I don't think he was really real at all. And if he is real, whose uncle was he anyways?" Elvis asked.

"I will tell you everything that I know tonight. Now, get everything ready; flashlights, weapons, holy water, and crosses. Whatever you can find that you think can help, bring it. It is best to be over prepared than tortured by that demon.

Both boys swallowed hard and nodded as they sped away. In Ray's mind that would probably be the last time that he would ever see them. He also knew that if he did this alone, he would surely perish.

Jack strolled down Capetown Avenue slowly whistling a sad sounding circus song. In his hands he grasped a torn paper bag; a bloodstained sleeve dangling out of the tear.

"Your home Johnny Boy, what's left of the memory of what never existed. Your wish, as pathetic as it is, is complete." He dropped the bag on the doorstep of the quiet suburban home, turned and then he was gone.

"Jack, Jack, Jack…. Your irony can only take you so far in life, and in death." Bruce spoke as he looked down on the bloody clown that bowed before him.

"Do you know why you were chosen? Why you were spared hell and brought to that special place where wishes are granted?"

"Bad wishes." Jack whispered under his breath.

"Yes, bad wishes. I have helped everything from the dying and decrepit to Ling Ling the panda who is so fugly that no other bear would dare touch. Yet, I found pity in you. You Jack, are the most undeserving creature that I have ever known that has muttered the words I wish. That's why I like you."

Bruce stood, his suit pressed and shoes shined; out of place yes, but stylish none the less.

"You complete your task. Undo your doing and you will enter the gates of heaven. I promise you." The clown stood, eyes sparkling as he stared at his saving grace.

"You fix the paperwork. Pay off who you need to pay off. I will complete what I have started and once in heaven, I will be your agent. But I have to go to heaven. Promise me that."

"Sweet, pitiful Jack, you will enter heaven I assure you." Bruce jotted some notes down in his book of wishes and closed it softly.

"Bye, bye Jackie." And at that moment in time, Jack was gone from the Wishing Plane and back inside that old house staring down into the courtyard where little Ray stood carrying an old plastic tackle box.

The wind blew gently tugging at Ray's windbreaker as he stood in the middle of the yard staring at the upstairs window.

They're not coming. The words wounded him as they turned over in his little mind. Ray began the short journey to the door. Shadows danced on the outer walls of the building. Limbs from the trees warning him with their swaying branches, but warnings were not acceptable tonight.

You murdered four innocent boys Jack, I promise, you will never kill again after tonight.

Upstairs in the room where Jack had slaughtered the youngsters, where he had carefully cleaned each carcass, Jack awaited. There was no use in hiding and trying to pounce on the child. Unlike the others, this child had come looking for him. Jack could smell it also. The last piece of the puzzle was about to be placed and when placed, he would be sin free.

Ray entered the unholy house. Ragged curtains adorned every window and dust blanketed the entire house as if it was its way of protecting itself against the purity of life. Ray looked right and then left and then towards the stairwell.

He could be anywhere, but where is he?

"I'm up here you little shit!" Ray swallowed hard but spit wasn't even forming he was so terrified. He walked over to the stairwell and without hesitation began making the climb. His whole body tingled as if being pulled, as if his destiny had been found. A calming found its way into his shaky little legs and his unease over the situation began to settle and fade away.

"Second door on the right boy! Don't make me wait. I don't have time to wait." Jack sat there on the bloodstained table and with the flip of the wrist, flung a tiny piece of bone in the air and caught it with his mouth.

The crunching stopped Ray cold at the door. He had never heard bone crunching before but that is exactly what he imagined it to be when his hand reached for the knob.

"Hello?" Ray asked knowing damn well that Jack waited on the other end.

"Hello Ray. And how is my little snackable today?" Jack's smile was genuine this time. It shown from underneath the smeared makeup and it was even uglier than the one that was painted on his face.

"I must say that I was getting a tad bit worried about you. I mean, your friends have already come and gone, they thought that you had abandoned them."

"My friends?" Ray glanced around the room nervously.

"They were here? You let them go?" Ray's eyes were starting to tear but his will held them back.

Jack closed his colorless eyes as if replaying the scene in his twisted mind.

"Yes, I let them go. I explained to them that you had set this whole thing up. I told them that you had been feeding me young boys and that they were the last two on your sick little list. They were so very scared when I removed their skin and sliced into their muscle tissue with my steely knives. They *hated you* Ray. In their last dying thoughts, it was you that they cursed, not me." Jack laughed as he reveled in his own twisted thoughts.

"That's a lie you old bastard. I know all about you. My mom told me that you were nothing but a coward who raped women and were sent to prison. That you were so ugly this was the only way that you could ever get a real woman."

Jack stood up abruptly. His feet caused the room to shake and thunder as his weight came down.

"Your mother Ray? Is that what she told you? She didn't happen to tell you that she was one of the women that I had raped did she? She didn't happen to tell you that by the time that I had finished with her it was she that was painted like a clown. My makeup covered her whole trembling body. And you know what I *left* that whore of a mother of yours? I left y*ou*, you little shit. I raped many women that summer and I left little parts of me inside each and every one of them."

Ray's tears fell for real this time. He loved his mother so much and he had known that his dad wasn't his real dad, but no one had ever told him this story before. This sounded too sick for this freak to have made up.

"You're my father? Why would you want to hurt your own son? You're supposed to love family. Why would you hurt my mother or me?"

Jack looked at the sad child with sheer hate. How could he have spawned such a weak creature?

"Because she had that certain *something* Ray my boy. And why hurt you? I'm not going to hurt you Ray. I am going to eat you. Every last drop. You see, I have been granted a pass to get into heaven if I can undo some of my past mistakes. You see, years ago I spilt my DNA inside a few unlucky females and I figure that if I consume the very DNA that I spilled it would be as if the crime had never existed. They were all of my children, and you are the last. I wish that I could say that I was sorry, but right now, I'm just hungry." Ray dropped his tackle box and fell to his knees.

Bruce sat behind his mahogany desk as the blood covered clown made his way down the marble set floor. Little bloody footprints were left behind him as he dragged his full body up to Bruce, master of the dark wishes.

"You have done well clown. I have nothing else for you here. You have cleaned up your mess and I have your papers that will allow you through the gates of heaven. Enjoy my friend and I thank you for the entertainment that you have bestowed."

Jack smiled and took his paperwork work with a trembling hand. It was real. The envelope that held the documents were sealed with golden wax.

"Thank you for this." Bruce smiled.

"No, thank *you*."

Jack stood outside heaven's gates gripping the envelope as an angel approached bearing a warm smile.

"Well hello my friend. And what do we have here?" Jack held the envelope out in front of him and the angel took it from him and smiled.

"So you are the one Bruce has called us about? Well follow me and we shall get you processed."

Jack approached the beautiful gates and stepped through. It felt so good, like perfection Jack thought. There was a scent in the air that filled his nostrils, it was sweet and euphoric.

"I am going to *love* it here." Jack said intoxicated by what lay in front of him.

"Ok, Jack, just go through those doors and the judgment committee will make their decisions." The angel smiled and opened up the door.

"Oh and don't forget your paperwork."

Jack entered the doorway and made his way down the marble set hallway. All too familiar he thought as approached the mahogany desk that Bruce sat behind. A smile graced Bruce's face.

"Welcome to Judgment Day." Bruce said loudly and proudly.

"What the hell is going on here Bruce?" Jack asked?

"You are being judged my friend. God won't even deal with the likes of you. The jokes are sent to me. You raped women, you spread your evil seed and it was up to us to either let the seed grow or destroy it before it bloomed. You were the devils tool when you decided to rape those girls. You were ours when you destroyed those tiny clown spawns. I'm sorry Jack. There is no other place but the fires of hell that await you." Jack held up his hand holding the envelope.

"But I have papers." Bruce studied him with sad eyes.

"You have papers to allow you into the gates of heaven. You entered. Now, you must go and meet your destiny."

"Well I will see you in hell, Brucey." Jack snarled.

"No Jack. You will see your demon children in hell. And believe me, they are all waiting on you, and they are all very hungry."

The floor opened and the flames wrapped around Jack's body burning into his flesh and soul.

"They are all so very hungry Jack."

Paperwork

Benjamin Bussey

It's just something you do when you're bored, isn't it?

Granted, many view it more as an 'Office Party' kind of thing. In those instances, it's more likely to be the gluteus or, if you're lucky enough to have an exhibitionistic female or two in your section, the mammary glands that are pressed against the Perspex and fondled by the sliding white light. But on this day, as typically unexceptional a Tuesday morning as one might expect, it was just me, without so much as a drop of cheap white wine in my system, brain matter dissolving into the walls of my skull as I unfolded yet another A3 document face down onto the cold screen, pulled the weighty white plastic door down and pushed the button, counting down the interminable ten to twelve seconds the machine took to mull the idea over before it finally decided, oh alright then, to spit out the reduced to A4 copy.

Then came the inevitable dry-mouthed moment of doubt, the fervent prayer that the correct settings had been used and the facsimile was not missing half the image or reduced to illegibility. If it had not, then the trusty *Official Copy* stamp was ker-chunked down in any convenient empty corner. Or, if it had, the process would have to be re-started from scratch.

I'm sure you can understand why I was bored. It's only after thinking hard about it that I remember I had been in the job for one year and eight months, give or take a week or two. For all I knew at that moment, it might have been two weeks or twenty-two years that I had been employed by the British Biological and Biomechanical Superannuation Scheme, in the Office Services section, in the capacity of administration assistant. It was every bit as thrilling a job as the title suggested. The BBBSS head office took up one whole storey, eleven stories up, in a damp concrete monolith on the peripheries of an exhaust fume flavoured industrial district. Nothing within but desks, computers and filing cabinets; nothing without but parked cars and tarmac. There wasn't really anything to complain about, but not a lot to get excited about either. Sure, it gave better hours, more money and way less stress than the pub, the restaurant or the shop floor. But in exchange... monotony. An unbreakable wall of cotton wool enveloping the very soul, keeping you clean and sterile and *numb*.

Occasionally I'd try to convince myself that it was indeed work of value. Someone has to do it; someone has to ensure that Britain's biologists and biomechanical engineers, as well as the clerical/administrative staff of the laboratories and research centres, have a secure pension. Once or twice I tried to make myself believe that I might even, in some indirect way, be contributing to a cure for AIDS.

Usually the delusion looked like it might take hold for all of about two heartbeats. Then *whoomph* – the cotton wool enveloped the soul once more.

And so, the office plebs drank bitter coffee, flavoured with dusty milk substitute. We found little things to complain about, and vent to one another when management were out of earshot. The men would talk Fantasy Football League, the women Heat magazine.

So in not so much a fit as a lukewarm blur of boredom, I slumped forwards and pressed my face against the glass of the photocopier, and hit that unmistakable big round green button marked 'Copy.'

It was probably down to that anaesthetised mental state that I didn't immediately break into violent hysteria when, after a few moments of mechanical juddering and whirring that I almost completely failed to notice, I found myself face to face with a six foot paper man.

I don't mean a man who came to deliver paper. I mean a man - a tall, strongly built man - whose body was made out of paper. From the neck down he was completely white, the bleach-bright pearl of untarnished printer paper. His head, for the most part, was similarly clean and colourless, except for the dull grey and black mess of his face; a lifeless image with splayed-out features, bleary eyes, flattened nose, mouth slightly agape.

It was my face: the face that had just met with the photocopier. My boredom had given birth to a solid three-dimensional entity.

And solid it was, broad-shouldered and thick-bodied: muscular, if there were indeed muscles within the paper shell. There was no mistaking that it was made entirely of paper, yet I had no doubt that, were I to prod the creature, it would scarcely move. It might well have been carved from marble, yet it was clearly paper, and it was clearly alive, and looking at me. It was looking at me, through a photocopy of my own barely conscious eyes.

And it just stood there, as good as motionless. I wonder now which of us looked the more lifelike.

Guy leaned back on his chair in the time-honoured manner of the tough kid at the back of the classroom, on two legs as opposed to the oh-so conventional four; this despite the fact that his chair, like all the others in the office, was on wheels. Ah, Guy. Guy. Was there ever a being more aptly named? Chewing the end of his biro like it was liquorice; he passed a glance in my direction as I took my seat opposite him.

"Looking a bit pale there, Carrot."

I have red hair. You never would have guessed. I rubbed my tongue around my teeth and gums in the vain hope of working up a little saliva to whet my throat. I swallowed nothing.

"Guy, something kind of weird just happened at the photocopier. He chewed the pen and smirked. Spit sloshed in his mouth.

"Oh yeah? What was that? You find a nice nudie photo of Melissa from HR?" *Honestly, you intimate you find someone attractive just once...*

"No, Guy. I mean, something that was, well... I don't really know how to put this. Something that – well, something that kind of, well, really, does, I mean, go beyond the realms of the physically possible. Kind of thing. You know."

From the look in his eyes you'd assume I'd just broken wind after a particularly potent curry.

"No, Carrot. I don't know. Please enlighten me."

Strange to say it, but I was actually rather relieved when my big paper replica came walking around the corner and spared me the trouble of providing any semblance of an explanation.

And I also cannot overstate my joy at seeing that smug bastard I had been condemned to sit opposite for so long, being, for the first and perhaps only time, lost for words.

"It came out of the photocopier," I shrugged. It took a few attempts for Guy to get the words out.

"It....it's got your fucking face!"

"Yeah, well, I photocopied myself because I was bored," I shrugged again.

By now I was sufficiently accustomed to the bizarre sight of the paper man that I began to take more notice of other people's reactions around me. From the look of things, the entire office had stopped dead on the spot, dropped whatever they were doing, and were now staring agape at the strange thing hovering over my desk.

It was rather disconcerting to be so close to the centre of attention. Somehow, I found that bothered me more than the fact that an organism whose very existence defied the laws of nature was standing right in front of me.

The paper man still just stood there. He seemed at first to be looking only at me, but gradually became aware of the many eyes upon him. His paper head, still wearing my black and white face, crumpled slightly at the edges as it turned to survey the office. Bit by bit, the gobsmacked administrators moved a little closer. Still the paper man barely moved from the spot, no emotion apparent in the midst of such fascination.

It was Delilah from Accounting who first found the courage to step directly up to him and place a hand on his body. First she touched his shoulder, then, when he seemed not to mind, his cheek.

I waited for the questions, the questions that I too wanted the answers for:

Is he solid? Is he really made of nothing but paper?

Can he talk? Can he think?

Is he alive? Where did he come from? How, why?

Is he dangerous? But the only question came from Guy.

"You said you photocopied yourself? And this is what came out?" I swallowed again. There was at least a faint drizzle of saliva that time, for which I was grateful.

"Well, I guess that's what happened, yeah. I mean I just photocopied my face, and, well – this was the result."

Two ticks later, the queue to the photocopier was longer and less orderly than the one outside the cafeteria on pepperoni pizza day.

I've never been a big one for speaking up. People tend not to pay a great deal of attention whenever I attempt to. It's become force of habit, really, that whenever the urge arises to make an objection and give the assembly a piece of my mind, a psychological block pops up and suppresses said urge quicker than you can say "probably not the best idea." No surprise, then, that I did next to nothing to deter anyone from pressing themselves down on the photocopier and spawning their own paper clone, even though every fibre of my being knew that it was not the most sensible of things to be doing.

But what can you do? People get bored working nine to five. Any distraction is welcome, the more novel the better.

Marie from Leavers, Big John from Finance, and Anita and Sharon from Retirements all stood before me in duplicate. Their copies, like mine, were mostly inexpressive and stationary (there's an office related pun in there somewhere, I'm sure), seemingly content to do nothing more than hover nearby their flesh and blood doppelgangers.

Soon enough Claire from HR, Sanjeev from Accounts and Neil from my own department also had their own life-size paper pals, and it was steadily becoming apparent that the little alcove that housed the generally quiet and lonely photocopier was not quite spacious enough to house all these new visitors. And so, two by two the denizens of the office and their newborn clones wandered off to different places, and wherever they went the hubbub grew, the intense curiosity, the seemingly inexhaustible novelty.

Bemusement became fascination, which in turn gave way to obsession. Eager to search the possibilities, Chantelle from my department, about whom Guy had made enough of what were officially regarded 'inappropriate' comments in the office to land him a formal caution, became the first to yank up her top and see what would be born from a photocopy of her breasts. The result, I noted with oddly detached interest, was still a fully formed paper body, but faceless; the only feature this time was across its chest, a pair of squashed grey breasts, bulging over the cups of a frilly black bra. This was clearly a disappointment to the many onlookers hoping to see a figure with a tit-face, but didn't deter others from following suit. Soon there were paper people with nothing but a bottom, and one or two with only a right hand, middle finger extended.

Laughter rang through the office. Never was a sound so hard and sharp heard within those walls, outside of the weekly security test of the fire alarms. No one wanted to know how, or why, or what any of it meant. They were all too busy revelling in how strange, how wonderful, how extremely non-boring it was.
In short, no one was thinking about work anymore.

"Er, hi, guys? Excuse me; can I have everyone's attention please?"
The scene was of sufficient concern to lure the section manager from his office for a moment. God knows it took a hell of a lot to drag him out of his fully furnished fortress of solitude.

He had to repeat himself a couple of times before all heads, flesh and paper alike, fell silent and turned to face him. Must have been something of an unnerving sight.

"Well, uh, I'm not entirely sure what all this is about, I'm guessing some charity event I wasn't aware of; and so, while I'm sure it's a great thing all you guys in fancy dress are working towards, I must remind you that there is still a day's quota to get through. Now, if we could all return to our workstations?"

Jaws didn't quite drop, but they certainly hung a little looser than beforehand when, as soon as the section manager finished his sentence, each and every one of the paper people turned and headed to their desks; that is to say, of course, the desks of those whose faces (or breasts, hands or posteriors) they wore.

Strange that it took that for a wave of unease to finally sweep through the office.

The biting tap dance of fingertips hitting keys rang out loud and grating. The paper people were getting to work. Stepping closer to my own duplicate and looking over his pristine white shoulder, I could see that he was indeed doing my job, and doing it correctly, and doing it a damn sight more efficiently than I tended do. It was plain to everyone that these things got down considerably more words per minute than we mere humans, and they did so without conversation, without getting up for coffee, without slipping away for extended pee-breaks, and certainly without sneaking online.

A strange look swept over the section manager's face: an even greater degree of smug self-satisfaction than was normal. Amongst the staff, the mood was different. Unease gave way to dread, which gave way to panic. This was an invasion.

Neil from my department was the first to act. Gently but directly he strode over to his desk, where his duplicate sat typing away, immersed in its work. He struggled to find the words, as well one might.

"Alright mate, um, yeah, it's not like I don't appreciate this or anything, but, you know, you don't have to do my work for me."

The paper man gave no sign of hearing a word. Still his fingers pitter-pattered over the keys without interval.

"Look -" Neil went so far as to place a hand on his duplicate's shoulder.

"Look, I'm serious. This isn't your work to do. This is my work."

Still no reaction. *Pitter-patter-pitter-patter.*

Similar scenes were cropping up all around, cautious hands touching paper backs and shoulders, hushed desperate whispers: "don't you realise, this is my job, you can't take my job from me!"

It was Terry from Retirements who broke the unwritten peace treaty. Crying out,

"*Just get the fuck off my desk, will you!*" he grabbed his duplicate around the waist and dragged it from the keyboard with all his might.

The paper face that spun around to meet him was no longer an innocuous flat photocopy of his own. It was a huge, exaggerated, caricature of his face, frozen in absolute fury.

Paper arms swung out at Terry with the force of a pair of wrecking balls. They beat him down and pinned his back to the floor before he'd even had time to register the shock. And the worst was yet to come.

The distorted, enraged paper face opened its mouth and from that gaping hole into nothingness, there came a torrent of thick paper pulp, gobs and gobs of it, rank and viscous as paper mache garnished with a hint of stomach acid. It hit Terry full force in the face, his startled open mouth filling with it, his skin sizzling and fusing with it, his throat clogging up with the rancid newsprint vomit. And before Terry had a chance to struggle free, the stuff hardened, solidified, encasing a face forever locked in sheer terror, allowing him no escape, choking him to death.

Similar scenes were popping up in the four corners of the office. The paper people were, it seems, taking a moment to leave the work to one side as they stood before the desks as one, an impenetrable barrier between us and our work stations.

Those of us not yet struck knew well enough to back off. Now this was what you called a hostile takeover.

Over at the far end of the office nearest the exits, the Payroll team tried to make a run for it. The duplicates were a step ahead, two of them barring the door, spraying their hideous bile all over the handles – jamming the locks, trapping us inside. They turned to face the would-be jailbreakers, their mighty paper forms as ominous as brick walls, as oppressive as riot police in a playground. Like cattle they herded us, pushing us into a tightening circle in the centre of the room, giving us no way out –

"Here! In *here!*"

Never in my life did I think I would have been happy to hear the jarring, nasal tones of Guy, as he gripped my shoulder and yanked me backwards, along with at least four random others. I had been mistaken; there was an unguarded door. The door that lead into the section manager's office, barely a yard behind us.

A mighty paper body blocked our path before we had moved two steps: the one with Chantelle's tits. Far from the soft touch of I had on occasion fantasised about on her human counterpart, these breasts were lethal stalactites, grazing and tearing into whatever body was nearest, which unfortunately at that moment happened to be my own.

I fought her off with all my might, such as that was; and to my muted surprise, so did the rest of my fellow human administrators. Chantelle's duplicate flailed and thrashed, furious arms swinging, slashing vicious paper-cuts into my chest – and across the throat of a guy from Retirements, who it pained me to realise I couldn't remember the name of. His blood sprayed all over my face, thick saltiness seeping through my pursed lips.

"*Push*!" Someone bellowed. "*Push!*"

I don't know who yelled the order, but I obeyed regardless. I pushed, I shoved, I kicked for all I was worth, as did we all and the duplicate fell hard through the doorway, crashing onto its back on the salmon carpet of the section manager's office. Next came a flurry of movement, body after body rushing into the shelter of the office, mine somehow among them, me, the one always left behind; then slam, and tearful mutters of "I'm sorry" against the glass to the countless co-workers still trapped out there.

While at least seven or eight bodies held Chantelle's struggling duplicate down on the floor, I watched the scene on the other side of the glass as though it were a televised disaster site. The lifeless bodies of my co-workers, faces caked in regurgitated paper mache, slowly began to quiver. The flesh, already badly singed, was melting away into nothingness, blood and bile seeping into the thin beige carpet tiles.

The acrid paper pulp that had choked them to death, however, did not dissolve: it bubbled, and thickened, and spread. Soon enough, the few scraps of corpse that remained were entirely encased in the gunk. No, not encased: *cocooned*. I knew what that meant before the first corpse rose to its feet, but I kept watching anyway, watching as one by one my deceased co-workers rose up again, not as human beings, but as duplicates: the living dead, in paper.

The newly risen duplicates marched forwards, obeying some order unheard by human ears, and stood guard around the office, barring the doors, black and white photocopy faces watching the living. Then the first batch of duplicates returned to the desks of their flesh and blood originators and silently got back to work.

Pitter-patter pitter-patter.

I held my chest tight, an imaginary comfort blanket in the place of my tattered British Home Stores shirt. The paper cuts stung like a bastard, but they didn't feel too deep. I didn't dare look down to check. There had been enough disturbing sights those last few minutes: the sight of my own blood would probably have been sufficient to topple me over the edge. That said, the harsh salty taste of the Retirements guy's blood on my lips was oddly comforting.

"Come on then, you paper-titted bitch! Start talking!"

Guy. It could only be Guy. While five others held down the duplicate by its writhing limbs, Guy was squatting down over her, with what was presumably the first thing that might pass for a weapon in his hand: a stapler.

"I'm not kidding, bitch!" He must have rehearsed the routine for years.

"Start talking!"

"Guy, have you heard any of these fucking things demonstrate the power of speech?" spat Clarissa from Retirements.

"No. But up to a couple of minutes ago we'd never seen them spew that – that *shit*, did we? Now she'd better start explaining what's going on, or it's staple time." There were a few guffaws and mutters of derision.

"What?" Guy snapped, cranking up his schoolboy hard case act. "Who's got a better idea? We don't know what these things are, or what they want, so I say we do everything we can to find out!"

"What about the section manager?" It was Melissa from HR, the one I had a little crush on. "They listened to him before, maybe they'll listen to him now!"

See, intelligent too. Sigh.

"Ah," groaned Sanjeev from Accounts, "he's out there. And he looks a little too busy turning to pulp to help us right now." There were general hisses of *"shit"* and *"fuck."*

"Anyone else?" Guy roared. Christ, how long had he been waiting for a moment like this? "There's nothing else for it! They're not going to listen, and they're not going to talk; unless we make this one talk!"

"With *staples*?" some guy from Finance laughed. An even uglier than usual smile spread over Guy's mouth.

"She's made of paper, isn't she?"

And then Guy started. He pressed a staple right into the duplicate's neck; it broke through the surface as easily as it would any piece of paper.

The duplicate didn't make a sound. So he tried it again. And again. Then some of the others started joining in, grabbing whatever they could from the section manager's desk: more staplers and staple removers, hole punchers and stamps. They shoved staples in and tore them back out. They punched holes in her hands and feet. When she tried to thrash free, at last opening her mouth not to talk but to let rip the dreaded pulp, they blocked her mouth with as many desktop articles as they could, pens and pencils and post-it packs, and roughly tore off strips of tape to keep the mouth good and closed. The fact that this would, of course, prevent any possibility of the duplicate being able to talk was neither here nor there. She was to be punished. She was to suffer.

Then, some bright spark decided, she was to burn. Starting a fire indoors is not too smart at the best of times. When you're trapped in an enclosed space eleven stories up with no way of escaping, it's right up there with dropping a child over the side of a cross-channel ferry to see if it'll swim.

That didn't stop whoever it was from thumbing a lighter to life and putting it up to the tortured duplicate's armpit, whipping up a wave of flame that crept over her torso like a tarantula, leaving a wasteland of ash in its wake. Still the duplicate made no noise, but this was hardly moot when the many living beings in the vicinity were breaking into panic, coughing, crying *"put it out, put it out!"*

Then, wonder of wonders, the smoke alarm roared into life, and the sprinkler system came on.

And for a glorious minute or so, I thought we'd won. For though the glacial water was soaking us to the bone, it was also seeping into our paper adversaries, breaking the surface of their paper skin and turning it to the very mush they spat in our faces.

They flailed, they tried to get away, but they had trapped themselves in here, and had to pay the consequences. All around, administrators held their hands high and cheered in victory. The recent torturers even felt secure enough to open the section manager's door and join in the jubilation. The paper people were defeated, leaving nothing behind but steaming puddles of pulp. The office was ours once more.

But then I noticed how the puddles were slowly drifting into one another; how they were merging, solidifying, and growing, and growing…

Crisis far from averted.

Where there had been paper people, there was now a paper primordial soup. And it was rising, as a single, enormous entity. A mighty blob, so large as to almost touch the ceiling and so wide as to take up the width of the office, and it was only getting bigger.

Everyone screamed. Everyone panicked. I saw no reason not to follow suit. The monstrous pulp slid over everything: desks, computers, swivel chairs, waste paper baskets, Guy… and I felt a brick slip down my throat as I realised it was not only enveloping but *absorbing* all in its path, just as it had absorbed the bodies of the dead. The slithering mass churned, its surface here and there betraying splayed out images of faces and body parts, both physical and photocopied.

Munch, munch, munch. It had one purpose only; to consume all in its path.

Things are hazy from that point, but it must have been about then that I lost my footing. I can assure you, the floor is not where you want to end up during a stampede. Foot after foot rushed violently across my frail form, my brittle back, my already lacerated chest. Bodies flurried past my dazed skull like a torrent of rain, each indistinguishable from the last. All balance, all focus in my mind was gone as a warm, viscous sensation came washing over me, enveloping my body, my face, rushing up my nose, into my mouth, ears and eye sockets, cutting off that precious oxygen I'd gotten so attached to over the years. The screams were muted. The lights went out.

Had I the strength within me, I would have kicked and screamed and cried to the pit of my guts. But I had no air to scream, no muscles to kick. Every inch of my body, inside and out, was being consumed: softening, churning, turning to pulp.

Looking back, I'm not sure how long ago it was. I don't really have too strong a sense of time these days, if indeed I ever did. I don't know what time or what day of the week it is. I don't see the light of day, or the dark of night.
All I see is the screen before me, the keypad at my fingers, and the processes waiting to be done.

Looking down, I see my pristine white fingers dancing over the glossy black keys, instinctively hitting the right ones in the right order. I don't even need to think about it anymore. I certainly don't need to speak anymore either. Come to think of it, I can't remember the last time I ate, slept, took a piss or a shit. None of that seems a big deal these days. Not when there's work to be done.
In the peripheries of my vision, featureless white figures pass by now and then. I don't turn to look. Not my concern. They know what they need to do, just as surely as I do. Got to get through the processes; then there's the document retrieval; then the scanning, and maybe even some photocopying. And as soon as all that is done, there's always more.

I don't even remember what I was thinking about just now.

Forget it. No time to dilly-dally. Back to work.

Labyrinthine Gore

Dave Rex

Part I - Blood Money

It was underground, the Labyrinthine Gore. Not just literally as in securely well within the Earth's dank, stinking bowels, but illicit as in invitation only and you better keep your fucking mouth shut. The invitations, sealed by scarlet wax with the depiction of a circular labyrinth pressed firmly into its meat, were not extended to the mere wealthy.

Oh no. They went to those sick with wealth. The CEOs of oil companies, the war profiteers, the media moguls, the upper echelon of those with the means to topple entire governments ad libitum. In essence, the nation's elite. And they all gathered, of course, to wager on and keenly bear witness to the most uniquely barbaric form of entertainment titanium briefcases of dirty money can buy.

The crowd sat stadium style within a space twenty feet above - and forming a semicircle around the perimeter of a massive labyrinth, sealed within a clear dome. It was akin to Rome's legendary Coliseum and the sport below would soon prove just as brutal and bloody as any in Roman history.

Like a mighty Caesar, a well-dressed man, whose decidedly large frame suited well his booming voice, addressed the crowd from a large platform set within the gap of the semicircle of anxious onlookers.

"Ladies and Gentlemen," he began with microphone in hand,

"The betting windows are now closed. To those of you new to our home beneath home, what you are about to witness this evening will be unlike anything you have witnessed before. You were invited here this evening because you possess the one thirst that cannot be sated any other way. Tonight, I guarantee that your eyes shall drink their fill. The rules of this contest are simple. Below you are four men and three women. All of them have been thoroughly tested and found to be in pristine health. All will attempt to reach the center of the labyrinth. One will survive and go home with ten million dollars. Will it be Steven, Brandy, Mark, Susan, Lucas, Dora or Charlie? Who will win, who will place, and who will show?"

He spread his great arms wide as he finished,

"*Let the games begin!*"

Part II - Seconds Flat

The lavish display of fireworks lighting up the otherwise dark space above their heads, spurred on the roar of applause from the audience to a deafening level. Of course, the seven young men and women - early twenties all - trapped under a soundproof dome like laboratory rats, heard nothing but the thump-thumping of their own elevated heartbeats as a wide and thick concrete door grated and slid shut behind them. Each studied the other and then their surroundings, puzzled by the fear of the unknown. Each now stood in a claustrophobic six foot diameter room. Each was separated from the other by clear walls on their left and right crafted from the same material as the dome which encased them; soundproof and sturdy, which they all quickly discovered after a tiresome bout of kicking, pounding and yelling. Each looked alert, energetic, strong and nimble. Each would soon be forced to test the limits of these traits.

Outside the great dome, the sound of the applause had died down considerably. Strange music began to play. It was a recording which blared over the loudspeakers. After a half dozen or so tink-tonks, everyone in the audience was clapping along to what they recognized as *Pop! Goes The Weasel* as played when cranking a Jack in the Box toy. Some also laughed and others who knew the words even sang along; as though in some macabre way, rediscovering their inner child.

"Ev'ry night, when I come home," they sang with glee, "The monkey's on the table. I take a stick and knock him off..." The music paused just before each of the Labyrinthine Gore's newest contestants rose gradually in unison, only to slam back down again before rising even halfway.

"*Pop!*"

Suddenly the floor from under Brandy's feet sprung upward and slammed her headfirst into the concrete ceiling above. Like an accordion, her slim body folded into itself, bones cracking and crackling for an instant like aged birch logs on a campfire. Her gore exploded outward in every direction, splaying against every wall like an abstractionist artist gone mad with passion.

"*…goes the weasel.*"

Part III - Hell's Passage

That familiar *tink-tonk-tinkity-tonk* music started up again, as did the smattering of singing and clapping along. As the second verse neared its end, the walls before each contestant again began to rise. This time all the remaining contestants bent over and rushed under the openings without hesitation, except one. Susan stood shaking, staring at what remained of Brandy.

"She was my best friend", Susan uttered softly as tears streaked her pretty, ashen face. The others all now found themselves in the same wide, open corridor. They were all also now able to speak to one another and to Susan from under her still rising wall.

"Get out of there!" some urged. "Hurry! Come on!" others shouted. But she remained frozen in rapt fear and sorrow. The wall came slamming down. The weasel was about to pop. The game would be over for sweet Susan…if not for the New Balance sneaker she thrust under the opening, jamming the solid stone construct in place inches above the ground. Several of the others hurried to the base of the wall to try and lift it, then came the rest, and with visible strains and audible grunts, the wall budged upwards the few extra inches Susan needed to shimmy under and out.

The group gathered and most took a knee as well as a moment to catch their breaths. Lucas spoke up first by introducing himself. The rest followed suit.

Mark had chosen to remain standing.

"Now that we're past all the 'get to know your neighbors' shit, there's ten mil waiting for *me*...somewhere around this rat trap." he said as he started down the center of the wide corridor. Flames shot up randomly from a length of checkered grates under Mark's feet and licked violently at his sandal-covered feet. The acrid smell of burning suede and the sudden, intense pain of searing leg flesh were all the incentive the nimble man needed to zigzag his way through the blazing obstacle.

Mark made it to the end of the corridor and spun around,

"See, its cake! Just be fast on your..." He froze, wide-eyed, his sentence cut off as something blurred not past him, but *through* him.

Part IV - Unsated Thirst

The others jumped up in horror as Mark's body split lengthwise from crown to base, only to collapse in two like so much dead weight. The remaining contestants approached the grate-covered corridor before them and soon discovered that flames ceased shooting up. Still, the grates were scorching red with heat and they sped across to where Mark lay splayed on the ground. The object which passed through him making the swift, yet precise slice swung more slowly back into view with far greater clarity. The bulk of it was an enormous circular buzz saw, like a pizza cutter with jagged teeth; mean looking, glinting steel and now painted with the blood and bits of meat and bone from its latest frenzied feeding.

The single, wide corridor split into two narrower corridors, one that forked to the left, the other to the right. Lucas and Dora started off down the right corridor.

It seemed an eternity had passed as they moved ever onward and they both now wished for something, *anything* to happen just to break the escalating tension. Finally, they turned a new corner to find a door. They ran to it with renewed energy and hope. Careful to avoid exposure to the opening, they opened the door together, half expecting poison darts of some kind to spring out from within. Sensing no immediate danger, they entered a room lit only by the graceful glow emanating from outside the door. The room seemed bare apart from a single water fountain at its center, another door at its opposite end and a string of vents lining the ceiling of the sterile room.

The door sealed shut behind them as the deafening sound of industrial evaporators kicked in. Within seconds, essential moisture was ripped from their pores. Dora's body screamed in thirst as she sprinted towards the fountain. Lucas yelled over the din of the machines for Dora to stop, but she couldn't hear. Already taking several greedy gulps, she doubled over and coughed violently until her blood, the liquefied remains of her internal organs, retched outward onto the once spotless floor. She collapsed, writhing a bit in her own gore before moving no more.

Part V - Shattered Hopes

Steven, Susan and Charlie chose the left corridor and soon found themselves in a most unusual room. The room was cylindrical and spun casually in one direction like a merry-go-round while full-length funhouse-style mirrors lined the perimeter and spun erratically at every angle in the opposite direction. A giant, strobe-lighted disco ball hung high above, also spinning wildly. Music began to play seemingly from everywhere and lights bounced rhythmically on the reflective surface of every mirror as The Bee Gee's *You Should Be Dancing* blared from nowhere. Bewilderment soon turned to disorientation as the three contestants swayed and stumbled to maintain their footing in the revolving room.

"This is some fucked up shit," noted Steven after having tripped several times over his own feet and landing hard on one knee. He winced as he struggled to get up, and decided staying in one place wasn't getting him any closer to the prize money or out of this twisted excuse for sporting amusement. He strained his eyes against the blinding strobe lights and the spinning mirrors to see what could only be the door out of at least this *current* nightmare. He moved as swiftly and steadily towards the exit as his one good knee would allow.

It wasn't until Steven half-stood little more than a foot before the exit that his vision finally revealed the truth. What he saw now was a thick pane of glass blocking the exit beyond. He turned to face the other two in the room who themselves were searching ineffectively for an exit.

"Hey! I found a way out, but we need to break this glass with something." Steven turned back to the glass obstacle and touched it to gauge its depth. The glass gave just a little to his touch just before shattering inward utterly. He screamed as thick shards pierced his entire exposed body. Several of the crystalline daggers dug deep into his face, one even gouged the corner of one eye socket, popping the eyeball out. Its spongy mass clung to a nearby mirror like a glob of fresh bird guano.

Part VI - Biting Remarks

Susan and Charlie made their way to where Steven lay, clutching his face and crying in agony. Susan looked down sorrowfully at Steven and then stepped carefully over him. She lurched at the touch of his weak grasp about her ankle.

"Please, kill me," Steven pleaded, one side of his grotesque face streaked with tears, the other streaked with blood from the spurting eye socket.

"I...I can't," Susan whispered as tears of her own began to show. Then she saw a steel-toed boot come crashing down on a large glass shard that had been jutting out of Steven's forehead.

"This ain't Oprah, bitch." She heard the words coming from Charlie, but her eyes were glued in shock to Steven's last throws of life.

"This is ten million mutha-fucking dollars!" Charlie grabbed her arm and gruffly escorted her out of the room, crunching gore-splattered shards underfoot on the way.

Susan took one last look at Steven's limp and lifeless body and allowed a soft "sorry" to escape her trembling lips.

"What the fuck you got to be sorry 'bout?", huffed Charlie. "Your bony ass just better not slow me down. That's all I got to say."

They made it nearly halfway down the next corridor before triggering a long trap door just up ahead.

"Why would a trap door open ahead of us instead of directly underneath?", Susan asked, grateful that it did nonetheless.

"How the fuck should I know?" Charlie mumbled.

Susan heard stone grinding on stone behind her and craned her ashen neck to see what was making the horrible noise.

"I think we better run," she whispered as she tapped urgently on Charlie's shoulder.

"Don't tell me what to do, bitch. I..." Charlie looked behind him and saw a massive stone rolling pin adorned with hundreds of angry spikes and barreling towards them both.

"Shit! Run!"

They sprinted and leapt over the opening in the floor. Susan made it, landing painfully on her stomach. Charlie missed the jump and now clung to the edge of the opening. Susan looked on in horror as the *Rolling Pin of Death* chewed at Charlie's back like a cheese grater before falling to the depths of the floor opening.

Part VII - Crocodile Tears

Susan started off down the corridor, but stopped when she heard Charlie.

"Pull me up!" he demanded between clenched teeth and yelps of agony. Susan possessed a lot more strength than her pale, curvaceous body belied. With each of her soft hands wrapped firmly around Charlie's wrists, she pulled doggedly, and gradually he got close to escaping whatever awaited him at the pit's murky bottom. That is, until he was suddenly jerked downward and almost ripped from Susan's resolute grasp.

"Jesus! Fuck!" Charlie cried over an echoed splash of water from somewhere below.

"Something's got my foot!"

"Hang on!" It was the loudest Susan, the wallflower, had ever spoken.

"Just don't let go for fuck's sake!" Charlie was now sweating profusely and experienced a sense of desperation like none he had ever felt before.

He glimpsed down at the black, beady eyes and then the huge, elongated snout of a crocodile clasped firmly about his foot, almost up to his calf. The croc itself dangled above its home, determined to get a meaty snack for its efforts. It chomped down even harder as Charlie shook his leg wildly. Finally, the tender flesh from Charlie's leg tore loose and then cartilage snapped audibly and he was free of the croc…as well as his right foot.

After much struggling and little help from Charlie, Susan pulled him the rest of the way up. She propped the whimpering sack of worthlessness up against a wall and tore a large strip of cloth from her fashion-challenged plaid skirt. Charlie silently admired the creamy and shapely view below her waist as she bundled his new stub wound in the cloth. He winced loudly despite her great care and again a soft "*sorry*" escaped her trembling lips.

"What did I tell you about that…?" Charlie reached out to scratch a foot that was no longer there and blushed, feeling foolish. "…that 'sorry' is shit, bitch?"

"The name's Susan. *Suuu-Zen.*" Her irritation was finally beginning to show.

"Yeah. Whatever. Just give up one of those fine shoulders." He clasped a hand over her left shoulder and leaned much more heavily than a good balance called for as they made their way onward once again.

Part VIII - Sorry Charlie

Lucas emerged to the right of Susan and Charlie, and all three contestants now found themselves in a rectangular room with a closed cage towering just ahead. Within the cage sat an ornate treasure chest which all knew contained ten million dollars.

Something else was inside. An abhorrent creation by God's own cruel hands opened the cage door and locked it behind him, storing the key on a ring, strapped to his tree trunk of a left thigh. He was human, though barely so. His slouch was pronounced as was his musculature. He was eight-plus feet tall and at least a quarter ton of solid, twisted, hirsute brawn. His bulbous dome was helmeted by the carved out bloody head of a massive bull. He wielded a remarkable double-bladed battleaxe the size of a lamp post and gave the illusion, not coincidentally, of the fabled Minotaur; half burly man, half beastly bull. All rage and willful destruction.

A sword, broad of blade, lay at Lucas's feet. He picked up the weighty weapon with both hands and roared at the creature as he charged. The abhorrent creation turned to face his puny challenger and returned the roar tenfold. At the last moment, Lucas lowered the broadsword and sunk its blade deep into his opponent's thick thigh. The beastly man bellowed again, but not before swinging his mighty battleaxe, severing Lucas's head from his shoulders. His body slumped to the ground in resigned defeat as gore spurted jets from his neck.

The monstrosity turned to Susan and Charlie, issuing forth another roar; a dare for either to approach, likewise they would die brutally. His heightened fury made him forget about the broadsword still protruding from his thigh.

"Sorry Charlie", Susan whispered as she shoved Charlie towards the Minotaur-like man's right. Charlie skidded along the stone floor, crawling and screaming briefly before one side of the double-bladed battleaxe split his skull in two.

Susan had the precious few seconds she needed to sprint to the distracted beast-man's left, grab the key and unlock the cage.

By the time the creature faced Susan, she had one hand on the treasure chest and the other showing off a middle finger.

Skin Deep

Stephen Morgan

Jack slumped against the wall of the bookstore, tired and regretting the entire day. He removed the bottle of scotch from a brown paper bag and tore off the seal. He wiped a trickle of sweat off his forehead with his shirtsleeve. Only mid-May and already the humidity was killing him. He needed to call Claire. His watch read after ten. AA had ended at nine. Not that he'd gone. Not that she would have believed him if he had.

He took the first mind-clearing swallow of scotch. Why, of all times, had Claire decided to quit the bookstore now? Two weeks ago, he thought he had left her at home to read her Bible or pray, but instead she had been to a job fair, scouting for a teaching position. A week later, she had her first interview. Today, though he urged her to pray about this, make sure It was what God wanted; she had given her notice and accepted the job.

"I can't just sit back and let my life slip by," she had said. "Maybe you shouldn't either."

To top it off, their new store manager, Patricia, had called him into her office to discuss his performance. Clearly, she said, something was wrong. He didn't say anything. What could he say? She was one of those New Age types that believed in everything without really believing in anything. Finally, he just couldn't stand it anymore. He stood up while she went on about the value of "sharing with your co-workers" and left without a word. She called after him on the intercom

"Jack to the manager's office," but he just kept walking.

Now, he wandered to the back parking lot, wondering if he still had a job. He lifted the bottle for a second drink.

Some rank smell assaulted his senses. He glanced at the dumpster and waved his hand under his nose. What had they thrown in there? *A dead body?*

A figure emerged from behind the dumpster, dragging something large.

Was that Larry? It was. Short, dark-skinned, bald and recently promoted to Assistant Manager Larry. Ambitious prick, Jack thought. *Working late to move up the ladder. And dear Jesus, with a body in tow.*

Jack recognized the victim immediately. The rolls of fat spilling over her pants. The double chin threatening to break into a third.

Patricia.

She moaned and scrabbled at the ground, but Larry unsheathed a knife and drove it into her belly. Her arms shot out like pistons. Her jaw dropped. Jack yelled for Larry to stop, but all that came out was a thick gurgle. His tongue felt swollen, his throat raw.

Larry sliced up through Patricia's ribs, then cut a deep T-shape through her chest. Blood spurted out of her mouth. Jack's stomach heaved. He fell to his knees and threw up what little scotch he had drunk. The yellow bile burned his throat. He wiped his mouth and went to crawl behind the corner, but too late. Larry had seen him. Larry smiled as though he had not a care in the world and continued to pull the blade down through Patricia's midsection, never letting go of his hold on Jack's gaze. Jack dropped the bottle and ran, not stopping to look behind him until he cleared the six blocks between the dumpster and his home.

He slammed the door shut, bolted it and slumped onto the kitchen floor. As far as he could tell, Larry hadn't followed him. He shoved himself against the door, clasped his hands together and prayed for safety. Hours later, the sun rising, Claire walked into the kitchen, her light blue robe pulled tight. She rubbed the sleep from her eyes.

"There you are. Where were you?"

"Not what you think," Jack said.

She knelt down and kissed him. She licked her lips and frowned.

"Tastes like what I think." Despite his calamity, his heart sank at the hurt look on her face. She went to the fridge and took out the jug of milk, as if this day were no different than the rest.

"I tried to find you. Patricia said you just left." She poured coffee into his favorite mug: big and stark-white, with Jeremiah 31:33, I will put my law in their inward parts, and write it in their hearts, etched in small cursive letters along the side. When he didn't take it, she set it on the floor beside him and took a seat at the table.

"Jack, we can't afford for you to lose your job. Listen, I talked to her after you ran out yesterday. I think if you just go back…

"I can't go back," he said.

"You have to. Just apologize. Maybe she'll listen to you."

"She's dead," he murmured.

Claire gulped. "What?"

"Murdered," he said. "Dead."

She glanced at the door, made sure he had bolted it.

"Dead?"

"Larry killed her," Jack said.

"But why would Larry?"

"I don't know!" She came next to him and held his face in her palms.

"You sure?"

"What do you mean?"

"I just… You've been drinking a little. Maybe you didn't see what you think you saw."

"She's dead," Jack said. "Dead! Oh, God…" He swallowed back tears, but he couldn't help himself.

"We have to call the police." Claire furrowed her eyebrows, unsure, but finally nodded.

"Ok." She picked up the phone and dialed the police.

At seven in the morning, a policeman escorted Jack and Claire to the bookstore. They pulled into the front row of the parking lot, empty except for the morning crew. The policeman motioned for them to stay where they were while he checked out the scene. Jack took Claire's hand. It felt cool to the touch.

"Maybe I should quit, too."

"Just quit?"

"Don't you think God might be giving me a reason? I could apply back to Seminary," he said.

"Jack, that... That would be great. But... you really think they'll take you after what happened?"

"Everyone gets rejected."

"Jack." She crossed her arms.

"Their preacher disagreed with you about the purpose of the Trinity and you told him to go to Hell. That kind of thing gets around."
He shook his head. They'd talked about this a thousand times.

"Hey," the policeman called. "You sure you got the description of your boss right?"

"Yeah," Jack yelled. "Why?" The policeman pointed his thumb to something inside the store. Once staring inside the windows, Jack did a double-take. Claire came up behind him.

"What's wrong?" Then she saw.

Inside, Patricia moved through the aisles, directing the morning crew with dramatic gestures.

"You said she was dead," Claire said.

"I know what I saw," Jack replied. Patricia saw them, opened the door, and popped her head outside. Somehow, she seemed even fatter, her skin hanging off her body in loose bags. The cop holstered his gun.

"Your name Patricia Evans?"

There followed a round of polite apologies and a short explanation from the officer before he gave Jack an angry stare. The officer told them he would still check around the back of the store, but if that was all, he wanted to wish them a nice day. Patricia let them into the store and locked the door.

"Claire, I think Thomas could use your help in the cafe."

Inside the cafe, Thomas, a goatee on his chin and that sleazy grin in place, waved at Claire.

Claire nodded. She glanced at Jack. She wanted to be with him. But Patricia glared at her, sending her on.

"Jack," Patricia said. "I need to see you in my office."

"I really need to help shelve the books…"

"*Now*," she said, and in an uncharacteristic move took his hand and led him into her office. He gasped. Her hand felt like ice.

She closed the door, let his hand go, and offered him a seat. He took it, grateful for the chance to be off his shaking legs. He rubbed his hands, unable to shake that icy sensation. *Cold,* he thought. *Cold as a grave.*

What had happened? He'd seen her killed. He knew he had, and the one explanation for his mistake, a heavy night of drinking, hadn't happened. Was it possible Claire was right? Had he started to lose his mind?

Patricia poured two cups of coffee and offered him one. He cringed and set the cup on the table, too hot to hold.

"Now, as you can see," Patricia said. "I am alive and well. So no more talk of murder, all right?" Jack nodded.

"Good," Patricia said. "Now, on to the real matter. It's bad enough you left our meeting without a word, Jack. I could fire you for job abandonment. However, Claire insists you're worth a second chance."

She sighed and held up her cup of steaming coffee. She inhaled the steam and smiled.

"I wanted to promote you, Jack. You're a good worker. But you don't seem to care about advancing. You don't seem to care about anything, really." She gulped down the scalding hot coffee and refilled the cup. "I think we know what the problem is."

"What's that?"

"No need to invade your privacy, Jack. Just listen. Claire tells me there's a... 'meeting'... tonight. Be there. I'll give you the day off to think about it. That's all." He stood to leave.

"Oh, and Jack," she said. "I shouldn't say this, but... life's precious. Not everyone gets the chance to make something of themselves. Don't let it go to waste."

He left her office steaming, all thoughts of last night forgotten. What right did she have to tell him what to do? For all he knew, her wisdom came from a purple crystal. Certainly not from anything holy. He stopped by the cafe to tell Claire he had to leave. But he didn't see anyone except a customer waiting at the counter.

Jack checked the stock room and heard Thomas whispering with that silky, slightly husky voice he only used on women.

"That's your life line. It's long. My God... There's something inside you." Jack glanced around and saw them smile at each other like Thomas had spoken some shared secret. "Something about to burst..."

Thomas cradled Claire's hand, tracing her palm with his manicured nails.

"There's a customer," Jack said. Thomas smirked at Jack. He took his time before dropping Claire's hand.

"Don't worry, Claire," he said. "I'll get it. You two need to talk." He then left.

It wasn't what it looked like," Claire said.

"What did it look like?" Claire shook her head.

"Nothing, nothing. What did she say?" Jack stared at her. Finally, he just said, "She gave me the day off."

"Oh! Ok." She reached into her apron and took out her keys. "Just take the car. I'll find a ride home. I know you need to go to your meeting." She started to walk off, but turned back around and kissed him on the cheek.

"I don't know what's going on, Jack. But if you just go to the meeting, I think they can help you. Promise me you'll go?" She smiled and kissed him, this time on the lips.

"Just do what you have to do. I love you."

He walked off, rubbing his arms. He hated how cold they kept the stock room. Even Claire's lips were like ice.

And despite himself, he went. After an hour of staring at the clock, smoking while they chattered about their addictions, Jack guzzled one last cup of black coffee and whispered a 'thanks to God' that the meeting was over. These were real addicts. He didn't understand why Claire had asked him to come. They had some desperate hole to fill with whatever their addiction was. It didn't matter what it was. They just had to have it. And that just wasn't him. He didn't need to drink. *He'd prove it.*

He went to the nearest bar and sat at the counter. When the bartender asked him if he wanted something, he ordered his favorite, a scotch, no ice, and let it sit. The smell intoxicated him, but he didn't drink a drop.

"That's your line of experience," someone said in the booth next to him. "I'll bet a lot of people don't recognize how much you have to say, if they'd just listen."

Jack turned his head to see Thomas, in full pick-up artist mode, continue to examine, then in mid-analysis shove away some young, chubby girl's hand. Intent now on ignoring her, he turned to the rest of the group sitting with them: a jock and his buddy in the corner, some other tall, blonde and wide-eyed girl at the end of the table.

The fat girl pouted, upset Thomas had deserted her. She held her hand out. "What does this line...?"

"Hey," Thomas said, raising his eyebrows. "We're having a conversation here, ok?" He turned back to the rest of the group. "Now, what were you guys saying?"

The jock said something Jack couldn't hear. He just saw Thomas nodding enthusiastically, murmuring, "Yeah, yeah. I dig." As though on a timer, Thomas stopped mid-sentence and pushed his way out of the booth.

"Excuse me, I just saw another friend," he told them. Jack ducked his head but too late, Thomas saw him and approached as though he had been the life-long friend he'd been dying to see.

"Jack, let me ask you something," Thomas said. "I'm writing a book. A Life-Coach on Life-Mastery. What do you think it's going to take to wake these people up?"

"A book? Who published you?" Thomas shrugged.

"I'm a man of some importance. Some people realize this. Anyway, we've all got a life. All this time. All this opportunity. Why don't any of us do something with it?"

As much as he despised the man, Jack didn't have an answer. For the first time, maybe wished he did. He laid his head on the counter, beaten down by the thought that this man, however destructive, at least pursued his ambition. While Jack? He wallowed at the bookstore, only dreaming.

"I think your friend's looking for you," Jack said.

Thomas couldn't resist a look at the girl he'd left behind to confirm that yes, she was pouting and pining for him to come back. He smiled.

"Jack, listen. I know you're mad that Claire likes me. But you've got to admit, it's a clever way of helping you."

Jack's jaw dropped. "You're helping me?"

"Yeah, yeah, I dig," Thomas said, as though it had been Jack's idea. "If she's going to cheat on you, it's better that you know now."

"She's *not* going to cheat on me." Thomas shrugged again, lifting his hands, palms up, as though he were a misunderstood saint.

"I'm just saying... I can tell when a woman's boundaries are down. And it was easy. Too easy." He looked from side to side, like a rock star checking to make sure he had a hungry audience.

"She's missing something, Jack. You're her husband. It should be you she gets it from." Jack stood up.

"You don't know anything about what she needs. And I'll thank you not to be thinking about my wife's 'getting it'."

Thomas stepped back, hands up in mock defense.

"Hey, no need to get so defensive. Just think about what I said." He grabbed Jack's hand and shook it hard, his long fake fingernails digging into Jack's skin. Jack gritted his teeth, as much in pain from the nails as the cold, clammy feeling of Thomas' hands. Thomas let go and returned to the girl in the booth.

She melted into his returned affection as he snaked an arm around her waist. Jack wanted to tell the girl what Thomas was: just another addict out for his fix, and she his victim.

He reached for the glass of scotch and a drink of courage, but he saw a smear of blood on the glass and dropped it. It shattered on the floor, spilling the scotch across his shoes. The bartender leaned over and asked,

"Hey, man, you all right?"

A line of blood trickled from where Thomas had pressed his fingernails into his skin. Jack shot a look of such terror at the bartender the man stumbled back.

"I didn't drink any of it," Jack said.

"Ok, man," the bartender said. "You got it. On the house, all right?"

Was he losing his mind? First seeing murders where there were none, now seeing blood where there were no wounds? He dropped a bill on the counter, no thought to the amount, and left the bar.

He raced home and found Claire in bed, already asleep. He pulled the covers off her and picked her up, into his arms.

"I know it's late," he said. He pressed his face into her hair and inhaled the scent of her jasmine shampoo. "You want to know where I was?"

"No," she said, still half-asleep. She smiled and kissed him, opening his mouth with her tongue. "I can taste where you weren't." He smiled at her answer, but her mouth felt wrong, so cold.

But it wasn't her. It was him. A sob shook him. Everything felt cold and distant.

"Jack, what's wrong?" He pressed his face into her shoulder and let the tears come.

"I don't want this. I don't. I want to get better." She caressed his face, his eyes, and wiped away tears he hadn't realized he had shed.

"It's ok," she said. "You'll be fine." She pointed to the Bible by their bedside.

"You've got help in more places than one, you know?" She kissed his eyes, licking away the tears. He groaned, an urgent need rising in him, and pushed her onto the bed.

"Jack, what are you...?

He covered her mouth with his. It had been months since they had made love. Too much on his mind and too drunk by the time he came home to think about it. But she grabbed his hair and kissed him, as desperate for this as he was.

They made love, no care for making the moment last, only the desire to put warmth back where they had grown cold. When he came, Jack almost left his cock in her, but at the last moment he pulled out, spilling his seed on her stomach.

Afterwards, Jack went to the bathroom to piss. A line of blood streaked his penis. But that was impossible, it was the wrong time of the...

"Oh, shit," Claire said, leaning against the bathroom doorway. "I guess I started my period."

"But you're not due until the end of the month," he said.

Claire laughed. "Jack, you're the only man that would pay any attention to that kind of thing. I'm just stressed out. Let's get some sleep.

They talked until the early part of the morning, made love again, then slept until noon, finally agreed on the issue. Claire would forget about the rest of her two-week notice. Today, they would both quit.

He couldn't continue to work there. And neither could she risk one more day of it. The Bible warned them that people of different yokes could not mix. Why had they pretended otherwise? Was it any wonder he had begun to see visions of blood and demons? This place and its people weren't right for them. They would work the rest of today and tonight would tell Patricia to never expect them again.

Tomorrow, Jack would send his application and apology to Holy Trinity Seminary. The rest was in God's hands.

As they walked into the store, Claire said,

"I need to talk to Patricia. Just to explain what's going on." Jack put his finger to her lips.

"Hush," he said. "Let me take care of it. Promise me." She nodded.

"Ok."

Claire kissed Jack's cheek and went to help in the cafe. Even the sight of Thomas, smug smile and hug in place to greet Claire, couldn't ruin today.

The day went without incident. He returned old and damaged books to publishers with barely a glance at his co-workers. When they left, he sat behind the table where they unloaded boxes of received books, grabbed a copy of The Screwtape Letters and read until he heard Patricia announce over the loudspeaker the store would close in ten minutes. Then he went to her office to deliver the news.

He turned the cool metal handle, but noticed the door was already ajar. A foul smell choked his nostrils, the same scent of decay he remembered from the murder behind the bookstore. *If it had been a murder.* He pushed the door open another inch.

"Goddamn," Patricia said. She removed her blouse. A flap of skin hung off her left side, exposing rotting meat from her neck to her ribs.

"They never last long enough," she said. She rummaged in her purse and withdrew a needle and thread. She made quick, familiar work of pulling the skin taut and sewing it back in place. Once finished, she dabbed the blood and pus from the wound, put the blouse back on and sprayed a heavy perfume on her entire body. In an instant, this beast confirmed everything Jack knew and everything he had feared was true.

He backed away from the offices and opened the hallway door. He whirled around. Jack bumped into Thomas on the way out.

"You ok?" Jack considered warning Thomas, but thought better of it. He just kept walking. If the beast had a mind to find a new skin, why not kill two birds with one stone? He returned to the warehouse, shaking. He sat behind the table and held his head in his hands. Overhead, the lights flickered.

Why had it let him live? It knew Jack had seen the murder, had reported it to the police. Though that hadn't gone well, he would have expected it to at least remove the danger of exposure. Instead, it had done nothing to stop him. Or had it? Its game was illusion and grief. With or without alcohol, everyone now saw Jack as unstable, an addict barely hanging onto reality. If he attempted to warn them, Lord knew they would discard his advice like ordinary flotsam.

But wasn't that the burden of God's chosen? To serve as Prophet and archangel, his visions secret, his popularity sacrificed for God's good? They had a chance to see what he had seen and make something of their lives before the demon robbed them of the opportunity.

Like Noah, he couldn't force them to listen. All he could do was make preparations for those God had chosen. Those like him. Those like Claire.

And the rest?

They sealed their fate. Look at what had happened to Patricia! A New Age junkie that would regret her decision to look away from God for the rest of eternity. God gave no second chances. Jack wouldn't waste this one. He ran to the cafe.

"Claire, time to go!"

But the cafe was empty. No sight of Thomas or the Claire. The lights shut off, enveloping the store in darkness. He ran to Patricia's office, a sickening suspicion dawning in him.

Inside her office, he found the empty, bloodless husk of skin that had once covered Patricia. He gritted his teeth, desperate and confused. Where was she? And if the demon was no longer Patricia, who had she possessed?

He remembered Thomas running by, his decision to let Thomas go, sure if the beast wanted a new skin, it would take him. His eyes fell on the security video, broadcasting views from every corner of the store. In the warehouse, the self-professed gift to the world, Thomas, stood over an unconscious Claire. When Thomas unsheathed a knife, Jack murmured, "Oh, God," and ran. Jack charged into the warehouse and tackled Thomas. They rolled over Claire and tumbled across the concrete floor. The knife skittered away. Jack pinned Thomas down.

"Claire," Jack yelled. "Wake up!"

Thomas cocked his head with a look of genuine puzzlement. Then he laughed: a deep and rumbling sound.

You don't understand," Thomas said,

"No," Jack said. "It's you that doesn't understand. You've probably been at this longer than I've been alive. It's made you stupid."

It felt odd to stare evil in the face. The demon had done good work this time. Jack couldn't detect a single stitch in the skin.

"We were going to leave," Jack said. "But I can't let you threaten her. Not my wife." Again, Thomas laughed.

"You're an idiot," he said, all pretense at kindness forgotten. "That's not your wife!"

Claire groaned, waking up. Blood pooled around her head from where Thomas had hit her.

"Wake up, honey," Jack said.

"That's not your wife!" Thomas said. "Whatever that... thing is, it killed Claire and put on her skin."

"I'm not stupid," Jack said. "I saw Thomas go into her office."

"I turned around to come to talk to you," he said. "But Claire passed me. I'm sorry, Jack. I wish it had been me."

It wasn't true. It couldn't be. There hadn't been enough time. Thomas pointed at the growing pool around Claire's head.

"Where do you think the blood came from? She didn't finish stitching herself up before I knocked her out."

"You're trying to trick me," Jack said.

"Check her neck," Thomas said.

"What?"

"Check her neck!"

Jack's lip trembled. His hold on Thomas lessened. Thomas wrenched his left arm out of Jack's hand and moved to shove him off. Jack, all doubt removed, punched Thomas, breaking his nose.

The beast groaned, choking on the still fresh fluids of its new face. Jack reached for the knife while it was distracted. But the knife was gone.

Claire stood over him, tapping her foot. She waved the knife back and forth. She scratched at her neck, fingering a flap of skin not yet sewn together.

"Claire," he murmured. She shrugged.

Not the one you knew." Jack jumped off Thomas and retreated to the back of the room. Thomas rubbed his nose.

"It's hard enough keeping these things in good condition," he said. Claire offered him her hand and helped him to his feet. "Without those fuckers breaking them to pieces."

"It'll never heal," Claire said. "You may as well just get a new one." She gestured at Jack.

"I don't understand," Jack said. "How can you both…"

"Of course you don't understand," Thomas said. "You think this is easy? He tugged at the skin around his neck.

"You think it's easy to jump into some wasted life and turn it around?" The skin around his neck and head came off with a soft, wet, sucking sound, revealing a face that looked all too human underneath: exposed, pulsating muscle, aching for a face and identity to put a name to its core.

"But only some of us get a chance. Meanwhile, we have to watch people like you waste their lives." He hefted the knife, testing its weight.

"At least this way, you'll die knowing you made something out of yourself."

Jack rubbed his hands against the cup of coffee. His hands felt so cold these days. He needed to visit Claire's grave. But her family had confiscated the body and refused to tell him where they had buried her. He could guess where. There were only two cemeteries in their home-town and one belonged to pets.

Sherrie, the group leader, said,

"I want to thank you all for coming. Let's go home. I'll see you all here next week." The AA members clapped. Jack joined them. It felt good to be a part of their group.

They filed out, nodding to each other, murmuring polite gratitude, forgotten the moment they hit the street. Jack didn't mind. Most people were just bare souls looking for some way to connect. At least he had found a way, even if it was for a short time.

"Hey, Jack, wait up," Sherrie said.

Jack pointed to the pot of coffee, still half-full. "Not going anywhere until I finish this off."

"Pour me a cup?"

"Sure," he said. She drank a sip, frowned, and spit the coffee back into the cup.

"Jesus Christ, do I really make you guys drink this every week?" Jack took a long swallow.

"It's good," he said. "Warm." She laughed.

"Listen, I want to thank you for sharing tonight. I know it's been hard for you, especially recently. Losing your wife. That horrible investigation at the bookstore. I just want you to know. Some of us still believe in you. Don't give up, ok? You're finally starting to make something out of yourself. Last thing we want is for you to fall off the train again."

"Oh, trust me," Jack said. "That's the last thing I want, too. I was just accepted to Seminary, you know."

"Really? Jack, that's... That's wonderful." She gave him a sexy smile, maybe more than a passing interest there and reached out to shake his hand. He accepted. A strange look came over her face. She pulled her hand back, suddenly a little afraid.

"You're so cold, Jack. Maybe you should go see a doctor."

"Maybe I will," he said. Sherrie nodded. She walked away, at a loss for any more words.

Jack took another, long swallow of coffee. He pressed his free hand against the still warm pot. He poured one last cup and started out to the streets. Idly, he fingered the stitches along his neck, hidden by his collar. The only thing holding him inside this life called Jack. It couldn't last long. It never did. But for now, he had a life, and he meant to make the most out of it.

Harlequin

Sarah Basore

Pronunciation: hah(r)-lê-kwin • Hear it!
Part of Speech: Noun
Meaning: 1. A clown dressed in tights with a multicolored diamond pattern, such as is associated with the Italian commedia dell'arte. 2. Any clown or a buffoon.
See: "Helplessly Hoping" by Stephen Stills, performed by Crosby, Stills, Nash & Young.

Harlequin approached the simple, solitary cottage. A line of windows warmed the structure's stone wall, each square a reflection of golden sunlight, painting the walls with flame. Tilting his head in curiosity, Harlequin moved closer.

Heat from the panes leeched into his palms as he peered inside. The small room was whitewashed and meticulously clean. It held a lone human occupant, a woman with wild auburn hair framing her face.

She hummed a pleasant tune as she sat rocking in a primitive wooden rocker, its back and forth motions keeping cadence with her song. An enormous cat graced her lap. Smiling, she stroked its back.

Harlequin imagined the cool silky feel of the animal's fur under his palm, then shook his head in rueful remorse. Cats didn't like him anymore. Not wishing to reveal his presence, or at least not yet, he released a burst of silent laughter. How ironic, the animal's appearance. The black and white pattern of its coat was known as harlequin.

Could it be a sign from the gods? If an omen, he wondered if it portended of good…or evil.

His sigh carried on the wind as if it searched for her hearing. If only the woman would speak. The kindness with which she treated the animal communicated to him a nature of gentle integrity. A thought came to him and the possibility made him gasp.

Could this be the woman of whom the gods had spoken? She who would mean either his salvation, or his doom?

Happiness blossomed in his chest. Unable to contain his exuberance, Harlequin broke from his hiding place. He began to run and the fleeing became a dance as he twirled in circles throughout the small yard. It was as close to flying as he could come. His feet trampled multitudes of colorful wildflowers growing there in random design. Yellows, reds and purples died beneath the soles of his jester's shoes. Crushed blossoms formed his wake, as if his tights were melting, becoming puddles in the grass. His heart raced with the joy of the dance, with the possibility of freedom at last.

Unable to resist, once again he peered through the window. The cat met his gaze. It erupted in a fur-spiked hiss and bit the hand that once caressed it. The woman cried out,

"Fierce feline!"

She grabbed the struggling animal by its nape, took it to the open door and tossed it across the threshold. It landed on its feet. Regaining its dignity, it strutted away, head and tail held high with royal disdain.

"Go. Nurse your injured pride," the woman told it. "You are banished until you learn better manners." Her words caused him to falter.

Does she find it so easy to throw away love?

Heavy footfalls struck the path behind him. Panic flooded his stomach in a burst of acid. Harlequin moved back into the shadow of the now waning afternoon.

A man approached, big and burly, his expression sour upon an otherwise attractive face. Pride forgotten, the cat jumped the fence and escaped. Making haste, the woman stepped aside to allow the man entrance.

The man studied the living space with a critical eye, surely taking in the rumpled shawl on the rocker, the discarded book by its runner.

"Is this how you spend your day, reading and biding your time by the hearth? Lazy wench! Have you cooked my meal? Or were you fondling that cursed cat I saw, instead of tending to your work?" His booming accusations spilled across the windowsill. The woman cringed in the face of them. The sound of the man's voice tugged at Harlequin's memory.

That thunderous tone, oh so familiar. His brow furrowed.

"I - I'm sorry," she said. "Our larder is empty. You were going to bring us game." Her eyes widened with realization before the words completely left her mouth. The man lashed out. The blow echoed through the now claustrophobic room. Harlequin felt the sting against his own palm. The woman reached to the table and picked up a mug. Stoneware crashed against the doorjamb, close to the man's head. The man ducked. Scowling at her response, he stomped from the cottage and crossed the yard to go into the woods, perhaps to ponder his transgression.

Anger rose like an army of hornets to swarm Harlequin's chest. Rage buzzed in his head to accompany the sound of the woman's sobs. Harlequin sank deeper into the shadow to wait for the reign of darkness.

When night fell, Harlequin followed the woman's movements to the back of the cottage. Now the windowpanes were absent of light, as was the sky, save for two moons shining amongst the stars. Silent and stern, he watched her sleep. She rested alone in the bed.

A memory, no, *empathy*, filled Harlequin's emptiness. He knew the man would never admit he was wrong. The woman stirred. She began to moan, as if terror held her in its grip. Harlequin nodded. She had cause to fear. Her breathing quickened. He matched it with his own. Deepening his concentration, he pushed his mind toward hers. He hardened his heart and then entered her nightmare.

She was indoors, but the cottage was wrong. The walls met to clash in impossible angles. Shadows stained the whitewash. They lingered, grew taloned hands, reached for her, for him, and then faded away. The floor lurched up to greet them. It fell away without a sound.

Her cat crawled through an open window, fur spiked with purple and green, but still marked in harlequin design. It crouched beside the rocker. The woman reached down to stroke it. The animal recoiled from her touch, travelling away on centipede legs. It paused only to glare at him with chartreuse eyes. The woman turned.

Her visage darkened with anger.

"You! I don't want you here," she said. "Leave me.!" She saw him as the man. He thought it a just disguise.

"You murdered me!" she said.

And he realized, perhaps, he was in no disguise at all. Harlequin's mind sped back to his own body.

The woman tossed and turned, writhing in her sweat soaked sheets. *Did she remember?*

At last, her sleep calmed. Her breathing steadied. At last, she made it past the dream. Conflicting emotions swept through Harlequin, babbling like hoary specters to haunt him with indecision. The gods once told him interference would mean his *doom*.

But, if he left, his chance for redemption would be lost. Pity goaded him at the woman's plight, but restrictions bound him like Prometheus's chains. His eyes narrowed. His resolve hardened to mortar his will. *The gods made me what I am. But they cannot control me. I will stay. I will do what I must.* He returned to the flower strewn yard content with his decision.

Harlequin never tired, so he did not sleep to pass the time. When dawn broke over the horizon, morning found him at his post, waiting outside her front window. He peered through dew-kissed windowpanes and watched the woman eat a simple breakfast of fruit and bread. The man did not join her, for he had not come home. After cleaning up her mess, the woman returned to the rocker. A scowl hardened her face. She began to rock.

Back and forth she moved, with fierce determination. Black and white and ordinary, the cat entered the room through her open front door. Back and forth, the runners arced. The animal wisely kept its tail out of the runners' reach.

A shadow marked the passing hours as it crept across the floor and up the opposite wall. Still, the woman rocked. And Harlequin remembered...

Approaching his own cottage, centuries before, sod dappled with sunlight that shined through the leaves. He lumbered along like a bull, favoring his aching muscles in the aftermath of chopping wood for their fire. He'd found no game for his wife to cook, so it would be another night of her weak and tasteless turnip soup. Useless woman, could she not find herbs or roots to build up the slop's flavor? The acrid scent of turnips drifted to him on the breeze. His nostrils burned from the stink of it.

Rage sharpened his eyesight. He approached the weathered door, and the wood grain stood out like ridges on a mountainside. Leather hinges squealed as he pushed inward. His wife stood next to a huge kettle hanging over a fire. Whitish liquid bubbled inside, black iron cradled by an orange flame. She pushed auburn hair from her face and greeted him with a smile.

"Welcome, husband. I've prepared the soup, so you may eat and take your rest."

The axe weighed heavy in his hand. He'd loved her once, this strange woman said to be favored by the gods. Love vanished in the face of his ire. She ladled the mess into a wooden bowl and set it on the table. Holding out her hand, she said,

"I'll take the hare from you. I shall clean it while you break your fast."

His answer was the swing of the axe. His muscles bunched to make the stroke, but he felt no pain. She didn't get a chance to scream. Iron cleaved the astonished expression from her face. Blood spattered the room. It fell to flavor the soup. His wife fell to the floor, her life spilling from her body. Parched brown dirt drank its fill. He hefted the axe. Swung again. It struck her flesh with a meaty thud. Again and again he struck, until his rage was spent. He righted the chair and sat down in its worn oak seat as he stared at nothing and everything. Slowly, his reality came seeping back.

"I'm sorry," he whispered. He cradled his face in his palms. His hands dripped crimson accusations as he sobbed. His transgressions had brought him a punishment he only now thought just.

Doomed to journey the world forever, Harlequin searched always for the woman who would mean his redemption: the reincarnation of his wife. The scene enacted the day before, almost a mirror image of his tragedy so long ago. A smile traced his lips. Certainty girded his heart.

She is the one.

He stepped through the open doorway and made himself known. The cat yowled. Its fur puffed, making the beast appear twice its size. It tried to run, scurrying, its claws slipping, sliding until they took purchase on the floor. It fled to another room. The rocking stopped. The woman raised her hand to cover her mouth as her eyes widened.

"*You,*" she whispered.

"Do you know me?" he asked.

"No." Her forehead furrowed in a frown. "Yes. I feel as if I've met you before."

"As strange as it seems, you have. Centuries ago. I've come to help you, to save your life." Suspicion replaced the frown.

"Centuries? You must be mad. Besides, I need no help from one such as you." She paused, her gaze so inquisitive she seemed to be examining his very soul.

"If I am in any danger, it comes from you." He moved closer. Her hands clutched the arms of the chair. She half rose as if she were about to flee. He stopped in his tracks.

"I mean you no harm."

"My instincts, every fiber of my being, tell me otherwise."

"It is your husband you should fear." She sat back, watching him with wary alertness.

"What do you know of my husband?"

"I know he is cruel."

"Husbands and their cruelty to their wives, it is an old story."

"It is," he said, shame bowing his shoulders with its weight. "It was our story. We were married, as I said, centuries ago. I know now how much I loved you.

In a fit of anger I killed that love. Now I mean to make it up to you. There is a way I can ensure that your husband will never strike you again."

She rubbed her palms over her skirt, weighing risk against the hope of safety.

"Why would you do such a thing?"

"It would mean my redemption."

"Why should I trust you?"

"You have no reason to trust me."

She took a deep breath and released it with slow deliberation. Her fingertips came up to touch the purple bruise that colored her cheek.

"What should I do?"

"When he comes home, act as if nothing has happened. See he is seated and feed him his meal. I will do the rest." Harlequin went into the bedroom, to wait among the growing shadows for the return of his life.

The scent of herbs accompanied the odor of boiling turnips. Harlequin's mouth watered. Irony brought him a smile. For the first time in centuries, he hungered for turnip soup.

His mind drifted, mulling the future and its myriad possibilities. The sound of voices brought him back to the present. Twilight told him the day had passed. He heard the sweet tones of the woman - of his wife - and the deeper baritone of the man who had dared to take his place. Harlequin moved so that he remained hidden, but could watch through the doorway. He saw the man toss a dead hare on the table, turn and approach his wife. The man reached out as if to touch his wife's face. His hand dropped.

"I'm so sorry I hurt you." She raised her timid gaze to meet his. A tear trickled down her injured cheek. The man crushed her in his embrace.

Harlequin saw the stiffening of her stance. The hard lines of her expression. He could see the effort it cost her to soften that expression as, gently, she pushed the man back.

"Shhh, don't apologize. We must act as if it never happened."

The man started to speak. A shake of her head stopped him.

"Please, be seated. I've made your favorite turnip soup. Break your fast and I shall prepare the hare."

Watching the man, Harlequin began to match the rhythm of his breathing. He closed his eyes and focused his will. His concentration deepened beyond any focus he'd attained before. Using the full extent of his strength, he pushed his mind, his soul, his very being outside his flesh and toward the man.

Empty, his body revealed its true age. Moisture fled until it was nothing but a desiccated husk. No longer skin and bone, it crumbled, taking with it the faded remnants of a jester's suit.

He felt a jolt as he entered the husband's body. Still, he shoved, crowding the man's consciousness, down, down deeper inside, until the man was nothing but a sniveling wraith cowering in the corner of his mind. Harlequin's will closed that section of psyche, walling the man off from escape.

Now it was Harlequin's thoughts that drove the hand to take up the spoon. The man's face smiled with Harlequin's intention. He dipped the copper utensil into the soup. Raised it to his lips. For the first time in centuries, he took in nourishment.

The woman smiled. The sharp tang of cooked turnips burst on his tongue. He put down the spoon. Cupping the bowl in his palms, he lifted the soup to his lips and gulped its warm savor, drinking until it was gone. Harlequin belched. The woman watched as he sat back. The bowl tumbled from his hands. Liquid fire spread through his belly. Cramps roiled in his gut, stirring his entrails, stoking the pain. Clutching his stomach, Harlequin stumbled to his feet. He fell to the floor, writhing and screaming as the poison did its work. Hands on her hips, the woman stood taking in his every move.

"What is the old saying, husband? Something about killing two birds with one stone?"

Her revenge perfected, the woman laughed.

Beneath Frozen Graves

John Grover

The snow was red with blood.

Puffs of frosty breath escaped Brune as he stood and surveyed the scene. He panted heavily, patted his leather sack to make sure the stones were still there and wiped his battleaxe of ice.

"Such carnage," he whispered while flurries danced around his head. The remains of slaughter marred the hard snow in every direction—severed body parts, ravaged carcasses scarred with bite marks, hollow battle armor seemingly sucked clean of flesh, decapitated heads glaring at the overcast sky. Brune did his best to avoid their dead gaze.

A battle chest of fallen weapons was a thief's dream. What a price they'd fetch in a marketplace but Brune didn't have enough arms to carry it all. The stones and his other supplies were heavy enough. He thought at first a massive battle took place but counted only one banner. It was one army. What caused the destruction of an entire army?

Brune shook the thought from his mind. Matters of warriors were of no consequence to a thief and time was wasting. The clan of the blood moon sent their best after him.

He stepped over the devoured torso of what was once a man and ran. Fur-clad boots carried him quickly over frozen snow mounds and through the dead. Normally he'd sink down to his knees but this winter had been colder than the land of Espire had ever known. Months of frigid temperatures and snowstorms locked the world in a winter of desolation. Food was growing scarce, people were dying and there was no end in sight.

Brune held tight to his animal skins as another biting wind lashed across the horizon. He jumped over bodies and protruding weapons, when something latched onto his leg and sent him crashing down.

A warrior, barely clinging to life, climbed on top of Brune's legs. Horror washed through him as he noticed the warrior's missing lower half, entrails dragging through the snow. The warrior let out an agonizing scream.

"It devours all things," he screamed at Brune. He struggled to escape the warrior's grip but it held tight. The warrior reached for Brune's dagger and with hesitation Brune lifted his battleaxe in defense. He could think of no other way to end this.

With a sigh the warrior let go and died. It had ended itself. Brune rolled the man aside with trembling hands and caught a glimpse of a silhouette in the distance. One of the clan had finally caught up with him.

"Good trackers." Brune rolled his eyes and stumbled to his feet. As the form drew closer he saw bones decorating bloodied skins and furs, and blades in both of his hands. A howl pealed through the air.

Perhaps stealing the precious stones that adorned the statue of their God of death wasn't the best idea. What choice did Brune have? His woman and daughter were hungry and the stones could be traded for gold or food.

Brune raced across the white landscape but heard the crunching steps of his pursuer grow closer. They were known to be fast hunters but he never realized how fast until now. His heart slammed and his belly ached. His legs cramped but he pushed on, knowing full well more of them would join the first. A stream of spittle froze to his chin -there was nothing but vast emptiness ahead, and nowhere to hide. Moments later he heard another howl and rustling behind him. Brune turned sharply and the hunter was hurling through the air towards him.

The two crashed onto the ground and rolled over one another. The hunter crossed the blades strapped to his wrists over Brune's throat and pushed with all of his might, attempting to take his head off. Brune smelled stale breath, stared at jagged-yellow teeth and fire within blood-shot eyes. The hunter's nose was pierced with bone and his face was painted black with runes.

Brune used the handle of his axe to keep the blades at bay and kicked his foe off to the ground with his big feet. The two gathered themselves and clashed again. Blades met axe and sparks showered their heads. Brune's raven locks were protected under the makeshift hood of his furs, while frost coated the hunter's bald head. The hunter disengaged and landed a swift kick to Brune's gut.

Brune double over and coughed. The air snatched out of him, he backed away from his foe, who quickly moved around him in some bizarre dance. The hunter's wiry body twisted and turned until suddenly Brune lost sight of him.

A bladed arm reached from behind Brune and pressed against his throat again. Brune would not go down so easily, with brute strength he took hold of the hunter's arm and flipped him over his shoulders. The hunter landed hard and Brune then swung his axe with both hands. Shards of ice shot through the air as the hunter rolled out of the way and the axe plunged into the ground. Brune pulled it with all his might but it was stuck.

"By the Gods!" he cursed.

His adversary got to his feet and spun around wildly. Blades slashed across Brune's arm, cutting fur and drawing blood. Pain seared through him and he grimaced, his teeth gnashing. He bellowed angry grunts and his foe replied with a howl.
The hunter advanced but Brune's fist connected with his jaw, temporarily dazing him. A growl rose in the hunter's chest.

"I do no fear you!" Brune mocked. "Scream all you want, animal!"

The two lunged for each other, running at full speed. They collided again and with his weight advantage Brune ended up on top, forcing the hunter to the ground. One of the hunter's blades smashed a pile of ice and cracked in half. Enraged, he thrust his hands around Brune's throat and squeezed, his strength was shocking.

Brune's vision blurred, his breath grew short as the hunter shouted babble at him. A numb feeling slithered up Brune's spine as he leaned onto his side, suddenly he felt colder than the land around him. Flashes of his woman tore through his mind.

His rival's eyes glared as he leaned in on him. Out of sheer instinct, Brune bit into the side of the hunter's head. He pulled away with part of an ear clasped between his teeth. A trail of crimson shot across the snow and the hunter wailed in agony.

With a gasp, and a curse, Brune jumped to his feet, grabbed hold of the hunter and tossed him across the icy ground. The hunter slid into some rocks and stopped a few feet away from his intended victim.

The two stood across from each other, facing off one more time when a thunderous rumble caught their attention. The ground beneath them rocked violently. Brune looked down and watched the ground crack under his feet. He fought to keep his balance as did his pursuer. A screech resounded through the air and in a blinding flash of snow and ice a huge creature burst from the ground, scooping the hunter of the blood moon clan up in its massive maw.

Brune fell backwards, mouth gaping as a monstrous worm with white fur covering its entire body rose nearly thirty feet into the air. It caught the hunter in a circular mouth lined with razor teeth.

The hunter fought for freedom, his arms and legs failing until the worm swallowed his legs. A gurgled scream filled the air and a geyser of blood exploded into the pale sky. Seconds later the clan hunter was gone.

The worm reared back, a bulge eased down its body and vanished. Blood painted its white fur with scarlet blotches. It screeched and curled around to face Brune. His heart jumped into this throat, his arms twitched, he could find no eyes on the beast but he knew it sensed him standing there like a fool. The gargantuan worm plummeted downward and the entire land jumped. Brune tumbled off his feet, landed on his belly and gasped.

He immediately jumped up and ran like never before. The ground rumbled again and he peered briefly over his shoulder to see the worm squirming after him, seconds later it burrowed into the ground.

Faster…faster, the thief carried himself like the wind. Brune searched briefly but there was no sign of his battleaxe. In the distance he could see a mountain range. He made a straight line to it.

"Great beast cannot move under the mountains." Brune hoped as the ground roared and the sound of thunder echoed again.

A mound of snow rose up to his left, keeping pace with him. It turned sharply and cut in front of him. Brune dove to his left and out of its way, as the ground erupted like a raging volcano.

The worm breached once again, it wriggled to the surface and searched the area. It almost appeared to sniff the air but Brune could find no nose on the creature either, only a carnivorous mouth full of layers of teeth, two maybe three circles.

Brune, cut off from his route to the mountains, wondered if that was by design. He needed a new way to get there for it was his only chance of survival. He hurled himself up again and continued to his left. The worm followed, diving back underground.

In this direction Brune thought he saw a body of water. A vast surface glittered in the light.

Light? The sun finally appeared in the sky. After weeks of hiding in the gloom it had returned! Brune smiled as the light revealed a frozen lake.

"The Gods bless me," he quipped. "Keep following beast!" A new plan formed in Brune's head as he raced toward the lake.

"Sink beneath the waters beast. Sink!" He laughed aloud as he heard the creature burrowing behind him. He looked back to make sure the snow mound was behind. It grew nearer...

And nearer still...

Until Brune reached the lake and skidded over its surface. He was in the center before the ice began to crack and splinter in every direction like a spider's web. Brune beamed from ear to ear as the snow mound reached the edge of the lake and the worm started to surface.

"Come...come!" Brune shook his hands and stomped his feet but something was wrong. His smile vanished as he looked down and discovered that it was no lake he stood on...it was a pit. A scream raged from Brune as he fell through and slammed against solid ice. He slid at neck-break speed into the darkness below and woke hours later to the sound of dripping all around him.

He opened his eyes to see nothing but the dark. It was cold and wet. Brune shivered, dull pain washed through him. He felt around in front of him and but all his hands could detect was ice. He patted his body down for the sack and found it still strapped around his body.

"Thank the Gods." He bowed his head with respect. Reaching into the sack, he pushed the stones aside to search for an unlit torch. He found one and a bit of flint, taking them out he struck the torch once with the flint and flames came to life instantly.

Brune looked around and discovered he was in a cave with huge icicles hanging over him, dripping methodically. When he stood he actually noticed he was in a network of caves, tunnels, dark as pitch, twisted off into several directions. He chose the most straightforward route, the one ahead.

He made it halfway down the tunnel when he stopped dead in his tracks. His torchlight picked up a ghastly sight flickering in the shadows. Brune moved closer to find a body frozen into the side of the tunnel. Behind a tomb of ice, the half devoured body of a woman hung in eternal slumber, her anguished expression frozen for all of time.

Beside the woman was another corpse behind ice. This one was a man without legs. Brune choked back his vomit and pushed on, his feet nearly tripping over something hard in the tunnel. He shined the torch below and saw a skull leering up at him.

"*Its lair,*" Brune whispered. *Can this be? The creature set a trap to get me into its lair? Yes, it brought me to the pit by blocking my path to the mountains.*

"Help!" A voice called from the dark.

Brune rushed down the tunnel and found a young man hanging by his feet from the icicles above.

"Help me... please...before it comes back."

"I will try," Brune set down his torch and took hold of the young man's arms and pulled. The ice held tight.

"Use your fire..." the young man begged.

"It will take too long." Brune answered. "The beast is on my trail." He looked around and then pulled the dagger from his belt, his only defense left, and began digging.

"Faster...please..."

"I am trying. I will continue until..." A rumble echoed through the caves, interrupting his words. The white worm came barreling down the tunnel.

"I am sorry," Brune said as he dashed behind a cluster of rocks.

"No! I beg of you!"

Brune doused his torch and watched the worm squirm through the tunnel. Its body could not entirely fit in the cave but enough that it managed to bite the young man's arm clean off. Blood sprayed across the ground as his screams filled the cave.

After swallowing the arm, the worm secreted a clear fluid from its mouth all over the convulsing young man. Within moments the fluid froze solid, encasing the man and preserving the creature's meals; which it would undoubtedly eat at a future date.

The worm coiled its way through the frigid cave, nudging slowly down the tunnel. Brune eluded it for the moment but could not stay where he was forever. He appreciated being away from the lashing winds outside and the threat of frostbite, but the creature was in no hurry to move, perhaps digesting its recent meals.

How do I get back to the surface? Brune thought long and hard but could think of only one way. He pulled the dagger from his belt and ignited his torch. His arms trembled, he drew breath quickly and despite the cold, sweat soaked his face.

He sucked air and launched himself at the beast. The dagger found its mark, plunging deep into the worm's hide. Black pus spilled to the ground as Brune used his dagger to scale the mighty creature's body. An ear-piercing wail resounded and the beast writhed with fury.

Getting his footing, Brune pulled out his dagger, held onto the fresh wound and plunged the dagger into the body again, at a higher position. More black ichor flowed, the stench was enough to render Brune unconscious but he pushed on, climbing to the top of the worm at last. He ran away from the creature's head, all the way down its long furry body, fighting to keep balance, while it jerked and swayed, searching for the pit he'd fallen through. Brune figured the worm was big enough for him to reach the top of the tunnel and get out.

The worm twisted around and moved quickly. Brune almost slipped, hitting his shoulder up against the cave wall for support. His torch illuminated the way, icicles barely missing his head as he ran. Finally the creature returned to burrowing and snapped its body like a whip.

Brune sailed through the air and smashed through a host of icicles. He landed hard on his back, slid across a new cave, and hit a wall. Blood stung his eyes and seeped into his mouth; the ice tore into him, ripped his face and lanced his left arm. His entire body twisted in agony. For a moment, his sight went black. A hollow groan rang in his ears.

Brune lay there unmoving. His fingers wiggled a little and a salty taste laced his mouth. A voice called to him…fleeting…barely a whisper. It was his daughter's voice.

"Father, my belly hurts…" He stirred slowly. A leg… an arm…

"I am so hungry. Why haven't you come home?" Her voice dwindled into weeping.

"Layla," he groaned as the sobs grew louder. One eye popped open and searched the cave for his daughter. The weeping shifted into shrieking. Brune pulled himself up on unsteady legs and recovered the torch by his feet. It wasn't his daughter crying in the cave.

Brune hobbled over to a dugout hole in the corner of the cave and shone his torchlight. Inside the hole squirmed a nest of small white worms, about the size of serpents. The creature's young. He searched the cave for his dagger, found it and stepped towards the nest…

The wall behind him shook violently and crumbled, the white worm smashed through it and screeched at the stunned Brune. He eyed the young stirring beside him and realized he and the worm were one in the same. Both wanted to protect their family and would do anything necessary to accomplish that goal.

The worm charged and so did Brune, letting out a scream that echoed throughout all the caves. As the beast closed in, Brune wasn't quite sure if he fell or jumped out of the way, but he managed to sidestep the worm and catch it with his dagger again, tearing open its body as it burrowed.

Hot pus poured out, steam choked the air, and Brune held tight as the creature dragged him out of its den. His legs skinned the ice-covered ground before he managed to climb onto the beast again.

The worm curled around the icicles and stalagmites along the cave's floors and wedged itself. Brune continued to stab the creature again and again, blood sputtering over his hands and face, realizing it was having little effect.

Brune stopped, panted and looked up. Above him the icicles stretched long and sharp. Seizing his chance while the worm was stuck, he stood carefully and began chopping at the ice over his head.

The first icicle cracked and fell, lodging deep into the beast's flesh. Wails erupted as another dropped then another. The worm buckled, threatening to throw Brune off but he held tight, grabbing hold of one of the protruding icicles.

A rage-filled roar finally exploded from the worm. It thrashed wildly and loosened itself, smashing the stalagmites to pieces. It shot down the tunnels at full speed. Brune held on for dear life, the terrible speed causing his nose to bleed and his eyes to water.

The worm squirmed to the pit entrance and reared up, exiting half way. It rose high into air and bucked one last time. Brune soared into the air, screaming all the way down until the snow broke his fall. He lifted his head to see the worm, embedded with huge icicles, bare its teeth and screech at him.

A misty black cloud drifted from its mouth and dissipated into the air. Moments later it slammed down on the edge of the pit and sighed. Brune sat up and bowed his head with respect. The worm slithered back into its caves and tunnels, the faint sound of burrowing resounded in the distance.

Brune rose and walked on. He looked up and saw the mountain range ahead, and the newly risen sun as it breached the peaks. He knew on the other side of the range a large village awaited. He looked down at the leather sack still with him and patted it. He knew now that his family would be all right. The air was just a little warmer, and the snow a little softer. He looked back at the caves one last time and a smile curled over his face. *Family*, he thought.

Last Resort

Gayle Arrowood

Part I Jim Sparks

Buzzzzz! Buzzzzz!

Chris, the boss, jerked out of his chair. He grabbed the phone at his waist, then muttered,

"It's one of the victims' lines." He plopped back down in his seat. Each man had a cell phone with the same number. If Chris was ever in trouble for something that he or Jim did or didn't do, they'd hear about it on this phone.

Chris' eyes shot rage at Jim.

"Answer the F-ing phone." He stared at Jim and the five computer monitors as if he wanted to listen carefully while Jim talked to this Moran guy.

Before answering, Jim waited for a name, address, SSN, assets, net worth and hotlines history to appear on one of his computer screens. Neither the victims nor the other hotlines knew this one had caller ID and illegal access to the government's data bank on everyone.

Buzzzzz! Buzzzzz!

"Terrorism Hotline," Jim spoke gently as if he were a heavenly helping hand. "How can I be of service tonight?"

A full minute of silence.

"Somebody gave me your number. Fuck this has been going on too long. I've got to be dead, but can't be, hurt too much." The caller stopped for a labored breath.

On a second monitor, coming through the web cam phones, Jim saw this victim drooped over his dining room table where he kept his computer system. He fingered the 14K gold watch in his hand, fascinated by it.

Jim spread two fingers in a victory sign to Chris, winked, and quickly cut into the conversation, like he'd been dipping into the accounts during the last few days. The victim couldn't see this because the computer ran a program, whereby he saw a pre-recorded session of Jim's actions, but with Chris' face.

Every once in a while, the main office in this operation clicked into the monitors to make sure everything was going the way they wanted. They didn't know Chris had hired Jim. Chris had requested an assistant, but they turned him down.

"Let's see here. Practical matters first. What's your name and problem?"

"Phil Moran."

"I see you bought the web cam phone, like the other hotlines suggested. It's important we see each other. We need to be as close as possible for me to help you."

Jim went over some details, and he reviewed the caller's extensive case history with every hotline in the country. (All of them had 800 numbers.)

"OK, you started with Crisis Hotline, I believe. Do you recall what advice they gave you?"

"Leave immediately and get a divorce." The victim's shoulders sagged even further over the table because he knew the next question and dreaded it. Most hotlines started out the same way. Jim knew the answer before Moran said it, because a third monitor picked up Phil's thoughts.

"What was the fight about tonight?" Jim asked.

"The bitch bought a Ouija game for our computer and me. If I sat down and used the keyboard to ask it questions, the bitch would have been able to read my mind. If I knew the answer, she and the computer would know it. I can't afford that. She'd kill me."

"Are you saying she could have controlled you better if she knew your thoughts?" Jim asked.

"Yes! Everybody we know is talking about this damn game, so she had to get one." Phil let out a deep breath. "Ouch! My ribs hurt every time I breathe."

Jim's third monitor worked about the same way as the second one did. But Phil didn't have to touch the keyboard, just his watch. Then his computer transferred all thoughts of the victim to Jim's monitor. This advance had something to do with nerve endings and blood vessels. That's all Jim knew.

"Have you ever tried to leave?" Without waiting for Phil to answer, Jim asked,

"Is that ticking coming from the watch that the last hotline told you to buy a couple of nights ago?"

"Yeah! My first gold one. It was 60% less than the other ones. The hotline told me to check Norman's Jewelry. I couldn't pass up a deal like this. I'll be dead if the bitch finds it." Jim shot back,

"Excellent. You did a good job, Buddy. That's what your mother called you, isn't it? May I call you Buddy? We're going to become fast buddies before this call is over. How long has it been since somebody called you 'Buddy?' Too long I bet. It's time for a change. A step up and out of prison. This is the Hotline of Last Resort. We always get results. One way or another you're going to stop hurting this very night."

Buddy had no reaction to the comment; he was anxiety-ridden, like other victims.

Great! He didn't pick up on the threat. So far, so fantastic. Jack loved it when his comments went over their heads. *Now to get full control of the conversation and his thoughts.*

"Buddy, just keep staring at the watch. The way the gold shines right into your eyes. The way the second hand winds around the watch evenly, exactly." By this time, Jim was almost whispering.

"Do you see shine and precision?" Silence.

"Buddy?"

"I hear you." The victim sighed, hunching his elbows and muscular shoulders even further over the table as if he and it were one, like his thoughts and Jim's computer were one.

"Let it put you to sleep for a moment. Trust me. I won't let you down. You'll wake up when I count to five. And you won't remember anything about this call or the visitors you will have tonight, the ones who will make your darkest fantasy about Mary Jane come true."

"OK, OK! That bitch!" He scrunched up his forehead and closed his eyes tightly while waves of rage passed through him. Buddy trembled slightly; then he opened his eyes. He gazed around the dining room and parlor, all decorated in pastel to medium blues, colors he could only choose because Mary Jane had given him permission. But first, he'd had to get on his knees, put his head on the floor and beg her for so long his legs and back had cramped. At least, that's what the mind reading monitor flashed; a picture of Buddy on his knees.

Fantastic! Jim was in control. Buddy's right back to blaming his wife. Buddy might be difficult to hypnotize. Still, this man was his best chance. Jim had to make the decision immediately. One time in a hundred, did this type of nut phone a hotline. Jim was supposed to get them off the line as quickly as possible. They couldn't be totally controlled. *Too crazy.* Going ahead, Jim asked,

"Are you feeling all right? Your breathing sounds like broken ribs. Maybe you need an ambulance?"

Buddy's body jerked; the monitor showed that he suddenly remembered the phone resting on his shoulder and his watch in his hand. He put the receiver on the table, stared at it and a calm comforting voice wound through the air to his ear.

"Who am I talking to?" He whispered.

"It's me, Jim, the Terrorism Hotline. You called about your wife beating you black and blue with your own belt. That's what you told the other hotlines. Was it the same tonight, Buddy? I'm Jim, like an old buddy, think of me as your friend please. I want to help you out of your painful rut, and it can happen this very night. Wouldn't that fulfill all your fantasies?"

"Yeah!" Phil shouted, forgetting his wife was asleep in the bedroom, a woman he didn't dare awaken.

"Shhh...You'll wake Mary Jane!" Jim cautioned Buddy.

"Oh, sure..."

Speaking softly, Jim urged,

"Go back to admiring your watch, the blinding shine of the gold, the precise movement of the second hand. It'll make you forget about those broken ribs. Now blank out the pain by imagining you beating up Mary Jane."

Jim studied the screen and knew more about Buddy than even he could remember. Every stray thought, and sometimes more, came on the monitor, and Jim was an expert at putting everything together.

The victim's eyes descended to the watch and danced with glee as fantasies popped into his head and the monitor screen. They were the same ones he'd had for the last eleven years, no…since he was ten, the monitor says. Fantasies started up again, fully-steamed, the moment he met a face so close to his mother's, who died when he was ten. Over the screen came images of women, many women, all of them bloody and dead. Some with smashed faces. Others with cut up cunts and tits. More without hands. Blood everywhere. He laughed while he worked.

Jim's spirit soared over the fantasies. *This ass is hooked*, he thought. *I'm still flabbergasted at this mind reading machine. Shit! What it reveals.*

The night Buddy's mother died he had grinned into the darkness, before falling into forgetfulness. For one second, he grinned the same way he did the night she died, but his face quickly closed up again, like a wall between him and reality.

With glee, Jim pursued the victim he believed could destroy this network. Once this leg of the operation was gone, he'd be free and rich. He's already transferred half the money from their accounts to his.

"Keep watching the second hand and its shine; keep the fantasies. Your rage is totally justified. Tonight years of fantasies will come true. It's payback time! Is that what you want? To be a man again? Be the boss in your own castle?"

Jim's voice and the watch soothed the victim. He relaxed against the back of the dining room chair and snickered at the same fantasies again, as if he were ten.

Not once did Jim let on that he knew the fantasies. He was clever. And Chris had gone back to his work.

"F-ing! Would that feel great?" Buddy muttered. "I can't say the word. It'll wake Mary Jane. She has eagle ears over that word." His eyes were wide open. They danced with love of his fantasies and past murders.

"Good thinking. Now don't talk unless I ask you a question. Can you hear me?" Jim asked.

"Yes." The victim could barely be heard; his eyes stared at the watch, but Jim knew he didn't see it anymore. *His fantasies have control of him*, Jim thought.

"You'll have some visitors tonight. When they come, you give them everything: checkbooks, savings accounts, stocks, all your assets. Sign over the house and let the movers take everything, whatever they want. Understand?"

"Finally some relief..." Buddy muttered.

"Permanent relief, Buddy. This one's permanent. In return, you can do anything to your wife you want. Your visitors will protect you. At the end, you can kill her, like you dream of everyday. Understand?"

"OK!" Buddy muttered again. His mind went wild with what he could do.

"Now I'll put on music, and when it ends I will return and count down from five; on one, you will wake up, hang up the phone, and forget this phone call. Your visitors will be at the door, and you'll let them in. They'll take over. Do what you're told, everything you're told, OK?"

"Yeah..."

Jim pressed the "H" on the keyboard. Buddy was now hypnotized.

Part II Buddy

Soft elevator music began. Gradually over the next half hour, the music progressed to a wild abandon; the victim's fantasies rose higher and higher until his mouth grinned, eyes glistened, nostrils flared and vibrated. He trembled with excitement. Madness.

The same expression he had as he lay in bed staring into the darkness the night an unknown intruder had murdered his mother. Exactly the frame of mind he needed to act out his beloved fantasies, plaguing him since fifth grade. Eventually, Jim's recorded voice counted down from five.

On one, Buddy hung up the phone and stood up, planning to kill his wife. Before he could, he heard a slight tap at the front door. Without hesitating, Buddy hurried to the door and opened it. A freezing chill hit his face. It calmed him. The tone of Jim's voice floated in Buddy's mind as if it were a far off memory, as if it were the voice of Satan soothing him.

"Come on in, guys. It's great to see you," said Buddy. Five men, dressed in black with black hooded masks on their heads, stepped inside the foyer and stood beside Buddy. He could only see their dark eyes.

"Hi Buddy, you look all ready for the main event. Good! That's what we like to see." This man acted like the boss. He slapped Buddy on the back.

"Excellent decision you've made here. And what a house! Is it three or four bedroom?"

"Five," answered Buddy. "I repair antiques and make a fortune at it."

"That's what we like to hear, Buddy. We want to make sure you can afford us. Now for business. Let me tell you how it works."

The boss man took Buddy by the shoulder as if to speak confidentially to him, as if to keep him calm so everything could run smoothly.

"I only want to kill my wife," Buddy answered. "So give me the papers fast, so I can sign over everything I own guys."

"First things first, Buddy," answered the boss. "It needs to look like assholes broke into the house. We need to have rope burns on your wrists and ankles, hers too. So let us tie you up."

The boss slapped Buddy on the arm again.

"So we can get to work. Then you can give us a good show."

"No you don't. Nobody ties me up." Buddy pointed to his chest. "If you try, I'll have to call the minions from hell."

"Buddy, relax. Hey Bro, calm down. We're on your side. We'll untie you when it's time to sign everything over to us. Then you can kill her. Relax and trust us. We have a ritual to follow here. Now sit down in this dining room chair." One of the men hurried to get the chair and bring it to his boss, who stood between the living room and the foyer.

"I won't be tied up!" Buddy yelled.

"We have to. OK, you four get him down and hog tied," said the boss.

"Then put him in the chair and get the bitch."

The door was still open and Buddy was in the foyer. The dark shadows rushed against his face. The pine tree was bending from a strong wind, and the shadows rose higher as Buddy glanced out. He jerked when a single strong thrust of wind broke the tree trunk in half. The triangle it made with the ground reminded him of his wife's cunt. He'd hated it from the beginning. The way it grabbed him and threatened to never let go. Buddy felt trapped in there.

Shadows and spooks dove into the room. Buddy stood outside his body and watched the minions from Hell defend him. This is the way it always was. These spirits came to his aid. They soon turned from spirits to people, and they looked just like Buddy. *That was always amazing.* The four men moved fast towards Buddy. He felt a surge of energy that only the mad possess. He gave it willingly to his defenders, the minions. They needed this energy, not him. Only one minion fought at a time.

His jaw clamped closed and the minion grabbed the first two. They rolled on the floor with the ghost from Hell landing on the bottom kicking and screaming. The first two men grabbed his arms and the last two, his legs. The phone and its stand fell on one of the hooded men. He had to let go of Buddy's leg to push them off him. That gave the specter his chance. He kicked the other man's knee with his free leg. That sent the man sprawling against the wall and breaking a mirror. He slid slowly to the floor, the mirror on top of him.

The specter jerked the other leg and rolled both of them above his head and caught one man by the neck. He squeezed the Adam's apple as hard as he could. The man used all his strength to loosen the devil's hold. He even tried to angle himself with the wall to give him more leverage. The two remaining men yanked at the minion's legs, too. The spirits were insurmountable. In a couple minutes, the man had blood trickling down his chin and he'd quit fighting.

With his arms free, the minion grabbed two of the men's necks, one with each hand. He pounded their skulls together, hard and fast, over and over. Brains exploded and blood landed everywhere in the foyer and into the living room. Human tissue dangled from the overhead light, the furniture and Buddy. A couple pieces of flesh and brains spotted the couch. He looked down at himself and smiled. And the spots on the couch were like heaven. Will the bitch be pissed, he thought. *Hee! Hee!*

He knew he was one mother fucker. He laughed and his body jiggled. His shadows from hell always did an excellent job. He was so satisfied with their work. *Tie him up?* Nonsense! He tried to tell them. He had no choice, but to call his defenders.

He enjoyed the spectacle long enough for the boss and a wounded man to get to their sedan and burn rubber driving away. By the time Buddy ran to the door to catch them, they were already down the road and into the forest surrounding Buddy's house. Outside, he glanced around to see who was next.

When Buddy turned around, he grinned at the blood, brains, and bodies in his foyer. He'd forgotten all about Mary Jane. Naked, she raced into the living room with his belt in her hand, but halted, horrified and paralyzed. Her bleached hair was flat on the sides and straight up on top. Her green eyes, once vibrant, went dull. She stared at Buddy. He knew what she was thinking. He didn't need that damn game to tell him. *Not at all.*

The bitch thought he did it. He'll just have to show her what happened. The wind blew and chilled his neck. Again he was outside his body.

Here they are. Great! Pay back time. The same minion as before started toward her. She backed up a step at a time.

"You…You…this…no…no…" She swung around and raced toward the backdoor, screaming as loud as she could. Mary Jane only made it to the dining room. The creature from hell grabbed her by the waist and flung her down on the rug. He still held the rope. After he dragged her under the walnut table, he tied one hand and one leg to the table's legs. Running out of rope, he went back to the foyer where he found another long piece, soaked in blood.

As the minion ran back, he stumbled on the rope and fell. His cheek slid on the carpet, and he got a rug burn.

"The bitch got loose," he screamed. Up in no time, he grabbed her before she got to her feet. He forced her back down, tied her up again, and slapped her face.

"Quit calling me 'psycho,'" he shouted. "I'm not Buddy. I'm from Hell." This time, he pulled the rope so tight around her ankles and wrists, bulges appeared. She screamed louder. Big tears rolled down her cheeks.

"Please," she begged. "Don't kill me. I'll never beat you again." The creature whispered,

"No way, Mommy." He grinned.

"I'm not your mother. Please, can't you see? I'm Mary Jane.!" After slamming her face again, he watched her nose bleed.

"Don't you remember slapping my face bruised?" he asked. He sat up and listened a minute.

"The back door!" he said and hurried through the kitchen, looking all around. He reached the door and glanced outside, but he saw no one. He locked the door and went back to the dining room. She wiggled her hands and legs, trying to get loose.

He plopped down on her diaphragm and slapped her face several times. She jiggled slightly and passed out. Buddy ran to the kitchen for a pail of water and brought it back. He dumped part of it on her face. She jerked awake. Buddy's image was back in the living room again, where he hooted and howled.

Finally, the minion drew out his pocket knife. Very lightly, he carved the word, "bitch" into her chest. She wiggled, squirmed and sobbed. She even begged. The minion just kept on. Buddy laughed and cried out,

"Now do you see? It's not me who murders."

"Stop," she yelled. "I'm not your mother." She tried even harder to wrench her arms and legs free. Blood ran down her sides onto the rug, some puddled in her cleavage. She glanced down at herself and sobbed louder.

"Wiggle all you want, bitch. You're dead." The minion turned around with his butt and back towards her face. He ran his hands through her thick muff and divided the hair.

"There's that evil bugger," he said. When he grabbed the clit, he started sawing with the pocketknife.

Her body arched once and then she remained motionless. Neither the minion nor Buddy noticed. He finally held that little bugger up to eye level where he could take a good look at it. Buddy found himself on top of her. He examined the devil thing closely. He hadn't stopped laughing and giggling since the violence started.

He felt her pulse.

"Nearly stopped. Mother Fucker! She died too fast." He pounded her body with the knife. Before he finished, she looked like a pile of blood. Then he stood off where he could see the masked men and his wife. He clapped and danced until he fell to the rug, exhausted. A shot rang out, and Buddy fell flat on the carpet.

Part III Jim Sparks

Buzzzzz! Buzzzzz!

Two phones with the same number rang, one for the boss, the other for Jim, who was ecstatic over the call. They grabbed the cells fast. These had never rung before.

"Get the hell out of there! Moran killed three of our men and clipped his wife's clitoris with his pocketknife, then grinned while she screamed and bled to death. We sneaked in the back door and watched it all. He was crazy as a wounded cougar. I shot him in the head when it was over. Shit! What a show!"

After a few moments, the man continued,

"But then our backup tried to kill us: we got all four of them. A couple of miles down the road, some black car started after us. It's got to be our own. Fatso, you messed up so big we're all dead! Hear the bullets pinging ..."

Vaaaaaaaabooooooom!

Both men dropped their phones and went for the hardware. They rolled behind their chairs and desks, only looking out to get a shot. With the desks against the walls, both men were trapped. Neither one could move around in the room, nor reach the door.

They exchanged shots. Monitors shattered. Computers fizzled with sparks flying. When his gun was empty, Jim grabbed the one in his boot and waited. Chris fired away. Soon the clinkety clank of Chris reloading his gun echoed in the silence. Only Chris' hands were visible. Jim took careful aim and plugged the boss' trigger hand. Then Jim shot him in the forehead; he ended it by emptying the revolver into Chris' heart.

Out came Jim's lighter; he set the boss' pant legs and a whole lot of papers on fire. He stopped a few moments to watch it. Flames rose quickly, even before Jim barely made it to the door. He grinned at his work.

Once in the hall, he lit every McDoogle's bag he could find, like a kid arsonist. He found one every few steps. By the time Jim reached the stairs, a wall of fire raged swiftly toward him. He laughed and flew down the steps, touching concrete only once between landings. What a high! He was going for broke.

"Fuck!" He screamed when he heard the third floor give way, then the second, or was it the roof and the third, he hoped. He shrieked,

"Fuuuuuck! Not now! Billions..."

All of a sudden, Jim could make it. He was sure of it. The last flight of stairs, he leapt higher than ever. He felt so powerful he could have dived through the door to freedom. High on success, he sailed up above the stairs. Then the wall beside him exploded from decay and heat. A billion slivers shot into him before he hit the ground floor outside.

Q

Jade Eckert

Dave and Marcy O'Conner were planning on a dinner/breakfast at Denny's. It was something that they did every Thursday. Dave would pick up his paycheck before leaving the office, deposit it on the way home and walk in the front door and yell,

"Wanna go to Lenny's?" Marcy would call back,

"Denny's!"

It was their thing; dinner once a week at Denny's. Some weeks they would splurge and see a movie after. This week wasn't one of those weeks. Marcy had an early day the next morning so they would eat, come home, make love and sleep. They were still madly in love after being married ten years. No children, but neither was overly upset about their inability to have them.

Marcy was sitting at the kitchen table when he walked in. She had on a light green floral print summer dress that he loved. She looked so young. He kissed her and walked toward their bedroom.

"Let me change into some jeans and I'll be ready to go," he said.

"Ten-four. I'm ready whenever you are!" He laughed as he walked down the hall. She was a funny gal. He felt blessed they remained as close as they had through the trials of marriage. There had been hard times, but the good outweighed the bad. He used the toilet and changed into his jeans. Mary was at the front door when he returned.

"What the hell is that?" She was looking out the glass in the front door.

"What, babe?"

She turned and looked at him. Worry lines crossed her forehead. He stepped up behind her and looked out the window. A pile of something white, gray and red was in the front yard.

"Jesus, I think it's a dog. Go back in the kitchen and I'll go take care of it. It must have been hit by a car."

"Oh God, oh babe, that's bad."

Marcy had lost a beloved dog when she was a child. They would discuss things when they were just going off to sleep. The dog story had been the worst she'd told him. The dog had been struck and not killed immediately. It had suffered while she waited for her dad to get home. Her mother refused to leave the house and offer assistance and the woman who had hit the dog never stopped. Marcy was forced to spend over an hour with the dog until her dad came home and shot it. It had left scars on her, not visible ones, but deep, dark, closet ones.

"Go babe, I'll take care of it. Go on now." He shoved her gently toward the kitchen. She went and he opened the front door.

The dog was lying on the corner of their yard. As he neared he was sure it was a dog. A large, fluffy white tail was spread out behind it. It was lying with its head tucked under its chest, its legs weren't visible. It was as if someone had dropped it from above and it just crumpled. He found himself glancing up. Did he expect to see a plane circling overhead dropping out white fluffy dogs? He shook his head and knelt by the animal. There were no obvious injuries one would expect when flesh met metal. Its fur was covered by patches of blood and dark gray. Puzzled, he leaned over closer to get a better look at the patches. It appeared as if the fur was moving. The fact that the dog was covered by mosquito's entered his brain the same moment the dog lifted its head.

"Jesus CHRIST!" He fell back landing with his arms behind him. He began to crawl backward as quickly as possible, never taking his eyes off the dog. The dog seemed to smile. A lone mosquito flew from its mouth.

"What the hell?" he asked out loud as he continued to backpedal across the yard. The dog stood and shook like you'd expect a dog to do fresh from a bath or swimming hole. Mosquito's rose in a cloud. The dog took a step toward him and then fell. Dave saw the cloud come together and head towards him. There was something very wrong here. Dogs can't smile, and they sure the hell couldn't stand up, shake and take a step once dead. He got to his feet as the mosquitoes neared. He could hear the buzzing, but to him it almost sounded like voices.

"No way, you little shits, no way!" He took off running toward the house. If there was one pest that drove him nuts more than the common housefly, it was the mosquito. They lived near a lake and it never failed they would plan a nice outside activity and the mosquitoes would come in swarms. They tried everything to get rid of them: sprays, candles, it didn't matter. They really pissed him off. He ran up on the porch and turned to see where they were. The cloud was half way between the dog and him. He could see some were still around the dog, but the majority was headed his way. He burst into the house and slammed the door.

"Dave? What is it?"

Sweat was dripping down his chest. He could feel the wetness under his arms and across his back. He took a deep breath and wiped his face. Marcy came out of the kitchen, a look of concern on her face. When she saw him, she stopped.

"What is it? Is the dog still alive? Is it hurt bad? What should we do?" The questions came like rapid fire, one after the other with no time for him answer.

He didn't try. What the hell could he say to her to explain this? He turned and looked out the glass in the front door. The dog continued to stagger down the middle of the street. He couldn't see if the swarm was with it.

"The dog is fine and is on the way down the street."

"What? It was dead!"

"No kidding."

"It must have just been stunned. It's almost got to the Cooper's and was still going strong." This was true. The dog's gait had improved as it went down the street. It was going at a quick jog. He watched as it paused and lifted its nose in the air. The dog turned and seemed to look at his house before continuing down the street and around the corner. When he lost sight of the animal he turned to Marcy.

"Something weird, though." She had come up behind him and was peering over his shoulder.

"What's that?"

"It was covered with mosquitoes."

"Mosquitoes?" He could hear the doubt in her voice.

"Seriously, mosquitoes. I have no idea where they came from but the dog was covered. I ran back so they wouldn't get on me." He left out the dog scaring the shit out of him by raising its head and taking a step toward him. He had to save face after all.

"Why in the hell would they be on a dog like that? That many I mean?"

"I have no idea, but let's go ahead and go, I'm really hungry." She backed away from the door.

"Sure it's safe to go out?"

"I don't see the problem. It's not like the mosquitoes know we're hiding and are waiting around the corner. Really, Marcy."

"Don't make me sound stupid. It's just weird. It's too early for mosquitoes, that's all." It wasn't the bugs she was worried about, she didn't have to say it; it was all over her face. It was the dog that was on her mind.

"It'll be okay. Let's go." He opened the door and looked around. Everything was as it should be. Marcy followed him to the car and soon they were on the way to Denny's. Dave would turn left onto Main, straight for six blocks and then left on Gilbert. The same route every week and he damn near drove it without thinking. He was in traffic, ready to turn left onto Gilbert when Marcy gasped and he heard her window purr up.

"What the hell, Marcy?"

"There was a mosquito. It looked like the damn thing was checking me out. I didn't want it to get in the car."

"It was checking you out? Like trying to look down your shirt?" She jabbed him in the ribs.

"Don't be a smartass, I'm serious."

The turn light finally turned green and he waited for the Mustang full of teenagers to burn around the corner before he followed.

"Kids today, I swear." He turned to ask Marcy what she thought about the car full of teens and saw her close the vent on her side of the car. She reached the middle vent and shut it.

"Close your vent, Dave." He did as she asked without question; Marcy was a woman with her head on straight. If she said close the vent, there was a reason for it.

Denny's came into view and he turned in the lot and parked.

"What's going on?" She was pale. He could see a fine row of sweat along her brow where she had her bangs pulled back.

"You'll think I'm crazy..." He gave her his bullshit look, eyebrows scowled, forehead wrinkled; mouth turned down.

"Never happen," he replied. She cleared her throat.

"While we were sitting at the light about a dozen mosquitoes landed on the hood by the antenna and went into the crack in the hood. They were going in the engine compartment and the only thing I could think of was that they were getting under there to get in the vent system," she paused, "so they could get in here and get us."

He didn't think she was crazy, not even for one second. He thought she was right. His stomach felt like it was trying to exit through his feet. He nodded to her and looked out the window. Night was falling and the sodium arc lights in the Denny's lot were coming on. He could see swarms of mosquitoes circling in the spray of light. The thought of going out into that was more than he could take.

"What do you think we should do?" he asked.

"I'm not sure. . . I'm not very hungry for the Grand Slam right now." Dave smiled.

"I'm not either. Do you think it's in our heads?"

"I don't think so, something is going on."

Sirens rose in the distance and Dave turned his head toward the street and saw first a fire truck blast by followed by an ambulance and three police cars pulling up the rear.

"I want to go home," Marcy said.

"I think that's a good idea. Problem is, tomorrow is grocery day. I think we should run by the store and see what we can get from there. We'll need the basics at the very least." Marcy nodded.

"I need tampons, and I only have one left. We have to get those as soon as possible." He started the car. While pulling out of the lot he noticed traffic had become almost non-existent the few minutes they had spent parked.

It was a weeknight and on a usual night the streets would have been busy with families coming home from a dinner at a restaurant, soccer practice car pools and men home late from the office. None of that was taking place tonight. One light gray Chevy van was swerving down the street. Dave watched as the blonde woman behind the wheel batted at her head. At first he thought she was pulling her hair out and until she was right in front of him did he realize she was slapping at something.

"They got her," Marcy said. "Did you see her? They got her." There was no uncertainty in her voice. She made up her mind there were rogue killer mosquitoes on the loose and her and her man could be in jeopardy. She kicked into immediate survival mode.

"Let's get the hell out of here. Go to the market on Swan Avenue. It's closer to the outside of town. Maybe they haven't gotten that far."

Dave was half listening and half watching the spectacle up the street. A man was running through the intersection in the same direction the van had come from; the same direction as their home. The man was naked and waving his arms over his head. As he watched the man fell onto the curb a block away. He was immediately covered with a pelt of moving insects.

"Jesus Christ." He pulled out of the lot quickly before Marcy caught sight of the naked man. He headed for Swan Avenue. The rescue units had been heading toward the man. Dave was hoping the swarm was coming from that way and not all over town. They could stop at the store, get what they needed and then decide if an unplanned vacation was in order. He had credit cards and if the swarm hadn't spread they could go just about anywhere. Tampons and staying alive were the top priorities for the moment.

The streets were deserted of cars. It wasn't until three blocks up that they met traffic. It seemed things were as they should be on the South side of town.

Excellent. They could get Marcy's tampons and stock up and go to a hotel out of town for the night.

"The radio!"

Her sudden burst scared him and the wheel spun in his hands. He recovered but his heart was seriously pounding.

"Honey, I love you to death, but Jesus, easy on the sudden bursts of energy, okay? I about put the car onto the curb and for some reason a dead car is not sounding like a good idea tonight."

She wasn't listening to him; she was spinning the dial through static.

"There's nothing on. How can there be nothing?" Sweat popped out on his forehead. No broadcast in Los Angeles County? No way. There were countless stations coming from Los Angeles and the surrounding counties. It had to be the airwaves. The mosquitoes were somehow interrupting the signal. The stations couldn't be off the air because there was something wrong with the people. His brain couldn't wrap around that. Millions of people lived here. Millions. You couldn't simply wipe out millions of people with just mosquitoes. It was absurd.

"It's the airwaves, not the stations. They've been interrupted, that's all."

"Okay, that makes sense."

He drove without incident to the intersection of Gilbert and Swan. Across the street the market was lit and people were going in and out.

"Well everything looks okay over there. Let's get in and out as quick as possible," he told her.

"We aren't going home, are we?" She must have figured out which way the swarm was coming from, just as he had done.

"Probably not the best decision. We'll stay in a hotel or something farther inland. Hell, maybe go to Vegas."

"I have a case in the morning! I can't leave town. No way am I missing it. Fern will not suffer at the hands of that son-of-a-bitch again! I'll see him in prison for what he did to her, or die trying."

Fern was Marcy's latest case. She worked as a social worker for the county and Fern was one of the worst cases of spousal abuse she's seen in her ten years with social services. Marcy would fight the good fight.

"I know it means a lot to you, honey, but we're just going to have to see how things pan out. If they come this far, we're going to have to keep moving."

"The little fuckers!" She slammed her hand on the dashboard. The light changed and traffic began to move. Dave was in the lane that would carry him through the intersection and into the parking lot of the market.

Two cars were in front of him, none behind. He eased on the gas and began to pull through the intersection when lights shone in his rearview mirror. The lights behind him were on high beam. He flipped the little switch on the bottom of the rearview mirror to dim the lights behind him as he pulled into the intersection. The lights didn't dim much and he looked into the mirror. The car was coming up fast, too fast to be approaching an intersection. It was swerving. Flashes of the blonde woman swerving down the road came to mind and he began to honk at the car in front of him.

"What the hell are you doing?" Mary asked.

"Move, move, move, MOVE!" he yelled at the car in front of him. "Brace, Marcy!" he yelled to his wife. She stuck her feet straight out and high onto the floorboard and braced her arms against the dash. The car behind was less than a block away and the car in front was just through the intersection and going into the market parking lot. Dave knew that unless the driver behind him made the turn, he and Mary were in serious trouble. He put the gas on and was half in the lot of the market when the car behind him came screaming into the intersection. It happened too fast for him to see who was behind the wheel. No matter, whoever it was, they weren't going to make the turn. The driver tried to make it, Dave gave him or her that. He heard the tires growling and smoke came from behind the car as it began to slide. His eyes were glued to his rearview mirror as his car bounced into the lot. The car behind began to tip.

"SHIT, SHIT!"

The car in front of him hadn't gotten far enough in the lot to be out of his way and Dave ended up banging into its bumper. He didn't look from the mirror even as his car was recoiling from the car in front of him.

"Dave?"

The car behind teetered for a moment before losing the battle with gravity and tipped on its side. It slid hot across the intersection and into the back of Dave's car.

The force of the crash forced his car deeper into the trunk of the car ahead of him, pinning the two together. Marcy's head bounced off the seat rest when they were hit, but both their seat belts held strong. The car died. Marcy began to cry.

"Are you hurt?" His voice was shaky.

"I'm scared, not hurt. What the hell is going on?" He looked around.

"I have no idea."

Neither one of them got out of the car to assess the other people involved and the damage as they would have on any other day. Dave unfastened his seatbelt and turned around in his seat. The hood of the car behind him was crushed against his trunk. His back windshield was intact. He couldn't see any cracks, relieved her turned back around. An overweight, older woman dressed in jeans and a sleeveless red blouse got out of the car in front of them.

"She shouldn't be doing that." Marcy waved at the woman to get back in her car. The woman had a scowl on her face and was walking toward their car when she suddenly stopped and slapped her face.

"Uh-oh." Marcy said from beside him. He didn't bother to respond, he was waving frantically at the woman hoping she would see him and get back in her car before it was too late. He watched as the woman slapped her face again.

"She's in some serious shit here, Dave. What are we going to do?"

"Nothing we stay in the car. Do not open your door!"

He was serious. He would love to help the woman but there was no way he was going to risk Marcy or his own skin. They would stay right where they were windows up and vents closed, thank you very much.

The woman was looking into the street behind their car. Dave glanced in the rear view mirror but all he could see was the crushed trunk and the hood of the car that had hit them. He looked back at the woman. She was lifting her arm and pointing toward the street. Mosquitoes dotted her face and arms. She didn't try to bat them away, whatever was in the street had her full attention. Dave's hand went to the door handle unconsciously. He was going to get out and see what the hell was going on. Marcy's hand on his thigh stopped him.

"Don't go out there. There's nothing we can do. Neither one of us have any kind of medical knowledge. We can't help." She was right and his hand fell from the door handle. Whatever was going on was going to have to go on without him. The woman from the car in front of them was wiping at her face and spitting.

"Jesus, they're in her mouth."

The woman panicked and began to run for the market. She made it half way across the lot before the gray cloud engulfed her. The huge cloud of millions of writhing mosquitoes had come from behind their car and Marcy began to scream. Dave grabbed her and hid her face on his chest. She didn't need to see this, but Dave found himself unable to look away. The woman was covered with the bugs. She went to her knees first before falling over and trying to crawl toward the market.

Dave shut his eyes as Marcy cried into his shirt. When he opened his eyes the majority of the cloud was gone. The woman was face down on the ground covered with feeding insects. He leaned forward to see if he could get a better angle and Marcy whimpered. He sat back and closed his eyes. They were in some serious trouble if help didn't come soon. They had no food or water. He'd heard somewhere the human body needed a half a gallon of water a day to survive. He wasn't sure how accurate it was, but it sounded about right. Hell, humans were mostly water.

"Babe, do you have any water?" he asked.

Marcy sat up and got her bag off the floor. She pulled out a bottle less than half full. She handed it to him and took a tissue out of her purse and wiped her face.

"Do you have any food?" She stopped wiping and looked at him.

"What are you trying to say? We're going to be in here for a long time? No way, Dave. No fucking way."

He looked around. Apart from the woman on the ground, no other people had been by. He turned and craned his neck to try and see if there were any cars on the street. He could just make out a corner of the street around the wreckage. Nothing was moving.

"Nothing is moving. No one has come out of the store since the accident. I imagine they have the doors blocked by now. I would. There's no one on the street that I can see. We may be here awhile until help comes."

"How long is awhile?"

Marcy was fact oriented. If he told her he would mow the yard soon, she wasn't satisfied, she wanted a day and time she could count on him sweating with the push mower in the front yard. 'Maybes' and 'I don't knows' weren't in her vocabulary.

"I don't know, babe." He took her hand in his, hers was cold, his hot. He closed his eyes and thought about it. There was nothing else he could tell her. He didn't know. How in the hell had this happened? Thoughts were tumbling through his mind. They were going to die because of mosquitoes? The woman in the red sleeveless shirt won't be going home with dinner for her family because of mosquitoes? Just where in the hell had the mosquitoes come from anyway? Sure, there were lakes around but the number of mosquitoes that had just passed by defied reason. Was this some sort of attack from someone else? A biological warfare experiment dropped from a plane into fresh surface water where the secret, deadly mosquito eggs had grown and flourished and then had waited for the signal to attack?

"Dave?"

Or maybe it was our government. Maybe they decided to do a little spring cleaning. Instead of using mustard gas and torture like Hussein, use something they couldn't be blamed for.

"Dave?"

It would be just like them to do something like this. He wondered how many cities were going through the same thing.

"Dave?" Her voice loud in his ear. He opened his eyes.

"Just woolgathering, babe."

"Dave, the woman, look at the woman." He did. In the time it had taken him to try and figure out how the world, or at least greater Los Angeles, was going to become a memory, the woman in the red sleeveless shirt had stood up and walked to the door of the market.

"Jesus! I thought she was dead!"

"I know. It took her awhile to get to her feet and make it that far. She's better than she was when she first got up. Stronger somehow."

"Just like the dog."

The woman was merrily banging on the door of the market as if someone inside was going to be stupid enough to open it. As he watched, incredibly, someone did just that. The door opened enough for the woman to slip through.

"Maybe we can get in there! There's food, water and everything we need! We'd just have to wait for the troops to arrive!" Marcy hollered in his ear. Dave hadn't taken his eyes off the front of the market. The door remained closed and as he watched splashes of red wash over the door.

"Dave! Let's go!" He turned toward Marcy, shaking his head.

"Honey, no," he said quietly.

"Why not?"

He took her face gently in his right hand and turned her head toward the market. The red was outlined on the door by the inside light of the market. It was unmistakable what had happened. The woman had gone in and mayhem ensued. They wouldn't be going into the market.

"Oh shit," was all Marcy had to say.

Mosquitoes were visible in the lights of the parking lot. Dave wondered how the driver of the car behind them fared. Most likely not well; not from the impact of the crash, but by what had driven the driver to cause the crash in the first place. He craned his neck around to see if he could see anyone else. Marcy gasped and he turned back to the market. The doors were wide open and people were spilling out. One old woman still held her purse over one arm and her market basket over the other. She was shoved aside by a large man in jeans and a chambray shirt.

The old woman went down on one knee and was shoved over and trampled by the remaining people trying to get out.

"No, oh no, no, no. . ."

Dave didn't respond. He shoved Marcy's head down and squished down as far as he could to be out of sight. The people, in a panic, could try and get in the car, leaving them vulnerable to the mosquitoes. Dave locked the doors. If people saw them alive and safe in the car, they may rush over and try to get in. Marcy's frantic breathing was in his ear.

"It's okay, babe. I just want to stay out of sight."

He stayed crouched over for more than a minute before he couldn't stand it anymore and had to look. He lifted his head and peeked over the dashboard. Most of the people from the market hadn't made it far. The man in the jeans that had knocked over the old woman was about ten feet from where Dave sat. The man was face down. Mosquitoes circled over him, landing, drinking their fill and leaving. The old woman that had been knocked over was getting to her feet. Dave watched as she picked up her purse and limped back into the market, leaving the door open behind her.

"What's going on?"

"The man that knocked over the old woman is the closest. He's covered. The old woman got back up and went into the market, but she'd left the door open. There were several more people from the market in the parking lot. No one but the old woman has moved."

"Shit! What are we going to do?"

"I don't know."

"I'm really hungry. It's stupid thinking that, but I am. I have a few mints in the bottom of my purse, want one?"

"No, babe, you go ahead." He heard her rustling around. He was watching the market. If they could somehow get in there and hide in the cooler then they might be safe. Mosquitoes weren't out in the winter after all. They didn't like the cold. If they could make it in there, they could grab food, water, Marcy's tampons, everything they would need to hole up for awhile. Plus, the cooler would be airtight.

He thought about all the people in houses with a torn screen, a small crack in the bottom of the door, a forgotten open window in the basement. Mosquitoes were so small! It would be impossible to think of everything, every place that one could get in. The market was a good idea but nothing more than a fantasy. The old woman was in there and God knew how many more people she was busy infecting, or killing, or whatever the hell she was in there doing.

"Water, water everywhere. . ." Dave turned his head.

"What?"

"You know that line, when the people were stuck in a boat on the ocean and they were thirsty and there was water everywhere but they couldn't drink? I'm just thinking of the market. There's everything we need in there, but we can't go in. It's right there!" Marcy said, motioning to the market.

"I know, I know. I'm thinking."

"We should have stayed at Denny's." He couldn't argue with her, she was right. They would have been indoors and able to hide, but what about the cracks between the doors? A mosquito would have no problem squeezing through the crack, or a hundred if they took their time and went in an orderly fashion, and Dave thought that's just what these mosquitoes would do. It was clear this was some kind of planned event. Someone somewhere, was sitting in a nice room waiting as the nightmare unfolded. Were they laughing, knowing that people were dying and the ones inside were just sitting ducks because 'the infected' were killing those that were not?

The man closest to the car lifted his head. Dave ducked and as he did so he forced Marcy down.

"What? What, Dave?"

"Shh, the man just woke up. I don't want him to see us."

They sat in silence until the knock came. Dave's stomach dropped. He had expected it, but it still surprised him when it came. Dave lifted his head and saw the large man standing next to the window.

"Hey, buddy. Open up." Dave shook his head.

The man smiled and slammed his hand against the glass. Marcy began to whimper. The glass held.

"Stop. We're not coming out. My wife is hurt and we're waiting for help."

The man crouched down and looked in the window. Marcy leaned over and clutched her stomach. Dave looked at the man's eyes. They were lifeless. Whoever the man had been, he was no longer. The man opened his mouth to speak and as he did so a mosquito flew out and batted itself against the glass.

"There's no help coming. Look the fuck around. Everyone's dead, now let me in or I'm going to come in anyway. Either way, it's your choice."

He waved his hand at Marcy; she needed to be quiet so he could think. He sat there staring straight ahead as the man circled in front of the car, sliding over the hood to Marcy's side. The man punched his hand against Marcy's side. A fine crack appeared in the glass and she started to scream.

Instinct took over and Dave started the car. It was a good American car and started on the first turn of the key. Dave rammed it into drive and floored it while blowing the horn. The man by the car screamed, held his hands over his ears and exploded into a cloud of mosquitoes. The mosquitoes fell to the macadam dead. The tires were screaming as the woman's car they had hit began to move.

"Dave!"

The car shook with the effort and he let up on the gas and put the car in reverse. He eased back into the car that had hit them from behind. The car slid. Now they were getting somewhere! Dave put the car into drive and pushed against the car in front. They were going to get out of here! A couple more pushes and he could go around the cars and out into the street and out of this damn parking lot. He put the car in reverse and pushed the car behind them out of the way. Free of both cars he put the car back into drive and looked at Marcy.

"We have three quarters of a tank. . ." he stopped. There on Marcy's right cheek was a mosquito. A small one, light gray in color, feeding on his wife. It was high on her cheek, where he liked to kiss her. He didn't know how it had got into the car; the crack in the window was so small! But there it was, on the face of the most important person in the world to him. In that one moment all he had to live for was gone. He blew the horn and the mosquito fell dead onto the front of her light green floral summer dress that was his favorite.

"What, Dave? Why'd you stop? Let's get out of here!" He watched as she rubbed her cheek. She didn't know what he knew. She didn't feel it bite and pour its poison into her. He turned off the car.

"Dave?"

"Let's just sit here a moment."

"Why? Let's get the hell out of here! Why'd you turn off the car?"

"I just want to tell you how much I love you." A mosquito crawled out of her hair and rooted itself on her forehead.

"I love you, too. Now can we go?" Her eyes were slowly starting to close.

"Dave? I don't feel so well." She fell forward onto his shoulder and he pulled her close to him and began to cry. He kissed her forehead and talked to her about the good times they'd had as he rolled down the window.

The Child Villain

Danielle Ferries

Moonlight splintered through the branches of a dead oak, shooting patterns across the grass. Tally Todd, a strange child with an unusually sour disposition danced as she followed the light, enjoying the swishing sound of her new dress as it brushed against her legs.

Struck by lightning before she could walk, her long hair was the palest of fine silver. In the light of the full moon it shone around her head like a halo, as fair as her heart was dark.

When the shouting began, she stopped dancing to listen. The parents were talking about the man again, their voices travelling clearly on the frosty night air.

"It's the last straw," one of them shouted.

"He has to go," another joined in.

"We've had enough," someone said and their voices converged into one.

The man's name was Garler and he'd moved into their street six months ago. He had no wife or children and no place living in a neighbourhood like theirs.

He was making their lives a misery and they wanted to get rid of him.

They were sick of being told how to live their lives, raise their children, drive their cars and water their lawns. He'd even tried doing it for them. They didn't want to hear him dole out his own opinion on keeping women drivers off the road and children inside their houses where they couldn't be seen or heard.

Her dad's voice was the loudest. She heard him yelling that his child was being affected by this; she couldn't play safely in the street anymore.

Tally smirked.

Stupid parents. Talking about it wouldn't get the job done.

She saw something move down the road and crouched behind the hedge. Her eyes narrowed to slits as she watched Garler walking up the hill towards his house. His long beard decorated his chest like a wide necktie and leather sandals encased his feet, covered by long grey socks. Even on a cold winter night he wore shorts, his legs as pale as his bald head.

Her smile widened to a malicious grin. *Make him pay. Horrible man.*

This afternoon he'd broken her kite in half and thrown it into the gutter. Then he'd yelled at her for playing in the street and told her to keep off his property. She closed her eyes and pictured him being lowered into a vat of hot oil, his head and bare legs crisping like fried chicken.

Make him pay. Horrible man.

She heard a door slam and opened her eyes as Rufus crossed his front yard. She motioned him over, watching as his pudgy legs struggled to carry him. When he reached the hedge she grabbed his hand, pulled him down beside her and pointed at Garler.

"Watch him coming."

"I'm sorry about your kite." Rufus puffed.

"The only one going to be sorry is him," Tally said as she stood up. "Are you ready? It's time."

"Now?" Rufus sneezed, which brought on a bout of coughing.

"Keep quiet. You don't want to wait any longer, do you?" *She'd do it alone if she had to.* Rufus shrugged.

"It's cold tonight."

"It's perfect tonight. The parents will be in their meeting for ages. It's going to happen. And then we'll all be happy again." Tally eyed him.

"You're going to help me, aren't you?"

"Of course I am."

"You're my best friend Rufus. You know I wouldn't make you do something that was wrong, don't you?"

"Uh huh." He nodded. Tally smiled.

"You know what you have to do." He nodded and wiped his snotty nose.

"I'll meet you at our usual spot." Tally insisted.

"Can't we talk about it here? I don't like going into that house at night." She nodded in the direction of the parents.

"We need to meet at our spot. If we stay here someone might hear us."

"Why can't we walk together?"

"Because someone might see us," Tally rolled her eyes. "We need to do this properly. You don't want to get caught now do you?" He shook his head.

"Remember what I told you." Rufus sneezed again and wiped his nose on his sleeve before taking her hand for their secret handshake.

"I won't forget."

"When it's done we'll have hot chocolate."

As she hurried across the street to the derelict house a bird swooped and circled around her head. She raised her arm and the bird landed on her hand.

"I was wondering where you were," she said as it ran up her arm to sit on her shoulder.

Frederick, a raven, had been her pet for as long as she could remember. He was missing an eye and his feathers had lost their sheen, but he was a faithful friend. The abandoned house loomed out of the darkness, a menacing and hostile reminder of its neglected state. No one had lived there since the Reverend fell to his death from the front balcony six months earlier.

She'd never liked the Reverend. She hated the feel of his clammy fingers on her skin every time he'd greeted her before church.

Horrible man.

Tally sensed a strangeness about the place the first time she'd gone inside. Exploring its dark recesses gave her a sense of being a part of another world, an unholy world where nothing was as it seemed.

She listened at the front door a few seconds before she turned the handle and went in. Colder than outside, its macabre interior welcomed her, busts of people with weird shaped heads and odd items of furniture left behind all seemed to warm to her as she passed them, as if they craved human company.

From the front room on the second floor she looked out over the street and waited for Rufus. This was their private world, better than any stupid cubbyhouse. They'd painted a red circle on the floor and it was inside this circle that they made their plans.

Tally smiled.

Tonight Garler was going to sleep forever. He had it coming. The parents might want him gone from the neighbourhood, but she wanted to make sure he could never come back. He broke her toys and yelled at her. Yesterday he'd killed her doll.

Make him pay. Horrible man. He didn't deserve to live.

She jumped as a cat slinked across the floor and began to meow loudly. Frederick squawked and flapped his wings before he flew out the broken window.

"Stupid cat, look what you did." She ran to the window but Frederick had disappeared. The cat meowed again and she scowled at it.
The scrawny fur ball, indifferent to her, disappeared through an archway and was swallowed by the inky darkness.

She turned back to the window as Rufus waddled across the road and waved his fat hand at her. She saw him sneeze and hoped he wouldn't ruin everything. No one else in the neighbourhood liked him. If his constantly snotty nose and sneezing fits didn't turn them off his hare lip did. But he was the best friend she'd ever known.

Frederick flew back in and landed on her shoulder.

"Watch out for the cat," she whispered to him, eyes darting around the room.

"It's still in here somewhere." She waited for Rufus to come, silently stroking Frederick's feathers. Her plan couldn't go wrong. It was too easy.

When he finally waddled into the room and sat down inside their circle, Tally leaned forward and took his hands. Wild eyed, he listened as she explained the plan.

"Just get him down to the well. That's all you have to do. I'll take care of the rest." Her voice sounded unnaturally loud in the empty house.

"But what if he won't come out?" Rufus spluttered.

"You have to make sure he does."

"What if he won't come down the hill?"

"Then you fail." Tally's grip on his hands tightened.

"I'll be waiting. When you get to the well, hide behind the prickly bush. Wait until I need you." Rufus nodded.

"Okay then, let's go." She let go of his hands.

"You know what you have to do. Don't let me down." She stood up and dusted off her dress. Together they went down the stairs, her footsteps almost silent next to the clunking sound Rufus' corrective shoes made.

The street was empty and she nodded to him to cross the road. She waited and watched as he reached the other side and scrambled around for rocks. He struggled to his feet, his hands full, and began to throw the rocks at Garler's house. When she heard the chinking sound, she turned and started walking down the hill; Frederick still perched on her shoulder.

A dog howled in the distance and a siren sounded nearby, but it wasn't what she was waiting for. She stopped and turned, listening. She heard Garler yelling.

"Finally!" she smiled and kept walking.

At the bottom of the hill she took cover behind the old well. The stench of a rotting animal mingled with the odour of stagnant water and wet concrete. She covered her mouth and breathed through her hands while she waited. Frederick chewed a piece of her hair and she looked into the darkness of the well, marvelling at the secrets it might hold.

She looked up when she heard Rufus' squeals and saw him clip-clopping down the hill, hampered by his corrective shoes. A few feet behind, and gaining on him, was Garler. As they drew closer she could hear his voice clearly.

"Give it back!"

Excitement danced its way up Tally's spine and she stepped around in front of the well. Rufus had the garden gnome in his hands. It was the one with the big curious eyes that sat by Garler's letterbox, waiting to greet the postman each day.

Rufus reached her, wheezing and coughing, dropping the gnome at her feet. Poor Rufus. He looked like he was going to fall down dead.

Hot chocolate would warm them both up.

She nodded for Rufus to go, picked up the gnome and hung it over the well.

"Give it back you brat, or I'll skin you bare. I'll leave you so your own parents won't know you." He sneered at her. "Not so smart now, huh?"

"Smart?" Tally smirked. "A smart man wouldn't be down here."

"I know you. It's Tallulah Todd. Don't think I won't tell your parents about this." She smiled at him.

"Of course it's me. Who else would it be?"

Time to pay. Horrible man.

"You've got something of mine and I want it back. Then I'm going up there and tell your parents what you're up to."

"Do you think they'll care?" Tally wanted a swarm of bugs to fly into his mouth and fill the large hole until he choked. Then she wouldn't have to listen to his annoying voice.

"Something has to be done about you kids. You run wild in these streets. Someone needs to put a leash on you. I've told them before. Maybe they'll listen to me now. They'll listen real good when I make an example of you."

He lashed out, but as his hand connected with her throat Frederick swooped at his face, throwing him off balance. His hands became tangled in his beard and he swore as he tried to right himself. Tally stumbled backwards and dropped the gnome.

As she hit the ground her ankle twisted painfully and she bit her lip to stop from crying out.

Garler reached for the gnome, a victorious smile on his haggard face.

"Push him in, Rufus!" She yelled. "*Now!*"

Rufus was coughing again and his wheezing was getting worse. It had to happen now so she could get him home before he got sick. The parents would blame her if he caught pneumonia again. They blamed her for everything else.

Frederick swooped at Garler again and he tried to duck away, his face contorted with rage. As he spun around, he waved his arms to steady himself and Frederick continued to flap his wings around the man's head.

Garler's hands opened and closed, desperately trying to grasp onto something. He reached out and she screamed when his hand connected with her dress. He gripped onto the fabric and she slapped at his hand.

"Rufus, help me." She struggled to her feet as Rufus stepped behind Garler. She threw herself sideways as Rufus shoved him. Garler fell and Tally screamed as she was pulled hard against his body. He had one hand on the side of the well and the other in a death like grip on her dress. He was going to pull her in with him.

"Rufus, help!" The inky darkness taunted her like a jealous cousin wanting her favourite toys and she strained to pull away. She couldn't go into the well.

She couldn't.

"Let me go," she struggled. "Let me go or you'll be sorry."

It wasn't supposed to happen this way. He was supposed to go in and then she and Rufus were going to run home for hot chocolate and sing about the man at the bottom of the well.

"I'm teaching you a lesson, girlie." He pulled her face close to his and she screwed her nose up as she breathed in his stale breath.

Rufus sunk his teeth into Garler's hand and she heard the agonised scream spew from his mouth, his breath making her sick. He released his grip on her dress and she fell back. Frederick landed on her shoulder as she hit the ground and she smiled at him. She wasn't going to die at the bottom of the well. The smile slipped from her face as the man grabbed Rufus by the throat.

"Let him go." Tally kicked at his legs. "He's my friend, let him go."

Rufus gurgled as he was reefed off his feet. His face opened up in a silent scream as he struggled and scratched at the edge of the well. They went over so quickly she didn't have time to grab him.

"*Rufus!*" Tally scrambled to look over the edge. Their screams became an echo as they fell deeper into the darkness and finally faded away to a hollow howl, a muted thud and a splash as they met the bottom.

A sharp pain stabbed at her heart and she fell to the ground as a cold dizzying sensation took over. Her Rufus, stuck forever at the bottom of the well.

It was Garler's fault. Horrible man.

Rufus would be so cold down there, no hot chocolate, no one to cover him with a blanket. She heard voices in the distance and looked up.

The parents were coming out into the street. Their meeting was over. She had to get home before they realised she'd been out.

As she pulled herself to her feet, her ankle began to throb harder and she clamped her mouth shut, denying the pain. She clenched her fists as she slowly made her way back up the hill, keeping to the darker side of the footpath. Frederick flapped his wings and came to rest on her shoulder. He pecked lightly at her hair and she smiled at him.

"You're my only friend now. Do you like hot chocolate?"

Would You Like Fries With That?

Ben Eads

Alice walked into Mega-Burger. The smell of greasy fast food was a comfortable, yet harsh reminder of her meager life. That same smell was ingrained in every article of her clothing, and every piece of furniture in the place, from long years of hard work at this sorry excuse for a paycheck. Her eyes studied the chairs and stools placed atop the tables, her mind worried about her child at the baby-sitter. Any daydream would do to forget this cruel existence, one she was afraid she would share alone tonight with the manager, Herb until closing time.

Why did he call me in for only an hour tonight? I don't like this one bit.

"Alice!" Herb called from the back of the kitchen.

"Hi, Herb. I'm on time tonight, just like I promised." All 300-pounds of balding, middle aged Herb came into view. He was panting, out of breath.

"Ya' bet your sweet ass you're on time baby." Herb's eyes studied her shapely body, her blue eyes amid a backdrop of flowing deep black hair.

"I guess I'll go run the drive thru, if that's ok?" But Herb's eyes kept him in a fantasy world Alice knew all too disgustingly well.

"Alice, you do what that sweet body of yours has to do." Out of Alice's peripheral, she could see him staring as she walked towards the drive-thru window.

I wonder if that baby-sitter invited her boyfriend over. Is she giving little Nathan the attention he deserves?

Alice placed the headset on; the foam ear piece slathered in Herb's gravy-like sweat chilled her ear. She watched the car approach in the drive-thru-cam, fiddling with the stuck 'talk' button.

"Hello?" boomed through her headset.

How many times am I going to forget that creep is damn near deaf?

"Welcome to Mega-Burger, home of the best beef in Texas. Can I take your order please?" She turned the volume down to a tolerable level.

"Ummm... Yeah. I'd like an Ultra Mega Mouth, with a large chocolate shake."

"That'll be $6.62, please pull around." Then right behind her soggy ear,

"Ya' forgot to ask them if they would like fries with that! How many fucking times do I have to remind ya' about the fries?"

Alice saw the young men in the Cadillac outside her prison, watching Herb berate her. Herb swatted her ass with that same, filthy hand for the one millionth time.

Please tell me they didn't see that. I don't mind the yelling, but he touched me...

Alice choked back tears handing the food out the window. Frightened, unbelieving faces stared back. After they left, Alice broke into deep sobs. Fat, but strong hands grabbed her shoulders whirling her around.

"Ya' know why I keep pushing ya', Alice? Hmmm? My wife, the owner, loves the fries. Besides, the more food we sell, the more money we make. Can you get that through your pretty little head? Better shape up girl. That's why I called you in tonight. You'll see." Herb ended it with his trademark pat on her ass. Nothing she could do anything about. With Herb's old, wretched wife as the owner, and, the only attorney in this tiny town, there were certain things you accepted to get by.

"I'm sorry, Herb, I really am. Give me another chance huh? You know how tough the economy is. Nobody can find a job these days. I have a kid to feed you know?"

"That little snot nosed brat isn't my problem. Uh-uh, no Ma'am. Since ya' brought it up, if I hear that baby-sitter call here for ya' one more time, you're fired. Am I clear?" Alice nodded, dripping tears on the same sea green tile she stared hypnotically into for countless hours over the years.

Herb took her chin between his sausage-like thumb and stained forefinger.

"Pretty gals like you don't have trouble getting jobs, so don't give me that shit. All you talk about is how much money you need for this, for that. You know what you need to do for that raise, Alice." Herb massaged his crotch, emphasizing his meaning. Alice's stomach lurched, some of it made it into her mouth.

"Think about it toots." Another car approached the drive-thru cam.

"Thank...Thank you for choosing Mega-Burger. May, I take your... order?"

"Hey, Alice, it's Roy. Let me get two big Texans, and let me get an order of large fries."

"That'll be $8.56, please drive through."

"Alice! Ya' forgot to ask about the God damned fries again!"

"Roy asked for em' Herb! I swear." She found herself ringing her hands around in her apron.

"Sorry, Alice. Just mind it ok?" Herb said playing it up in front of Roy, handing the food to her. Before the drive-thru window split she saw a brief reflection of herself, the epitome of desperation with mascara smeared eyes.

"Hey Herb! After I wolf down these burgers, I'll be in to clean ya' burger grills." Roy exclaimed. Herb approached the window.

"We close in a half-hour, Roy. Best get to eatin' son."

"Yes sir." Roy stated, pulling into the parking lot.

Herb grabbed her wrist with that hand, the same hand that tried to probe where God did not intend, pulling her close to him, his other balled up to strike her.

"Girl, you out your tiny mind if you think you can get away speaking to me like that in front of customers. I'm not some God damned dog! You gonna mind me now? Don't you ever, ever cross me like that again woman." Alice nodded, staring at Roy's taillights, waiting for him to finish eating.

"Don't break down again. God, I can't think of anything that sickens me more than a woman breaking down and crying. You have a real issue with that. Might wanna address it before ya' lose your job."

"Herb, I have a lot of personal things going in my life right now. You know what pressure I'm under. Mother's dying of cancer, the custody battle with my ex, who still refuses to sign the documents. Why don't ya' just lay off me a little bit ok? I mean, I can't go on like this."

Did I just say that? Where did that come from? Wherever it did, it felt good!

"Why, Alice. I don't believe I've ever heard you speak to me that way. It turns me on. Why don't ya' keep going and we'll see where it ends up? Huh?"

Again, Herb massaged his crotch. Alice turned from the repulsive sight gagging.

"I'll give you something to gag on. There's about eight inches of man below this fat here. You ever been with a man like that, Alice? I doubt ya' have. Probably take a lot of that stress away you keep croonin' about."

They heard a truck door close; Roy walked up and knocked on the glass door, then entered. Herb turned to Alice, scowled, and went to meet him.

"You like close calls don't ya, Roy? We close in bout' a half hour."

"I got it covered boss. Just let me grab my tools. I'll be back in a jiffy." Herb half-ran towards the drive-thru meeting Alice.

"Wife's got me working too many hours. Doc says I need a break. Right, and leave my wife in charge? Fuck that noise. Maybe one day, it could be you and me huh?" Having smacked her ass again, he walked towards Roy, who was setting up.

Is that why he called me in like this? To talk about a new partnership?

Alice pulled her headphones off and walked to the kitchen, preparing to close for the night. Roy was hard at work cleaning the grills with Herb hovering over him like a vulture.

"Uh, ma'am? Best be getting everything put up so we can close." It took Alice a moment to realize this was directed at her, she forgot Herb acted nice when others were around.

"Yes sir. Food's going in the fridges, and the dishes in the dishwasher." It was hard for Alice to act. She hoped it appeared genuine to Roy, for Herb's sake.

"How we doing Roy?"

"It's not bad at all, Herb. Long as I keep comin' once a month. Won't be but a few minutes of my time keeping the fire inspector off ya' back."

"You're a hell of a man. And I appreciate your help."

"Much obliged, Herb. Say, you want to help carry that bucket back to my truck? My back is paining me something awful." It took him a moment, but Herb agreed.

Alice swept, searching with frightened, drained eyes for the least little thing that would set Herb off. The door opened, and the heavy footsteps of Herb approached.

"Alright little missy, time for us to discuss what I called you in for. You been avoiding it for years. Besides, your attitude tonight warrants it." Alice could see he was pale as a ghost, but there was something else, deeper, uglier.

"You know what relieves my stress?" She felt his hands for the first time caress her from behind. He squeezed her breasts, and pulled her to him. Her only safety blanket, the sea-foam green tile stole her focus.

"For three long years you've played hard-to-get. You want your job? Best show daddy how bad." His hands kept exploring until she could feel the warty flesh touch her own.

Look up Alice! Look up! Good God, you don't have a choice! Look up!

She did, and what she saw scared her more than anything her imagination could conjure. Yet it was soothing staring at the shiny, inanimate object, begging for her touch.

"Get on your knees and let daddy show you what you've been missin' all ya' life." Alice grabbed the butcher's knife, and turned, falling to her knees. To her surprise, Herb's penis was exposed, not nearly as large as he boasted. In one swift motion, she shoved the blade through his penis, severing it, and buried it up to the handle in his crotch. Herb's eyes bugged out in shock, his hands went for the knife, and instead he collapsed in a huge pile on the floor. A pool of blood was gathering from the spout she created, shooting in quick bursts, a few beads landed on her shoes.

Herb stared up at her, mouth agape, unable to form words. Betrayal was his face, but she knew different. The aroma of copper filled the air as more precious life juice squirted across the tile, creating a bloody sea. Herb reached up to her for help, knowing he would bleed out soon, with the same hand that went where it shouldn't.

It's not over. That hand, that dirty, evil hand. What does the good Lord tell us to do with body parts that offend?

"Pluck them out." She stated, searching for a cleaver. She heard the door open.

"Herb? It's Roy. You forgot to pay me for the month. Mind if I get that from ya'?"

"Alice... Someone... Please.... Help me." Herb quietly whimpered like the dog she always saw him as. Finding it, she asked,

"Do you ask for forgiveness?" The crimson flow did not ebb, it gained pressure. Flat smacking sounds, like quick kisses from a lover pummeled the tile. "Yes! Yes! I'm sorry! Just... Please, call an ambulance. Alice, I'm dying."

His lips were turning blue, signaling her time was short if she wanted him to suffer.

"Then you shall have it." She brought the cleaver down where that damned hand lay severing it, burying it in his thigh. He did not scream, he did not whimper. He only stared, from cold, pallid eyes. Alice gave the cleaver a good yank, producing another gush. Herb's eyes fell back, turning white.

That isn't all; his wife is a part of this as well. She covered it up these three, long years. Take the hand, you know what to do.

She picked the severed hand up, feeling it twitch and placed it on the counter. She waited for the fingers to stop jittering and brought the cleaver down, cleanly separating every digit. She carried them over to the deep fryer, and dropped them in. Dropping them into the hot oil brought back the countless memories of her, and her brethren doing the same in the pedestal filled with holy water at church. Her heart quickened at the realization she was being watched.

"Roy, I... He was gonna..."

"I know darlin', I saw it all." Alice held the cleaver up, shaking.

Don't let him take it away from you Alice. This ends here if it has to.

"So...someone finally had the guts to do it." Roy stated.

"Wha...what do ya' mean?"

"Between him and that horse faced wife of his, you know how many people they fucked over? How many lives they ruined? You ain't the only one, dear. Now hand me that cleaver, she'll be here soon. We don't want her to leave hungry do we?" Alice shook her head, a smile stretching across her white, gorgeous face in realization as Roy took the cleaver from her and got to work.

It took three good whacks with the clever to separate Herb's flab, and muscle from bone. First his arms, then his face, Roy didn't stop until Herb looked like a road victim. Satisfied, Roy took Herb's parts and began feeding them into the automatic meat grinder. Strings of bleeding, meat-worms were slowly pushed through the spout. Roy turned on the grill.

Alice watched Eleanor's Lexus pull in the parking lot. Her walk was that of authority, corruption, everything she hated. Entering, she adjusted her expensive dress, and approached the counter.

"I'll have a Mega Burger to go, and tell Herb to get his fat ass out here so we can go home." Eleanor demanded.

"He's in the bathroom Ma'am, he ain't feelin' so good. He may be in there a while." Eleanor stared at her, as if she were a cockroach.

"Would you like fries with that, Eleanor? Ya' know, we have a new recipe Herb is trying tonight, would you like to give them a taste while ya' waiting on the burger to fry up?"

"You know me well, Alice. I'll take two orders of them."

Alice fetched the fingers out of the deep fryer, inspecting them, ensuring they were to her satisfaction. She watched Roy flip an Herb burger on the grill as he, failed to stifle a childish giggle.

"Here ya' go Ma'am. What do you think?" Eleanor pulled the first one out, and placed it into her stiff-lipped mouth. Grease and bodily juices ran down her chin as she bit into it.

"Just how I like 'em'. Nice and crunchy. Alice, what is that delightful smell back there?"

"Oh, I would hate to ruin Herb's surprise, Ma'am. Just wait until you taste it." For the first time, Alice saw Eleanor smile in anticipation.

"Let me check on that special burger for ya'."

"You know I like em' rare, Alice." Eleanor's voice called out to Alice while her stomach roared with hunger.

"They don't come any rarer than this." Roy quipped, handing the plate with the Herb-burger to Alice. She could see the corners of Herb's lips sticking out of the buns, unshaven. Alice felt like a giddy school-girl again, alive.

"Here ya' go ma'am. We call it an Herb-burger. After all, he was the inspiration." Eleanor, salivating picked it up and took a bite. Her lips and mouth made loud smacking sounds as she devoured it, her eyes closed in ecstasy.

"Mmmm.... Between us, Alice, I think we finally found something Herb is good for."

"Yes, ma'am. I believe we have."

Wrong Way

Jason Kepler

"Damn, it sure is late", Luke muttered as he rounded another corner in a seemingly endless stretch of highway. Route 17 in this rural part of Florida is no picnic during the day, let alone pushing 3 am. As he passed another mile marker, green reflective paint flashed a lonely beacon of light in an otherwise black expanse. *He wondered if he was doing the right thing.*

Leaving home was a big decision and leaving the state was even bigger, but it was just what needed to be done.

"Across the street isn't a far enough horizon for me," Luke said out loud to no one. He really was alone; nobody thought it was a good idea for him to leave. That was why he was leaving. He didn't want to be stuck in this dead end town like the rest of the losers there, no sir.

Big dreams, big ideas, enough to carry him far away. Still that nagging thought in the back of his mind plagued him.

Maybe they're right. Maybe he isn't meant to go, just to stay there and be. Be what though? Gas station attendant, cashier at the Stop and Go, shoe salesman in the strip mall?

His eyes burning, Luke rubbed them hard with the palms of his hands until he saw stars behind his lids.

As he blinked to regain focus, he saw a person walking along the side of the road.

Pull over and offer a ride, he thought. Or did someone else say that.

"Hell no, you're just tired. Maybe someone to talk to isn't such a bad idea."

Luke uttered under his breath. Even as he was pulling off the road something inside him wondered why in the hell he was doing this.

Nobody picks people up anymore, what with all the wackos running around. And yet here he was, rolling the window down on a deserted stretch of highway in the early morning hours.

"Need a lift? Sure is a lonely time to be walking, huh?" The man turned slightly, slowly bending to the open window.

"Why not, these tired feet could use a break," he said as he opened the door.

Climbing slowly into the car, he groaned as if the weight of time was all on his back. The stranger settled into the seat.

"So, where we headed?"

"Out of here, that's all I know for now. But you're more than welcome to ride along for as long as you like. Did you have any place in mind?" Luke enquired.

"No, not really. Just time to finally get away, finally get away..."

That was all that was said for the next hour or so. Luke was too afraid to start some sort of conversation with a total stranger, who just sat there, staring out the window like the guy in that Kenny Rogers song 'The Poker Player' or something.

*Jesus, I hope the old guy doesn't kick off in the car. What the hell would I do with a dead body with no idea who he is or what the hell he's doing...*Luke's thoughts tumbled.

"I am a little bit thirsty." The stranger announced as distant lights appeared on the horizon.

"Well, we could stop ahead I guess, but we need to be fast. I want to keep going for a while before we stop, if you don't mind."

"No, no, that's fine. I'll be quicker than owl shit down the side of the barn on a hot Sunday morning."

Alright, what the hell does that mean? Owl shit? Are you kidding? Good job on the travel partner. Maybe when we stop I'll just leave him behind or something. But at the same time it doesn't feel wrong, you know, I'm not getting that creepy vibe from him. Maybe I'm just tired or something.

"Alright, be as quick as you can so we can get back on the road."

"Yeah, yeah," he said as he shuffled away towards the mini mart as Luke lit a smoke.

'Out of here, finally get away'. That was a weird way to put it Luke mused. I wonder why he said it like that. I mean, that's just how I feel, finally getting away from here and starting a new life. Where though, is still a mystery. I was kind of hoping for an idea from the old guy, but I guess I'll just keep heading north for a while. Where the hell is he? Man, I hope nobody wakes up early and finds out I'm gone. Sheila especially. But Mama, too. This is going to piss a lot of people off, but it has to be done. I'm sure they'll understand. Luke's mind wandered rampantly.

"Right as rain, my boy, right as rain. Ready when you are. Say, you alright? You look a bit tense?" The stranger approached Luke.

"No, I'm fine. Let's go."

"Oh and it's 'The Gambler', son. Mighty good tune, that!" he said as he settled back into the car, a slight smile dancing across his lips.

This time there was little silence.

"So, why are you leaving, exactly? I mean, is there a specific reason, or just to get away for a while?" Luke questioned tiredly. The old man thought for what seemed almost too long.

"Well, a long time ago I decided to pack my bags and leave this town. And that's just what I did. Boarded a bus out of the depot and was on my way to the big city, any big city, to make my fortune. Beat them all I did; yes sir, snuck out well before sunrise to ease the blow of my leaving. Things were going well too, right up until the bus broke down. Six miles from town, it just up and died. Just like my dreams. So I walked back home and into a shitstorm of problems. What the hell was I thinking, how could I just up and leave, what about my family and responsibilities you may well ask? Well all these thoughts made me want to leave even more. And I got my second chance, the big war. I signed up as soon as I could and hoped that I left soon. This was a sure-fire way to get out of town for good, possibly dead, but not stay here. And that was great, right up until Mama died.

Two weeks before I was to ship out. And being the oldest male in the family, I now had to stay home to take care of the rest of the family. It almost seemed like there was something keeping me here, not wanting me to go. Every time I tried, something happened to keep me here."

The look in his eyes as he turned away towards the window revealed the briefest glimmer of fear before he closed them.

But a fear of what? The way he was describing the "thing" that was stopping him almost made it seem real, some sort of tangible entity holding him to the town with some sort of purpose.

Luke carried on driving digesting the man's words.

"Well what made you decide to go now? I mean, why did you wait so long after the last time?"

"That's a good question, my boy. I don't really know, come to think of it. It's been so long since I've thought about leaving that the idea seemed silly at the time. Just after dinner the other night, Monday I think, I just got this feeling in my stomach. At first I thought it was gas, you know, but it felt different somehow. Kind of like butterflies, the kind you get when you talk to a pretty girl or something."

He turned, looking at Luke.

"I couldn't sleep that night, so I started pacing around the house. I felt as if there was something that needed to be done, some decision that needed to be made.

That feeling stuck with me until late into the night, when all of a sudden it just went away. Damn if it didn't just up and disappear like a fart in a windstorm. I tell you, it just made no sense."

That's funny, Luke thought to himself.

I spent the better part of Monday night and early Tuesday morning trying to decide if I should actually leave this dump or not. And I did have a lot of gas, come to think of it.

"And ever since then," the stranger continued, "I've had this feeling like it was finally time to go. Only problem is, I don't have the foggiest idea where I'm supposed to be going. Been working on that little nugget all week. I've been trying to remember some of the places that I wanted to go when I was younger, but it's been so long. Times have changed, people have moved on and things are a lot different than they used to be. So *why* now? Beats the hell out of me, kid."

"Well, tell me about some of the places you wanted to go. You must remember something. Did you want to go to the big cities? Which direction are you headed?"

Why in God's name do I care? Luke wondered.

Where are all these stupid questions coming from? Here I sit asking this old man to regale me with grand tales from his youth when I should be concentrating on thinking of a destination for myself! I can't believe I actually picked this guy up, let alone want to know his life's story. But there is a part of me that wants to know, needs to know what he knows. For some reason I want him to keep talking. Luke persisted to drive as the man continued to talk.

"I guess the biggest place I can think of would be New York. That was the biggest place in the world at the time, at least on this side of the country. Everything and everybody was there it seemed, and it was always moving. I'd seen a few pictures in books when I was younger, all the people and horses and trolleys clogging the streets! And those buildings! Those tall buildings reaching high into the sky? Hell, in my town the biggest thing around is the church steeple, and that's only about forty feet. I'm talking about buildings that went up so high that you couldn't see the tops! Could you imagine what it was like, the entire world's people coming together in one large place, doing things, well, I don't know what things, but it must have been amazing! That was the place for me, boy. That sure was the place."

My God, he's really creeping me out now. What he just described, almost all of it was as vivid if not the most realistic dream sequence I experienced not two days ago! I mean, almost exactly the same! But how? How is that possible? I've never seen this guy before, and I sure as hell didn't tell him about my dream!

"You okay, kid? You don't look so good. You're not going to barf or anything are you, because I can't handle that. No sir, you blow, I blow. Been that way for as long as I can remember, really. I remember one time with my brother..."

"I'm fine, fine. I just need to try and understand something. You said that things were trying to keep you here. What sort of things? I mean, it sounds to me like just a bunch of coincidences, bad timing and all that."

"Well it wasn't anything like a rope or something, if that's what you're asking. But it always seemed that there was a presence, something that was constantly saying not this time, my boy, as almost if to mock me. And it seemed to be worse if I got farther away from home. Pretty soon I couldn't leave the house without getting almost sick to my stomach with anticipation. But not because I was leaving, the anticipation of what was going to happen if I actually got away. I mean, I made up my mind weeks before it killed Mama, what the hell would happen if I got on that bus? I didn't even want to think about it. So I didn't. Until the other night, I'd given up on my dreams. But you changed that, my boy."

"Wait, what the hell do you mean I changed that? I changed what? I didn't do anything! All I did was get up this morning and go, that's all. How did that change anything for you?" Luke clutched the steering wheel.

He old man smiled a crooked smile, revealing a mouth almost full of teeth.

"You just don't get it, do you? You are the one! The one that can finally fulfill the destiny that I thought was mine all those years ago. I don't know why, but there was something different about today, something special. Couldn't quite put my finger on it until, just now. It feels like I've been walking that road for an eternity, aimlessly trying to find my way out of this hell that has been created for me. But then you came along and saved me! I don't think you understand just how important you are!"

The man started to laugh, a deep hearty laugh that brought with it a coughing fit the likes of which Luke had only heard from someone one step from death. Wiping tears from his eyes and a considerable amount of spit from his mouth, he turned back to Luke, and he could tell he was done with the laughter.

"Son, you need to remember one very important thing. No matter what happens, you need to keep on the path. Never give up your dreams, no matter how hard things get for you or for anyone connected to you never, never stop going. Once you finally get away, you'll be free. Free to live your life however you want with no one to tell you different. I'm not going to be here forever to guide you along, so you need to take up the responsibility. I've gotten you this far, now I'm going to have to go. My work here is done."

"Ok, wait just one damn minute. What the hell do you mean you've been leading me along this whole time? We just met this morning, how in the hell can you say that you've been helping me? All you've been doing is keeping me awake and talking this whole time!"

"You'll understand in time, my boy. All in good time. But for now I can only offer you one more titbit of advice. Don't go the wrong way. Whatever you do, don't go the wrong way. WAKE UP!"

"AAAAAAAAAAAAAAAHHHHHH!"

It must have been the scream that actually woke Luke from his slumber behind the wheel. As his eyes focused on the road ahead, he saw the line of cars crossing the lanes. He slammed on the brakes so he wouldn't crash into them.

A damn funeral procession! All the way out here in the middle of nowhere! Man, it's a good thing that I woke up when I did or I could have really been in trouble. Wait, wasn't there something I was supposed to remember? I was having the wackiest dream about some dude... hitchhiking... who looks a hell of a lot like the guy in the picture in the hearse! What the...?

As the line of cars disappeared into the rising sun, Luke realized that they were heading back to the town that he had just left only a few hours ago. A part of him wanted to go back, merely to pay his respects to the man who helped him on my way, but then the words of the old man echoed in his head and he then finally realized the meaning behind them.

Making the turn at the crossroads, Luke accelerated away from the town and the old life he knew was just that, an old life born anew.

City of the Dead

David Byron

Susan sat upright in bed, staring into the darkness with terror in her heart.

The taste of vomit was in her throat. Cold chills, cold sweats. Though she was awake with her eyes open, all she could see was the *nightmare.*

Her right arm ached from the act of slashing at her dream attacker with a knife and her belly ached with phantom pains from the attacker's teeth. He had bitten her belly, sinking his teeth in deep, sucking blood from her insides like a vampire. Her heart pounded, bile moved in her throat, and her nerves jumped and trembled like she'd been given a jolt of electricity. After he'd finished bleeding her, he'd look up into her deep blue eyes, blood dripping from his lolling tongue and say,

"I'm sorry, Susan. I'm so *sorry.*"

In her nightmares she could never see his face; he was only a shadow, a shadow with dark, shining eyes and pearly white teeth that gleamed like pearls in the pitch black of her room. The dreams were always horrifying and frighteningly realistic.

But the dream attacker hadn't been the only violent, blood thirsty phantasm to rob her of her sleep lately; there was the dream where she'd cut off her mother's breasts with a meat cleaver and ate them, her nose filling with blood and milk. And there's the dream where huge red fire ants crawled into her nose and mouth and ears as well as other bodily orifices - biting, stinging, drawing blood.

In another dream, she felt a strange, creeping, crawling sensation inside her belly, as if some small creature were moving around inside her, trying to dig its way out. Her dreams were sickening, macabre, even terrifying and made no sense whatsoever. At times she felt as though she were losing her mind.

There was no movement of fresh air in her small, cramped room tonight.

The room smelled like stale blood, and sweat. Trembling, she climbed off of her tiny cot and opened her window in search of air, but there was none to be found. The hot, stinking air shrouding the city of the dead smacked her in the face like the blood of her dreams, clouding over her oppressively.

She backed away from the window, sat back down on the cot, trying to force herself to be calm. No matter how many times the dreams came, she vowed not to let them get to her. They still seemed to terrify her. The aftermath would last for hours, even days, destroying her sleep.

I can't go on like this, she thought. *I have to sleep. It has to stop,* she thought. She hated it each time she took in a deep breath that still smelled like her room, repulsive like blood spill and sweat. *I can't stay in this room any longer.*

She got up slowly and opened her small dresser drawer, pulling out a suitable outfit for the weather. A pair of cut-off jeans, a thin t-shirt, fresh panties and socks.

She stripped off her thin nightie and dressed, stepped into her flip flop sandals. Then she got the hammer out from under the bed. She had begun doing what all of the other "residents" of the motel Vagabond had done; every night, before going to sleep, she nailed a block of wood to the floor against the door, so it couldn't be pushed open from the outside.

Then she'd use the hammer to pry the block back up, put the block and hammer back under her cot, then slowly open her door and peek out, looking for any unwanted visitors. She walked out into the hall now, which reeked of the usual familiar odors; sweat, urine, bad food.

Closing the rickety door behind her, she made sure it was locked then crept down to the third floor window and on to the fire escape. She climbed up to the roof, now feeling a lukewarm breeze blowing through her long dark hair, the air stagnant but fresher than it was in her room. Down below, the sounds of screams, yells, gunshots and sirens filled the night. Just another night in the city of the dead.

Susan sat on the edge of the roof, wishing there were stars. When she was a little girl, she used to sit on the roof of her father's barn and count them one by one, giving them names or locations of their own. There was: Milky Way Avenue, and Orion Street. Big Dipper Road and Aurora Borealis Drive.

She looked up at the sky tonight, wishing there were stars out, but all she saw was the thick, gray haze that always shrouded the city at night; a scarlet flame piercing the darkness where the corpse removers burned the freshly dead. She could detect the faint odor of burning flesh getting closer and knew she wouldn't be able to stay out there much longer. She closed her eyes, daydreaming of the old days way back, when she was young and beautiful and had many hopes and dreams.

"So...you gonna jump, or what?"

Startled from her daydream, Susan's teary eyes popped open, staring around the roof.

"Who...who are you?" she said, her heart beating faster.

"*Where* are you?"

All she could see was darkness punctuated by occasional flashes of neon light.

"I'm sitting over here," a man's voice said.

Susan suddenly could make out a shadow about ten feet from her, sitting on the corner of the roof, his back against the L of the low wall.

"But if you're gonna jump," the voice said, "Let me go downstairs first. I hate the sight of blood."

"I'm not going to jump," she said, standing to her feet and hopping down from the edge.

"Never meant to jump in the first place." She suddenly felt as though her privacy had been invaded like she was being spied on.

"Well," the voice said, "If you did jump, you wouldn't be the first one, not from this roof anyways."

"WELL," she said, in a stern tone of voice, "I didn't come up here to jump. I just came up here for some fresh air, that's all."

"Me too," the shadow said. "But good luck. The corpse removers were burning the dead earlier tonight, must have had a long, productive day."

Susan began walking slowly to the middle of the roof, feeling the small pocket knife her father had given her in her right front pocket. He'd given it to her a long time ago, it seemed eons ago when she was twenty-five years old and leaving home for the hustle and bustle of the big city life, planning to be a dancer/singer. She'd ended up being a high priced call girl, turning tricks for $1,000 a pop. She had made a good living until she reached forty. An aging hooker didn't make so much money in the city these days, especially since they dropped the bomb back in 2013.

Times were struggling and money was hard to come by. Life in the city sucked and so did her life. Her belly ached with hunger most of the time.

"I come here at night, when I can't sleep," she said to the shadow, as she neared the corner of the roof. "Or when I have bad dreams that wake me up."

"I don't like to dream," he said, and she could see him more clearly now in the light of a neon sign flashing from across the street. The sign was flashing: *COME IN AND SEE BIG ED'S MEAT!! - FRESHEST IN TOWN!! - SALE ON FRESH KIDNEYS, LIVERS, HEARTS AND BRAINS - COME SEE BIG ED TODAY!!*

The thought of what Big Ed was selling made her queasy and she had to force back bile in her throat.

The man was tall, slim, muscular. Long dark hair flecked with gray. A handlebar moustache, thick and covering his upper lip. She could see tattoos of some type on both his forearms, but couldn't make them out in the semi-darkness. He was good looking, though, and she was glad of that much at least. In her line of work, she'd rather to talk to someone good looking in her spare time, her private time, than some old pot bellied geezer with martini breath who was stepping out on his wife. She might sleep with them for money, but she didn't enjoy it anymore. Hell, she'd never really enjoyed it to begin with!

"I like to dream when I'm awake," she told him, lighting a bootleg cigarette. It reeked of cheap, bottom of the barrel tobacco scrapings.

"I come up here and dream of what I'd do if I had a lot of money. I could get out of this dead city."

He smiled, revealing his pearly white teeth. Susan hadn't seen teeth as white as his in years. *Yeah,* she thought. *This good looking fella has some money, all right. Maybe this won't be such a bummer of a night after all.*

"What would you do?" he asked her, looking puzzled. "If you had a lot of money...where would you go, what would you do?"

"Well, for starters, like I said, I'd get out of here," she reiterated and laughed.

"Got it all planned out already, huh?" He said and laughed along with her. He wasn't laughing at her, but with her. He seemed to be enjoying listening to someone talk about their dreams.

"Yeah, I do have it all planned," she said. "First, I go buy a couple of real good looking dresses and some new shoes. Then I'd buy me a new suitcase. Then passport..." He cut her off.

"Passport? You don't like it here in the good old US of A anymore?" He smiled as he said it, joking.

She smiled back and looked into his eyes. They were dark; almost obsidian, but gleamed like black pearls in the flashing neon. They were mesmerizing, almost hypnotic.

"No, I don't like it here. Why should I? There's nothing here but death, stink and disease. I heard that over in Australia they've built a huge complex in the outback, miles from any cities or towns. They say it's clean, disease free, and the food is great. Of course it's said to be expensive as hell."

"You play, you pay," he said, flashing her a dry smile.

"What's that supposed to mean?" She asked. The intonation of his voice sounded almost sarcastic to her.

"What I mean is, not to offend you, of course, but you strike me as the type that's wasted too much of her life to even dream about getting out of this town, unless it's in a body bag, or being charbroiled to a crackly crunch on one of those bonfires down there. Hell...a woman like you?! With that great body and knowing how to use it? You should have been stashing money back a long time ago, saving up for your dreams. But you blew it, didn't you? Drugs, alcohol, what not. Now...am I right, or wrong?"

Yea, you're right, she thought, now feeling very uncomfortable in his presence. Violated, spied on. *Yeah, you're right, whoever you are. Whatever you are.*

But I'm not going to give you the satisfaction of telling you you're right. I may be a WHORE but I've still got SOME pride left.

"You're wrong," she said, stomping her cigarette out on the rooftop with the sole of her sandal.

"So very wrong."

He just cracked another dry smile and lit a smoke. As he exhaled, Susan could detect a scent of cloves, possibly mixed with ambrosia. It smelled delicious, almost an aphrodisiac. It filled her nostrils, tantalized her taste buds...made her weak in the knees. It was a familiar feeling and she suddenly found herself feeling...aroused?

Dear God, she thought. *No, Susan. Not here, not tonight, not with HIM. You need the money, but get a hold of yourself.*

She tried to fight the feeling; she couldn't picture herself having some romantic interlude with a total stranger who'd just insulted her, good looking or not. His words had cut her to the bone, even if they were true. She did have feelings, human feelings, even if she was a whore.

"I don't think I'm wrong at all," he said, staring out at the neon as if she weren't even there. "I've been around too, you know. I know a liar when I see one. I can almost smell them, just like I can smell that stink of death and decay on the uniforms of the corpse removers as they pass by. It's a very distinctive odor. So is the smell of a liar. It's almost as distinctive as the smell of *death* - or for you, the smell of *sex*."

Susan wanted to pull out the pocket knife, flick open the blade and bury it in the man's throat. Her daddy, God bless his soul, had taught her that even a *small* blade could be deadly, if placed in the right spot. That thought was crossing her mind now and she so wanted to act on it.

But she wasn't a murderer. She wasn't cruel like this man despite his being good looking. He was probably well hung too and it would *feel sooooooo good, buried deep inside my aching, throbbing, dripping, pulsating sex. I'd get laid and paid. I'd get to eat some decent food, drink some good booze....*

Yeeeeeeessss...

Good in bed I'm sure...looks like he has money to burn. Get a hold of yourself.

Besides...he's an asshole anyways.

She fought to keep her cool.

"I'm not a *liar* and I don't like being called one by a perfect stranger, either. Someone who doesn't even know me, has never met me before. *I'm a liar?* Well, I'll tell you what, Mr. Studly Hungwell, you're a real asshole, and this conversation is over. *Good night.*"

It was hard for her to walk away; something seemed to be gnawing away at her insides, making her want to stay. As she turned to walk away, she heard him say,

"I'm sorry, Susan. I'm far from perfect and it's not that we're strangers...it's just we've only met."

She stopped dead in her tracks, her blood turning cold. She didn't remember telling him her name.

As a matter of fact, she thought, *her hand sliding down to her front pocket, I know I didn't tell him my name. Who...what, is this guy, anyway?*

She didn't know why, but she turned to face him; his face nothing but a pair of gleaming black orbs staring out of a neon haze. She could see he was smiling, and when she saw his pearly whites gleaming in the darkness, she realized she'd seen him before. Him and his pearly white *canines.*

He was the *dream attacker.* The man in her dreams with the big white fangs, who bit her stomach, sucked her blood from her womb then raped her; planted his seed. It all came back to her now; she'd been bitten in her sleep by a vampire, one of the lost souls in the city of the dead. He'd come to her night after night, feeding off of her, draining her blood as well as her soul whilst she slept. She'd awakened in her dreams, fighting him off to no avail.

He'd gotten the job done; had bled her, *impregnated* her, and now he was back to claim what was his.

His unborn child.

Her unborn child.

Their unborn child.

"I'm sorry, Susan," he said again, rising from his stoop and walking towards her. His hands were claws, his teeth sabers.

"I'm so very sorry, my love, to have to do it this way. But I knew how strong willed you were, knew you'd never give in to me willingly. So I came to you in your sleep, so you'd think it was just a nightmare. What other kind of dreams could you have in a city of dead people? A city of *Vampires*?"

He was almost to her now, his hands swelled, his fingers twitching. Susan stood frozen stiff like a dime store dummy, unable to move, barely breathing. Frozen in fear, heart filled with stark terror, ready to burst, but her mind still functioned:

Yes, I remember now...the fallout from the bombs...it turned people into blood thirsty butchers, crazy people, walking dead VAMPIRES. The whole city was full of them! I can't hide much longer. You can run but you can't hide anymore...the corpse removers will find you even if the crazies don't. Either way you're DEAD.

She willed her arm to move, sliding her hand down into her pocket...

Oh God...dear God, hurry - he's almost here...

She wrapped her fingers around the handle of the pocket knife and pulled it out.

"It's time, Susan...it's time to give me what's mine. Our child! He or she will carry on the bloodline, so my kind won't completely die out. It will be the ultimate sacrifice, but your death will serve a higher purpose and will enable us to go on living, no longer members of a dead world of walking, talking zombies...but *ALIVE AGAIN*! Isn't that what you want Susan?"

He reached out to her, wrapping his gnarled fingers around her throat, rubbing her belly with his free hand, gently, lovingly. He felt a tiny heartbeat, and she did too, as the fetus of a new day dying seemed to kick her as if it wanted to get out and meet its father.

Oh God...dear God...help me, please...don't...let...it...OUT! It will tear me apart!

She flicked open the blade with her thumb, feeling its sharpness, and turned it around in her hand, the blade pointed toward his chest...

Now! Stick it into his chest NOW!

He opened his mouth wide; his huge, saber teeth gleaming white and dripping with blood. He reared his head back, as if to strike out at her like a cobra.

She raised her arm and quickly thrust the small blade into his heart, feeling it burst beneath the pressure of her hand like an overripe melon, sending this vibrating sensation up her arm and around to her spine, feeling like a jolt of electricity. Her hair stood on end. The front of his shirt suddenly turned crimson, as his life's blood began to gush forth like water from a fountain.

He fell limp, dropping to his knees as she twisted the blade back and forth, making sure his evil heart was shredded. The gnarled hand gripping her throat went limp as well and fell to his side. He emitted a small, muffled, bleating sound like that of a sick dolphin. Then his eyes closed and he fell back and lay still.

Susan fell weakly to her knees, breathing in gasps, shaken and frightened beyond comprehension but alive. After a few seconds, she rose to her feet, dragged his body to the edge of the roof and tossed it over the side, watching it fall three stories to the hard, filthy concrete below with a sickening thud.

Then she turned, smiled, and climbed back down the fire escape, the siren of the corpse removal truck blaring and coming closer. The dream attacker's fate awaited him in the flames of a mass funeral pyre.

An hour later, back in her room, she undressed and lay down on the cot, closing her eyes, praying for a well deserved sleep.

As she lay in the darkness, she began to daydream again. She daydreamed of her dream attacker coming into her room as she raised the knife above her stomach, plunging it into her womb, ending the life that was forming there, snuffing out the tiny heartbeat as easily as the flick a light switch.

As the knife blade struck home, he screamed, falling to his knees and crying, howling like a wounded animal. She smiled at him, twisting the blade to make sure his seed was good and shredded.

The thought made her feel *good*. It made her feel so good, in fact, that she decided to really do it.

Afterwards, she fell into a deep, sullen sleep. And as she slept, her sleep was dreamless forevermore.

Alone

Stephen W. Roberts

Timothy Ferguson avoided the harsh goodbyes of his wife and children as he loaded his suitcase into the car. He had quickly packed a bag with the essentials and made his way out to the driveway, squinting slightly as the evening sun shined into his eyes. Tearfully, his family looked on in confusion and fear as to why he was leaving and *if* he would ever return.

Timothy and his wife, Carol, had their moments of greatness in marriage, but sadly those were rare and few between the fights. Even his young children, Susie and Will, knew the unsavory truth of their parents, but never before had either mom, or dad left.

All packed up and ready to leave, Timothy slammed his trunk shut and walked over to the driver's side door and opened it. He paused momentarily, for he felt himself growing weak. Deep down he loved his family, but he wanted nothing more than to be alone. The constant nagging and need for attention was quite often more than he could bear. He glanced over his shoulder one last time to take in what he was about to leave, though in the back of his mind he knew that he would be gone a day or two at the most.

"Ok Timothy, you've put on your show and made your point." Carol said.

Timothy sat down in his seat and began to close the door as if he had not heard her at all. He knew full well what was coming and in fact regretted that his children ever had to see this. *A father who wants nothing more than to be away from them and a mother without an ounce of pride left within her body.*

"Will you just stop this and listen to me?" Carol pleaded. "For Christ sake Tim, you can't just run away from another problem."

"Why don't you get it, why doesn't anybody get it?" Timothy asked. "Why the hell can't I just be left alone for awhile?"

"Because you have a family, remember?" Carol replied.

"Well, maybe I don't want one anymore." Timothy said, slamming his door as he put the car in drive.

"Yeah, go get another drink, you sorry bastard!" Carol's angry voice echoed in the distance.

Good riddance, to bad rubbish!

Overwhelmingly guilt ridden, Timothy watched his family in the rear-view mirror. He watched them watching him, as he potentially drove out of their lives. As they faded out into the distance, he clicked on the radio and grabbed a cigarette. The soothing sounds of classic rock and the delightfully gratifying taste and feel of his first cigarette in days relaxed him. Both of which are things that his sweet wife Carol didn't approve of, but that was none of his concern now.

Timothy did his best to put all of his troubles out of his mind, smoking cigarettes, driving fast and singing along to the classic tunes. Though his cell phone did vibrate from time to time in his jean pocket, he dared not respond. His mouth grew dry and his head heavy, so he decided to stop by the local liquor store for something to cure his cotton mouth and soothe the soul. A quick in and out without time wasted would be the plan, for Timothy knew that anything that reminded him of home might influence him to turn around.

Nothing reminded Timothy of home like the crushing craving for a drink.

Car parked, grocer's door pushed and chilled alcoholic beverage selected. Timothy approached the front counter with his whiskey in one hand and wallet in the other. He tried not to make eye contact, but knew it would be hard for he had shopped here quite frequently.

"A rough night tonight, is it now?" The bald old store clerk asked.

"You don't know the half of it." Timothy replied, handing the man his cash.

"Well, here's to a better tomorrow." The clerk said, handing Timothy his change.

Timothy nodded and forced a smile as he grabbed his small brown bag and left the store. Once back in his car he opened the contents of his bag and took a swig, embracing the burn, as he turned the key in the ignition. Foot to the floor, Timothy spun tires and peeled out of the parking lot. He laughed vivaciously as he drove off like a madman possessed with freedom and ruled by impetuosity.

The sun had nearly faded completely into nothingness, welcoming the luminous glow of the moon and an effervescent blanket of stars. For the first time in a long time Timothy felt content with his surroundings, for once he felt pleased to exhale yet anxious to inhale again.

Life alone was sweet.

Timothy kept to the back roads as to avoid all people and elude the cops who might want to put an end to his night of reckless fun. He knew that Carol wouldn't approve of his actions, but then again she always had a complaint or two about the way he drove.

His engine roared as he accelerated on every straight, just as his brakes squealed on every tight turn; Timothy had never taken such risks nor had such fun. The smoke from the cigarettes that he had been chain smoking was starting to irritate his eyes, just as the booze was beginning to make him drowsy; even though Timothy refused to pull over or go home.

On and on he raced as if being chased by an invisible force, one that was simply identified as his life. His own conscience wouldn't allow him to ever get too far away from the ones, which he without a doubt still did and always would love. Even if he were on the other side of the world his memories would haunt him by the second, until he rectified his mistakes. He turned off the radio and flicked a cigarette out the window as he opened the phone.

Timothy hastily dialed his home number on his cell phone and readily anticipated a pickup.

"Hello, Ferguson residence." Carol answered.

"Hello? Carol it's me, I just wanted to call home to say that I am sorry and that I'll be home soon." Timothy explained.

"Don't bother, you idiot." Carol replied. "The kids are in bed and could use at least a full night's sleep without your guilt trip."

"Carol, I just…"

"Save it, I'm not interested." Carol interrupted. "My kids and I don't need to be tortured in such a way, especially since the only problem is *you*. Nobody can ever love you if you don't love yourself…I just wish that I knew this before we ran our kids through the mud."

"Carol, please just…" Carol's phone clicked, which caused Timothy's cell phone to end the call.

How dare she hang up on me? The stupid whore and her foolish pride, the pride so undeserving to a wicked waste of space!

Completely beside himself and full of rage, Timothy threw his cell phone down to the passenger side floor board and stepped on the gas. His mind was hazy from the anger, alcohol and smoke; his heart, broken from the unexpected truths shared by his beloved wife.

Maybe she was right; maybe they don't need a dead beat dad like him, though they do need his funding. That's right; the attention hording slut would lose everything without his financial contributions, not that her qualifications as a school teacher would pay for anything if she hadn't chosen to become a lazy housewife.

Pedal to the floor and mind miles away, Timothy pressed on down the dark highway. The highway that had turns so sharp that were dimly lit, even with his high beams. A light humming sound generated from his rubber floor mats which shook Timothy's ears as it echoed through the car. He reached to the floor board in a hurry as to answer the vibrating cell phone, though he knew not what he would say.

The phone lay just inches away from his finger tips, his seatbelt and steering wheel restricting his reach. Timothy lunged forward one hard time, causing the seatbelt to cut into his waist and the steering wheel to turn. Finally, he had his phone in his hand. As he sat up to readjust himself he stared into an incandescent white light and his ears rung with the sudden piercing scream of his oncoming fate.

Timothy awoke an undetermined amount of time later, only to find himself laying face down on the snowy asphalt. His body trembled from the aching in his head. The bitter wintry sensation of the punishing manmade earth, pressed against his flesh. He rose to his feet to find that his car was gone. His head began to hurt even more so when he tried to think about what had happened to his car.

Why had he awoken alone in the middle of nowhere and of course why on earth was it snowing?

Unaware of what to do or which way to go, Timothy began to trudge on down the road.

He gave no thought as to which direction it was or if he recognized it at all, he just lifted one foot at a time. On and on he walked passing what looked like the same bit of forest scenery drenched in snow, though he didn't stop until his shoes begin to slip from underneath in a man-shaped portion of the road which the snow had not had the chance to fall.

What the Hell, am I going in circles? No. No, I couldn't be…I mean; I walked in a straight line didn't I?

Timothy wrapped his face in his hands, messaging his temples as he tried to make sense of it all.

I drove tonight, yes, that much I do remember. But why did I leave that late, did I have a fight with Carol? This body print in the snow obviously means that I've been lying there for awhile, or at least somebody has. I walked away from where I awoke so…

"Hello? Is there anybody out there?" Timothy asked at the top of his lungs. "Please answer me; I know you're out there. Anybody, please…"

There is somebody out there, right? This can't be my imprint in the snow, I mean; I walked in a straight line…didn't I?

"Didn't you?" A mysterious voice chimed in from behind Timothy.

Timothy spun on his heels to see who had been following him, but to his own surprise he still stood alone.

"No game now, I heard you speak!" Timothy grew furious, both with himself and whoever else happened to be around.

I did hear somebody speak, didn't I?

"Didn't you?" The same mysterious voice chimed in from behind Timothy again.

This time Timothy spun around even faster than before; this time catching his assailant, though losing all the oxygen from within his lungs. He met face to face with a man about his height, though seemingly a lot thinner and younger. He wore a large black cloak that covered his face, though a strand of blonde hair stuck out from the top of his hood, his toothy grin and pointy jaw stuck from the bottom.

"Who…who are you?" Timothy asked.

"Oh me? You know me. Hell, everybody knows me. I am the dictator of life and a direct influence on the world's pop culture, in fact I always have been." The mysterious man chuckled.

"It's funny how you people celebrate that which they fear the most; not that I'm complaining."

"I don't understand…" Timothy replied.

"I hate it when I have to spell it out…here, check this out!"

The mysterious man showed his sharp-toothed smile as he pulled his hood over the rest of his face. His body began to grow and distort from underneath his cloak, the cracking sounds of his bones sent chills down Timothy's spine as he backed away slowly. The mysterious cloak lifted into the air as if it were levitating instead of being worn by a man.

It flattened out together before taking form of a thin humanoid figure, one whose skeletal legs stuck out from the bottom and touched the ground. His large skeletal skull face emerged with empty gaping holes for eyes. Timothy quivered as he tripped backward and fell to the ground. He tried to scream and ask him to stop but no words would emerge. A smile stretched across the skull as if he had just heard a brilliant joke as he stood there, full formed in his cloak with his arms folded.

"Now do you see?" The mysterious skeletal man asked. "Do you finally get who I am?"

The mysterious man extended one arm from under his cloak as to reveal an hourglass, which caused Timothy's eyes to open wide as he watched the sand pour through to the bottom. The skull grin stretched wide and to Timothy's amazement he stretched out his other arm to reveal a long scythe. The grim skeletal figure extended his hand and hourglass at Timothy, pointing with one finger, causing him to crawl backwards on the ground.

"No…no, please…I want to live!" Timothy angrily gasped.

"It's time Timothy, you must come with me." The grim figure explained.

"Everybody has a time on this earth, now it's your time to learn that."

The grim figure raised his arms and the snowy atmosphere faded away, revealing a fiery crash involving an 18-wheeler and a car. The 18-wheeler was set ablaze and the car seemed to have rolled off into a ditch. The bend was sharp; nobody had a chance of survival on such a dark night in the middle of nowhere. Paramedics could now been seen working on a person in the car, as fire-fighters fought with all they had to put out the truck. Timothy climbed to his feet as the paramedics rushed by; he noticed that they were in such a rush that they blew passed without really seeing him.

The grim figure slowly crept passed the working firemen and stepped into the fire; disappearing momentarily until he emerged with the terrified trucker. They both walked over to Timothy, conversing too softly for Timothy to hear. The trucker then looked to the sky; his form fading as the grim figure dug his scythe into his chest. The trucker vanished before Timothy's eyes, which caused a chill to run down his spine as the skeletal man approached.

"We're not done here." Grim explained.

Grim pointed towards the car in the ditch. Timothy followed. Even this close to the crash, the paramedics walked through him as if he wasn't there, which caused Timothy to scream. The reaper pointed to a gurney which had a white male lying on it, which wasn't too out of the ordinary until Timothy realized that he was looking down at his own bruised, unconscious body. Grim held up the hourglass and showed him how the sand poured quickly, which caused Timothy's entire body to quiver with every speck of sand as it fell. Then it stopped all together as the reaper tilted his head, exhibiting how he can control time in any and all ways imaginable.

"Please, I can't die yet. I have too much to live for, too much left undone." Timothy pleaded as he dropped to his knees.

"Is that your only reason to live?" Grim asked. "Do you not have enough in your life to live for already? Do you only focus on that which you don't have?"

"I don't...you mean the wife and kids?" Timothy asked. "I do love them, but I regret to inform you that they don't feel the same."

The scenery began to spin again, causing the flames to vanish and paramedics to cease to exist as the snow began to fall again. Timothy couldn't shake the image of his own seemingly lifeless body on that gurney, though he still clung to the hope that it wasn't too late. Grim shook his skeletal head as if waiting for Timothy to gather on his own accord as to why he stood before death.

"What the hell was that? Damn it you, explain immediately!" Timothy turned angrily on the grim figure.

"You will tell me why I am here and..."

"Quiet you fool!" The grim figure said, forcefully knocking Timothy to the ground with his beaming voice.

"I will tell you all that you need to know, but disrespect will not be tolerated."

The reaper held up his hourglass and reminded Timothy of how he can easily cause the sand to flow at a normal rate or as fast as he pleases, which caused Timothy to change his tone. He climbed to his feet and followed the cloaked figure as they began to walk, though the snowy setting spun again and this time turned into an all white narrow hallway. The announcements crackling through the speakers and the green and blue scrubbed doctors rushing by revealed that they now stood in a hospital.

"This way, follow me moron." Grim instructed as he quickly rushed down the hallway. "Up there, just beyond that doorway." Timothy took a few steps passed death and immediately noticed his wife and kids rushing into a room, which no doubt was the room that his lifeless body laid. Timothy stopped in his tracks out of fear, the fear that his wife was telling the truth and that his kids would be better without him.

"They don't want to see me, trust me on this one." Timothy explained.

"No worries, they can't see you...trust me on this one." Grim said, pushing Timothy through his family and into the room.

Timothy began to cry as he looked down at his swollen body, which was being kept alive by a breathing apparatus among other things. He could barely keep himself together, though he lost all sense of control when he looked at his wife and children. The sight of his two sobbing children and the face of his wife, riddled with pain and perhaps guilt consumed him. Timothy was wrong, his family did love him.

"I was wrong about them, they do love me." Timothy said.

"Took you long enough to get it." Death explained.

"I don't understand, I mean, I thought you were supposed to be evil?" Timothy asked.

"I am not evil; it takes the selfish nature of mankind to see my much needed job as murder." The reaper explained.

"Please death, is it too late for me?" Timothy tearfully asked.

The skeletal reaper extended his hand to look upon his sinister hourglass of death, smiling as he watched the sand slowly fall.

"Why do you want to live?" Death asked. "Can you give me one reason to tell you how to go back?"

"I can give you three." Timothy said with a smile.

The grim reaper pulled down his cloak again and quickly shifted back into his young human form, smiling as he extended his arm toward the bed. Timothy looked at the young blonde version of death, the version that was about to return his life. He smiled as he climbed into bed and laid on top of his lifeless body, which immediately fused into himself. Grim vanished and his family rushed over as he immediately sat up in bed, gasping for air and writhing in pain. Carol left the room to get a doctor as Susie and Will looked on from the doorway which they slowly backed toward.

A doctor and a nurse rushed in and forced Timothy down to the bed, sticking him with a sedative to calm him down. Timothy felt his hard hospital bed begin to feel softer and softer as he began to fade.

He stared past the doctor at his wife and kids, smiling in the knowledge that all would be ok. Timothy knew not what was to come of him physically after the accident that had changed his life, but he also had a revelation. He knew what was now important to him. Timothy faded off with one truth on his mind.

He never wanted to be alone again.

www.ingramcontent.com/pod-product-compliance
Ingram Content Group UK Ltd.
Pitfield, Milton Keynes, MK11 3LW, UK
UKHW041257180426
11947UKWH00008B/544